9/91
G

Dark Winter

Dark Winter

H. B. BROOME

A DOUBLE D WESTERN
DOUBLEDAY
New York   London   Toronto   Sydney   Auckland

A DOUBLE D WESTERN
PUBLISHED BY DOUBLEDAY
a division of Bantam Doubleday Dell Publishing Group, Inc.
666 Fifth Avenue, New York, New York 10103

A DOUBLE D WESTERN, DOUBLEDAY,
and the portrayal of the letters DD
are trademarks of Doubleday, a division of
Bantam Doubleday Dell Publishing Group, Inc.

Library of Congress Cataloging-in-Publication Data

Broome, H. B.
Dark winter / H. B. Broome.—1st ed.
p.   cm.—(A Double D western)
I. Title.
PS3552.R6598D37   1991
813'.54—dc20   90-26996
CIP

ISBN 0-385-26568-9
August 1991
First Edition

10 9 8 7 6 5 4 3 2 1

For Lucille Enix and Sharon Jarvis

Author's Note

ONE DAY in the mid-1880s a nineteen-year-old Mexican boy named Elfego Baca, a self-appointed lawman with a mail-order tin star, attempted to tame the town of Frisco (later Reserve), New Mexico. The story of his one-man stand, which is one of the most extraordinary in the history of the West, was once widely known. Baca lived to write his own fanciful autobiography, but the events used in this novel are based on the works mentioned below.

J. H. Cook was an eyewitness, and his personal recollections are described in his book *Fifty Years on the Old Frontier,* published in 1923 by Yale University Press.

Another excellent source is the biography of Elfego Baca entitled *Law and Order, Ltd.* by Kyle S. Crichton, published in 1928 by the New Mexico Publishing Corporation.

The El Paso historian and writer Leon Claire Metz devoted a section of his book *The Shooters* to Elfego Baca. That work was published in 1976 by Mangan Books.

In this account, some things that did happen and others that probably happened are mixed with a great many things that might have happened—until the story turns entirely into fiction.

Unnatural deeds do breed unnatural troubles.

—WILLIAM SHAKESPEARE,
Macbeth, Act V, Scene 1

Dark Winter

One

THE FIRST COLD WINDS of winter swept out of the north and whistled over the scattered frame dwellings and the shingled roofs of the few buildings of Santa Rita, an isolated community on the Concho River in West Texas lying hundreds of miles from most towns large enough to be noted on a map.

Tom English reined Judge, an old horse, but still one of his favorites, toward the Lost Hope Saloon only to find it closed for repairs. A passerby seeing the horseman sitting in his saddle with a thick jacket buttoned to his chin, collar turned up, hat pulled down, told him, "John Hope's puttin' a new roof on it. Got 'er closed for a spell. But you kin git a drink right yonder," he said, pointing across the rutted dirt road.

Night had fallen and beckoning yellow patches of light fell out of windows where Tom looked. He pulled his horse back, crossed the way, and reluctantly tied Judge to the hitching rail beside four or five other horses which stood there, tails to the gusting north wind, heads held low, waiting patiently.

Overruling his vow never to set foot again in the notorious Concho Street Saloon, Tom entered, nodded at the bartender, and took his place at a lone table as far from the bar as he could get. He made sure not to walk between a light and any window, and when he took a chair he had his back to the wall.

Two hours later found him where he'd first sat down. He hadn't exchanged one word with any other customer, and none of them dared approach him. Tom gazed at the scarred tabletop and at a corked bottle, about two thirds of its contents left, and at his sweat-stained, dusty, curl-brimmed hat which rested off to the right side of his glass. He picked up the heavy tumbler—it held about two inches of dark liquid—and drained it.

"That's better," he said out loud to himself, feeling the room rock slightly before steadying. The heat down his throat and stomach had finally spread enough to calm his nerves. His revulsion at being here faded, but he still made a mental note, reminding himself that he hated this saloon. Not the people, just the place.

Large coal oil lanterns, suspended by thin chains, lit the bar and one of them cast a flickering glow across his darkly tanned face. Others in the saloon would have noticed a wiry, medium-sized cowboy, five foot ten, maybe a hundred and fifty-five pounds, a man of around thirty years of age with unusual eyes: cold as splintered ice and intensely blue.

A matter of particular interest to any observers would have been the fact that he wore matching Colt .45s in tied-down holsters. Even strangers passing through, not acquainted with a soul in town, would have realized who this man had to be.

The entire saloon had fallen silent when he'd first pushed through the batwing doors. After all, this was Tom English.

Gradually the cautious customers in the Concho Street Saloon resumed their conversations. They could see that the feared gunfighter had no interest in anything but his bourbon, so as the night wore on they relaxed.

Tom drank quietly and steadily, ignoring the people who kept glancing at him, trying not to show their curiosity.

The odors of stale beer and old cigars, of whiskey and of sweat, hovered in the air, but the harshness, the slightly sour smell of fresh smoke filtered through the room until it prevailed over all the others. Leaping flames made irregular light patterns on the other side of the room. The bartender, Chesley Upshaw, excused himself every half hour or so to feed scratchy dry-barked mesquite logs into the rock fireplace.

The chimney didn't draw well—maybe birds' nests blocked it—and curls of darkness moved into the bar as the year's first fire burned brightly. The blazing wood crackled as orange, yellow, and red flames hit sap pockets. Then miniature explosions threw bright sparks flying out, and many of these burned small black smoldering holes in the wide boards of the floor. A gritty, grime-filled haze from the smoke hung below the square embossed patterns of the tin ceiling.

Two girls from Miss Hattie's, a well-known house down Concho Street, stood near the bar with a few cowboys who had their hats shoved back. Tom glanced their way and recognized one of them, a young woman with tawny golden hair, named Flippy. His old friend Calvin Laudermilk had once introduced him to her. He had said that most of the cowboys on the Lazy E half-loved, or loved entirely, this dim-witted but very pretty prostitute.

Tom heard sharp words coming from the bar and looked that way, having difficulty focusing his eyes. So much liquor on an empty stomach could do this, he knew. He felt detached from the scene unfolding before him, as if he were a spectator in a theater watching the first scene of the first act commence.

A man with a pooch belly dressed in overalls, wearing a narrow-brimmed hat with no crease in it, seemed to be trying to work himself into a rage with some success.

Tom thought he'd seen him a time or two, and it took a moment to recall who he might be. Then he remembered: Lester Burgeon, a farmer who worked a small place some miles to the east of town.

Lester stretched his bloodshot eyes wide as he stated emphatically, *"I'm goin' to kill him.* Hugh Johnson has insulted me for the last time." White spittle formed at one corner of his thick-lipped mouth.

The angry man pulled a small Smith & Wesson revolver from a gaping pocket in his denim overalls and placed it with a resounding crack upon the recently cleaned surface of the oak bar.

Chesley Upshaw dropped his washcloth and looked up in alarm. He said, "Now, Lester, calm down. I don't know what Hugh may have said to you but . . ."

"Shut your mouth, Chesley. It ain't what he said, it's what he done. The son of a bitch run off with Hilda. The bastard stole my woman. That there is what I'd call an insult. And I know the law in Texas—it gives me the right to kill him."

Lester stumbled as he backed from the bar, brandishing the revolver manically over his head. In a high-pitched voice he cried, "I swear before God Almighty that I'm goin' to kill Hugh Johnson. He ain't goin' to shame *me.* "

He weaved to the center of the saloon, stopping ten feet from Tom's table.

"You're not going to kill anybody, Lester." Tom English spoke softly but the words carried. Everyone in the saloon heard them as they watched breathlessly, surprised out of their wits by Lester's words and actions.

"The hell I ain't," blustered Lester Burgeon, but he lowered the Smith & Wesson to his side. "I *am* goin' to kill him," he insisted lamely.

"No," Tom English said. He looked down as he poured two fingers of whiskey into his glass. "You won't do that."

Lester's face twisted as if caught in a spasm, and he rubbed the fingers of his free hand across his stubbled cheeks. Everyone in the saloon stared at him. Overcome by embarrassment, he hurriedly stuffed the small pistol in his pocket and snuffled. Then he staggered slightly and said as he turned away, "Well, I *ought* to kill him."

He turned toward the swinging doors, ashamed and furious, and stomped out of the saloon. The loose planks of the floor swayed and groaned at his passage, making the only sounds in the complete silence as everyone watched him. And then they heard the hollow thuds of Lester's retreating footsteps echoing from the board sidewalk in front of the Concho Street Saloon.

Tom listened as the townsmen and the cowboys resumed their conversations. Laughter broke out, making him wince. *Poor Lester,* he thought, feeling genuinely sorry for the man.

He sighed and said to himself, "This place brings back bad memories." He stared for a long time into his glass. "Lester will sober up by tomorrow and all that violence inside him will fade."

But he knew his own would not.

In the fog of the saloon's smoky air he thought of Julian Haynes, the only man he had ever truly hated. Dark winter wind pressed against the frame building, and a rafter near the roof creaked. He took another drink, trying for forgetfulness or at least numbness.

As he sat there he experienced a curious flash of awareness. He whispered, "I'll have to go after Haynes."

He didn't want to do this. He had to do this. He refused to think about it.

As he picked up the glass of whiskey, heat scratched his throat, and fierce elation flickered within him like pent-up lightning in a cloud.

Later he would decide that this was the night that the sickness settled upon him.

He went to the bar where Chesley Upshaw stood and paid his bill. "I feel bad about Lester," Tom said.

"Well, he brought it on himself," Chesley remarked. "He stole Hilda from Hugh Johnson in the first place. Now she's just goin' back home."

Tom's eyes came open and he lunged to a sitting position, startled, his right hand sliding the Colt from under his pillow.

The sound of lumber crashing off a wagon had waked him, and he walked stiff-legged to the window of his second-floor room at the Taylor Hotel to look at the confusion on the road outside.

"I'm freezing!" Tom whispered, standing barefooted on the dusty, splintery pine floor in his long-handled underwear.

A rooster in the distance strained out his earnest cry into the violet sky as dawn struggled through the darkness. The norther whistled between the cracks around the window. Through the wavy glass of the pane, Tom heard the sounds of dogs barking at a team of horses which had halted in the street while cursing men began reloading the drayage wagon in the shadowed gloom.

I don't believe I could bear city life, Tom thought.

His head pounded, his tongue felt dry and tasted as if he'd slept with a very old sock in his mouth. He turned to a wooden stand near the bed and poured some water from the big pitcher into a matching blue and white patterned enameled basin beside it. After splashing an icy shock into his face and running his fingers through his hair, he went to the window again, checked the sun's rim burning orange streaks in the eastern sky, and decided he'd somehow overslept.

Feeling guilty, he took the razor from his saddlebag, unfolded and stropped it a few times on the calloused palm of his left hand, a habit he had when traveling. He tested the edge with a cautious finger and then began a scraping cold-water shave, leaving a burning sensation but only a few nicks and cuts. After this he dressed rapidly.

He tugged on his spurred old brown boots, feeling their perfect fit, pausing a moment to wiggle his toes. He owned seven pairs of these, all handmade to measure. He'd bought some in Fort Worth, but in recent years he'd preferred the boots made right here in Santa Rita by Rector, the bootmaker with his shop on Concho Street. One of the few nonsinful places of business on his side of the road, Tom thought, smiling.

He did like a good pair of boots. And a good saddle. These were the only personal luxuries he permitted himself—not counting his horses. He always rode a fine horse.

Tom stood up and tucked his long-tailed gray flannel shirt inside his tightly woven wool pants, and fastened the gunbelt around his waist. He'd had this made specially after a close call. The loops which attached the holsters were a little longer than average, putting the gunbutts equal with each hipbone. After tying the scabbards' leather thongs around his thighs, the gunbutts flared out ever so slightly. Small things like this could keep a man alive. Tom took particular care of such small things, and he cleaned his six-guns regularly. Had to, since he practiced almost every day.

He sincerely tried to avoid trouble. Surely, he'd often told himself, there had never been on God's green earth such a reluctant gunfighter. Even so, newspapers like the *Chicago Weekly* and the pulp magazines and dime novels kept coming out with stories about him headed by lurid titles. Within a month of publication, he could count on having to go to great trouble to avoid glory-hungry lunatics or kinfolks of men he'd felled.

Most newspaper accounts said he'd shot from twelve to eighteen men. Their editors would have wanted to keep their stories believable. But the simple yet complicated truth was that far more blood had run. It horrified him to realize that he'd killed thirty-five human beings. But not *one* had been a "victim," as the newspapers kept phrasing it. In every case, the gunfight had been forced on him.

At times Tom brooded, sitting sick at heart in his chair late at night as Sally slept, feeling the revulsion and the sickness of past times.

When someone had the gall to ask him the repeated question "How many men have you really shot?" he'd react with coldness, concealing the spurt of anger. His only response was to turn and leave.

He had tried running away before, even changing his last name a few times, and that hadn't worked either. So he lived each day as if it might be the last, trying to savor every minute. Didn't have much choice about it.

No one knew how often he had these thoughts. Not even Sally, his lovely wife. He smiled as he thought of the woman who would always act like a girl, regardless of her years, a girl with laughing eyes who had one characteristic that he found uncommonly compelling: she loved him—he felt certain of this—as much as he loved her.

He thought of Ben, the baby, and of Rebecca, the now rebellious daughter, still furious because he hadn't put up his guns. This subject bothered hell out of him. He decided to think about it some other time.

Tom grabbed the jacket he'd bought in Montana. This long, fleece-lined coat with its woolly tall collar that a man could put up high to protect his ears had enabled Tom to live through the ice-age winters that clutched that far-north mountainous territory for much of every year. *That's another reason I won't mind giving up my part of the ranch on the other side of Black Horse, Montana,* Tom thought, but then he scowled. He sure as hell had never planned to sell that. Land once owned should be held on to, that was how Tom looked at it. But he had troubles in Texas, and there were times when a man couldn't have his own way.

Tom walked down the stairs, out onto the shedded-over board walkway, and dived quickly into the first door to the west, escaping from the breathtaking chill of the fierce wind. This was the entryway to George Henry's café which lay right next to the Taylor Hotel. As he approached, Calvin Laudermilk's voice rumbled out great complaints.

Calvin leaned back on his side of the booth, squaring his enormous shoulders, pulling his head back into the protective folds of his multiple chins. His great belly, strangely enough, was hard in spite of swelling to such an extent that his specially made shirts invariably strained at the buttonholes. He pounded his hands on this remarkable curve and proclaimed, "I haven't had a bite to eat since five o'clock yesterday, and if they don't git my breakfast to me quick, I'll be a goner."

Roaring with good humor, he cried, "Thelma, in the name of all that's holy, where on earth have you gone with my grits and eggs, my ham and biscuits? Have you forgot I'm near death? It'll be a terrible reflection on George Henry's reputation if the word gets out that a customer died from starvation in his café."

Thelma, a bone-thin waitress, bustled up with a tray she could hardly carry. "Just calm yourself, Calvin Laudermilk. I'm goin' to make sure you survive."

"A spoon will stand up in this coffee without touching the cup," Calvin said, staring at the thick black liquid. "George Henry burns up the damn beans in his skillet when he roasts 'em, and he has a heavy hand when he goes to boil his witch's brew." He screwed up his face in anticipation and took a sip of the scalding coffee. "God A'mighty!"

he croaked emphatically. "Now that's what I call *stout*. Whiskey and women and good coffee are alike, wouldn't you say, Tom?"

"What on earth do you mean by that?"

"You think you remember exactly what they're like, but nonetheless, when you experience them again they're brand-new and a surprise every time."

Tom watched with fascination as Calvin fell upon his breakfast without any signs of restraint, and then ordered, between mouthfuls, a repeat order. This arrived as Tom's fried eggs and toast appeared.

Jedediah Jackson came into the café and sat down with them without saying a word. The old lawyer had a white mustache that hung down a good two inches on either side. He had probing, clear eyes above an aquiline, aristocratic nose, and his skin, networked by fine crisscrossing wrinkles, looked like parchment. He rarely spoke until he'd finished his first cup of coffee, so while he began on this, he also adjusted his wire-rimmed eyeglasses, and examined his companions.

Calvin paused as he poured red-eye gravy on his grits. "I've heard talk of your behavior last evening, Tom. I'm surely glad that Lester didn't by some accident shoot you. After all your adventures, it would be a mighty comedown to get killed by a farmer."

"We don't joke about such things," Jedediah remonstrated, breaking his silence.

"Don't include me in any of this 'we' business," Calvin said with a snort. "My only way to survive in this weary world is to make jokes about everything."

The elderly lawyer ignored him. That was his customary way of dealing with Calvin. Nodding graciously at Thelma as she refilled his cup, he turned to Tom and asked, "How's the cattle sale going?"

"We hired twenty extra men, got the stock rounded up, and the drive is on its way to the Slaughter ranch. They've been on the trail for five weeks now."

Calvin chuckled. "I can't imagine how you could bear not to take part in the cattle drive, Tom. Just think of all that glamour, ridin' in the dust, throat parched, a saddle drivin' your backbone up through your skull. You're missin' out on one of the last great traditions of the Texas cow country. Must kill you to have to turn that over to all your cowboys. But *someone* has to stay behind."

Calvin's laughter was contagious and Tom smiled. "I'll miss all that dust, but I guess I've swallowed enough of it in my time. Besides, I've got to talk to more buyers and handle some paperwork."

"You ranch owners have to take on all the rough jobs," Calvin gibed. "Come to think of it, you're just crazy enough to enjoy ridin' around like a kid, wavin' your rope and hollerin' at the rear ends of thousands of cows and steers and bulls, and chasin' after those that try to get away."

"I honestly do, Calvin. It's going to be quite an experience. The men will take the cattle clear to Arizona, just past the New Mexico border. They'll have to circle around mountains and cross some good-size rivers."

Tom's eyes shone as he spoke. "It'll take quite a while to get there. For one thing, in Texas the drive will be through dry country and the herd will have to meander from one watering hole to the next. But I've told the men there's no big rush—just to try to keep from losing any more stock than they have to along the way. Scott Baker has always been my head honcho, he'll stay behind to look after all the ranch business in Texas. Osie Black and Ted Carrothers will spell one another as bosses on the drive. In the meantime, Jim Farr, who runs the old Clarke ranch for Sally and me, and Asa Coltrane, the cowboy who used to work on Hester Trace's ranch—he's our foreman now at the old Lazy E up on the North Concho—are in charge of the men taking care of the stock we've got left, along with the sheep."

Jedediah said, "I had the impression that this was the first part of a dispersal sale, that you were getting rid of all your cattle."

"No, I'm going to keep my best bulls and cows for breeding stock. I hate to sell off what's taken so long to build. Some of the bloodlines stem back to Jason Field's time. I'm keeping all of the damn sheep," he added, tight-lipped.

Tom lifted his head, aware of the uncomfortable silence, and smiled at his companions. "Sorry, just thinking about being mainly a sheep-herder for the next few years. But I'll hold on to my best Herefords. I'd never let them go."

He'd experimented with this long-backed, short-legged breed of white-faced red English cattle and considered them ideally suited for the Concho country where they didn't have to cover long distances to get to water. Herefords weren't at all suited for long trail drives, but with all the fences going up, those days were drawing to a close anyway.

Calvin Laudermilk broke into his thoughts. "Here I am, all set for some pleasant mornin' conversation, and I'm faced by a sullen man who's given in to a hangover." He waved his hands grandly as Tom scowled. "No need to say you're sorry. It's not necessary to apologize to me about your lack of sociability—I understand such matters—even if more gently bred folk, like Jedediah here, might not."

Embarrassed, Tom glanced over at Jedediah, a man he held in the highest esteem. He then turned back and remarked, "I sure never expected you to lecture me, Calvin." Addressing Jedediah, he said, "I'm sorry, I was talking to you about our cattle sales. My next step is to head northwest to Tascosa."

"The XIT?" Jedediah asked unnecessarily since Tascosa lay inside that ranch.

"That's right. I hope to complete a deal with them before I head out across New Mexico to join up with our men in Frisco. I've been in touch with the management at the XIT and expect to get a contract for a few thousand head."

Clouds dulled the day outside the windows, turning the bright morning dark gray. Tom looked at Calvin and Jedediah in these familiar surroundings, smelling the friendly odors of bacon, ham, and coffee, and it seemed incredible to him that he was going to leave all this behind. He decided that his friends couldn't have any idea of the anxieties he felt. They wouldn't know about his anger either or about any of the matters that stirred uneasily just below the surface.

Calvin had been looking at him curiously, and when he spoke Tom wondered if he'd read his mind. "When you ran Julian Haynes out of town last summer, I figured that was the best way for the feud to end."

He cocked an eye toward Tom, waiting for an answer. When none came, he continued, "I hope that was just whiskey talkin' when you told me the other night that you had to settle things with Haynes."

Tom's features hardened and he did not reply.

"Ain't like you, Tom, to seek revenge. You've never done that before."

"He was behind the death of Santiago Acosta, Calvin. You know that." His voice was very low. "And his men killed Santiago's son, Benito. They used me as the bait for a trap and slaughtered them along with Luís Batalla and Pepe Moya and Juan Suárez. Five men who'd been with me through all those hard times on the Lazy E."

He added simply, "They were like family. You're aware of that."

Calvin said, "Well, you downed Baxter, the top gun Julian Haynes hired. Why not take that as your satisfaction? He's a mighty powerful man. Once a real blood feud gets started, there's no tellin' where it might end."

He put his hand on Tom's shoulder. "You need to put all this behind you."

The old lawyer sat quietly, listening to them, looking from one man to the other. He had learned long ago when to offer advice—and when this was useless.

Tom said, "I can't let it go, Calvin. I just can't."

Two

FROM A DISTANCE men were awed by the unexpected sight of the great house which appeared out of nowhere. There might have been mansions this large in Madrid or even in Mexico City, but this lay in the midst of vast spaces off to the west of the tiny community of Frisco, New Mexico.

Blending into the rocky land and rough hills which rolled away from the imposing dwelling, a scattering of miserable shacks could be seen. Some had wooden roofs; others, made primarily of upright poles with mud chinked in between them, had been dug into the earth and had roofs of sod. The Mexicans called these *jacals*.

By each of these dirt-floored shacks lay a vigorously worked small plot of broken ground where the inhabitants struggled to grow frijoles.

On drawing nearer a viewer would see that the plaster which once covered the thick walls of the fortress-like home had for the most part flaked away, leaving scabs of whiteness here and there upon the exposed crumbling brown adobe blocks. Brown-veined with strands of hay and sticks which had been mixed with the original mud generations before, the walls faced the constant wind with stoic quietness.

Many of the heavy dull red Spanish tiles of the roof had fallen, and broken shards littered the hard, grassless ground.

At one side of the house a kid goat hung helplessly from a wooden rack made of two poles and a crosspiece at the top. Head down, the *cabrito* twisted in useless efforts to gain freedom, swinging back and forth while it bleated its wavering cries. Someone had wired its hind feet to the crosspiece and would return to cut the kid's throat, skin, and clean it.

A young Mexican girl sat cross-legged on the ground beside the dangling goat, holding an old blanket around her shoulders as she waited for the cook to come from the great house. She would observe the slaughter. The rare occasions for fresh meat came only when the *patrón* stayed in his home.

A skinny dog crouched beside her expectantly—waiting for the cook to plop down the whitish blue stomach, pink lungs, and coils of bloody entrails—their heat causing feathers of pale fog to drift from them into the bitterly cold air.

Smoke drifted sideways from two of the chimneys in the house—from the big central one and the small square chimney above the semidetached kitchen at the rear. The stinging wind blew a dark haze from these toward the south.

A saddled horse, covered with caked gray lather, waited patiently before the main entrance, reins tied to a hitching post. A few chickens, chased by three small brown children, barefoot in spite of the cold, swept past the looming house and disappeared toward a collection of shacks near the hill the locals called Pico Blanco. White rocks covered its irregular top.

The mansion had a massive front door made of four-inch-thick boards held together with rusting, hammered-iron decorative plates. When this swung back, sagging from hinges mounted on timbers sunk into the center of two-foot-deep adobe walls, a tiled entryway met a visitor. Past this, a planked hall led to a large room measuring twenty feet wide and forty feet long. An eight-foot fireplace with a rough-hewn mantelpiece above it lay in the middle of the interior wall. Five or six Navajo rugs, most with holes in them, all tattered and discolored, spread their wrinkled patterns on the floor.

Uncomfortable-looking chairs, black carved wood with frayed tapestry seats, and matching tables with elaborate coal oil lamps upon them sat around the room at random.

A visitor with his hat still on his head stood with his back to the fireplace, grateful for the heat thrown off by dry scrub oak and juniper logs which burned brightly behind him. He waited in the room, in the midst of the smells of smoke and dust, and moved closer to the fire.

"I'm sorry to bother you, Julian, but I'm damned worried. That's why I've ridden hard since I left El Paso." The speaker raised his hand as if to ask that he not be interrupted. "I know that you come to this place to be alone. But as I said, I'm worried. My mother was a con-

stant worrier, just like me. She considered it to be a form of prayer."
Normally a glib person, with a certain ability to express himself, he
knew when he should exercise restraint. He started to grin but bit it
off when he saw his hostile host glaring at him.

T. J. Hoskins pitched his hat over on a table and put his hands
behind him as he got even closer to the crackling fire. A man in his
early forties with wispy hair and a grizzled mustache, he had once
served as a judge. He had also held less reputable occupations.

"It feels strange being here again," he said. "When I was a youngster the only thing I could think about was getting away."

Julian Haynes waited without speaking. He looked powerful, with
an olive complexion, a shock of black hair, and a well-trimmed black
mustache. He lay back in the musky leather seat of a deep-cushioned
chair, the only comfortable one in the house. He'd bought it in Santa
Fe years before.

He stared through slitted eyes at his guest. In sunlight or in shadow,
he always did this—as if his eyes couldn't physically open. He looked
through dark lashes, and men who'd known him all his life, if asked
about the color of his eyes, could honestly say they didn't know.
They'd never seen them. Even his mistresses and the scared young
girls his men brought to him wouldn't have known, not that they'd
have cared.

When he was very young, other children had briefly called him by
the nickname of "Lizard Eyes." But it had been many years since
anyone had dared treat Haynes with disrespect. The Mexicans, old
and young, who still lived on the ranch near this house which had
been built by his maternal grandfather, Joaquín Estévez, called him
"patrón." They kept their eyes downcast in his presence.

After an uncomfortable silence, T. J. asked, "Where's your dad?"

"He's up in his room. Hasn't been able to get out of bed for some
months now. Macha tends to him." A muscle rippled across Haynes's
smooth-skinned jaw as he thought of his bastard half sister. He normally ignored the fact of her existence, just as he did that of his other
illegitimate half brothers and half sisters who lived in the shacks that
lay around the looming, crumbling mansion. Haynes saw no difference
between them and any of the other Mexicans on the place, the ones
who lived on frijoles, an occasional chicken or jackrabbit, and sometimes a stolen goat.

He had been reared on the ranch by his old father who lost his eyesight after drinking bad liquor. With studied deceit, Haynes obtained a power of attorney from him, and after that he sold most of the forty-section ranch to J. B. Slaughter, an act which nearly killed his father.

T. J. shifted his weight from one foot to the other uneasily, then moved away from the fire. He looked at his surroundings, remembering the first time he'd been in this room. He had wandered onto the ranch riding a stolen bony horse at the age of thirteen. They'd taken him in, and he'd been treated by Julian's dad with complete equality. Which is to say, the Mexican kids and he and Julian Haynes had regularly been quirted by the fierce old man, whipped until the blood ran. And now this ancient tyrant lay powerless in his four-poster oak bed, tended by a brown-skinned illegitimate daughter he would never acknowledge. Not that it made any difference. People said his mind was almost gone, and besides, he couldn't even see her.

"Did you say that *Macha* tends to him?" T. J. asked, wanting to talk about her. He decided not to pursue the question when he saw Haynes's face turn dark, his brows gathering into a frown.

I wonder when I first realized that he scares me? T. J. asked himself. *But I am afraid of him. He's a dangerous son of a bitch. He knows how I feel and he likes the hold he has over me.*

T. J. said aloud, "If it's all the same to you, I'll put up my gear and go unsaddle my horse. But after that, we've got to talk. It's serious."

"Chato will unsaddle your horse. There's little enough work for these parasites to do out here. Send word by the cook to him, and tell her to take the saddlebags to your old room."

T. J. turned to go but Haynes halted him. "Why'd you ride all the way from El Paso? You could have sent me a letter about any business matters that might be worrying you."

T. J. Hoskins hesitated as he stood at the open door to the hallway. Behind him lay the main staircase with its fragile wooden balustrade. "I'm not here to talk business."

Julian lay back in his chair, his face inscrutable. "Go ahead, tell me what's on your mind."

"Tom English will come after you and me, I feel it in my bones."

A penetrating, gargled bleat sounded, made by the kid goat as its throat was cut. A girl's wild cries accompanied this. The two men kept staring at each other. The girl began to laugh. They could hear her, despite the thickness of the walls, through the few windows in the dark house.

"He doesn't know about this place," Haynes said finally.

"I hope not," T. J. Hoskins responded, "since he swore he'd kill us."

"You got any actual news, or is this some kind of guesswork?"

"Joe Dobbins mailed me a letter. It came to me last week in El Paso."

"Who's this Dobbins?"

"One of the pack of gunmen we hired when we were running things in Santa Rita," T. J. said. "He stayed behind, works in a livery stable there. Guess he decided to change his ways."

"Get to the point."

"English is bent on revenge. He's on his way."

"Alone?"

"I think so."

"Good. Couldn't ask for anything better. No use worryin' about something like this. Best to get it behind us. English may be hell on wheels in a standup fight, but if he rides into these mountains, on my ground, he won't have a chance." With a scowl forming, Haynes said, "But that's too much to hope for. Not likely we'd be that lucky."

"Lucky?"

Haynes ignored his companion's sarcasm. "Why'd Dobbins go to the trouble to write you?"

"Well, I don't know, to tell the truth. Guess he hates English. Probably because he was close to Baxter, the gunslinger we brought in from El Paso to be the sheriff."

"I don't like to think back on those times," Haynes said curtly.

The two men poured themselves large glasses of whiskey from a heavy lead glass decanter on the dark sideboard. Above it on the wall was a large crucifix which showed a limp Christ hanging from brutal spikes that penetrated hands and feet. The bright blood painted on the crudely carved cedar statue stood out in the room which otherwise had no primary colors, only gray and white and black and old shades that had long since faded. A pale winter light seeped in from the windows as T. J. sat in an uncomfortable tall chair facing Haynes.

People who have spent more than thirty years together, whether they love or hate one another, often sense what the other is thinking. Haynes and T. J., without speaking, shared a particularly unpleasant experience.

Within their memories they saw and felt the menacing approach of a sandstorm, the air turning yellow while black fearsome clouds boiled in the west. Wind blew down the streets of Santa Rita, Texas, and dust flailed against the windows of buildings. Reuben Baxter, their chosen top gun, had stood on the gallows they'd built to hang Tom English, taunting him after he'd been freed from jail. Calling him out, knowing that English had never been known to back down.

Concealing themselves within a large number of spectators, Haynes and T. J. had stood spellbound, hypnotized by the drama unfolding before their eyes, watching as the trick failed, as Tom English, tripped by Baxter's throwing open the trapdoors beneath his feet, had reacted faster than sight itself. And again they saw the horror: Reuben Baxter hurled backward off the scaffold, blood and cloth erupting from his chest as twin Colt .45s exploded simultaneously.

T. J. spoke first. "We should'a killed English when we first had him in jail. Before that fat man and the Indian busted him out. And before that lawyer friend of his got him off scot-free. If we had, we wouldn't be in this fix."

"You've always been a worrier, T. J. For one thing, English thinks you and I are back in El Paso. The three sections of land I kept with this house is known around these parts as the Estévez ranch, after my mother's father. I've been gone so long no one connects the name of Haynes with it at all. The only reason I've kept it is to have a hideout."

"Is that what you're doing now, Julian? Hiding out?"

Haynes shot a look of complete loathing at his old companion. "You know better than that. This is the only place I can go without most of my bodyguards. I come here now and then to relax."

"Your being here might have something to do with Macha, couldn't it?" T. J. asked maliciously.

Electricity crackled between the two of them and T. J., losing his nerve, looked down submissively, trying to conceal his alarm.

Haynes stared fixedly at T. J. Then he relaxed and sank back in the cushions. Speaking softly, in a carefully controlled way, Haynes said, "I told you what happened between us. She's just another Meskin slut that Chato Verdugo brings to me now and again."

"But she did bear your son."

"I don't claim any bastard as my child—any more than that randy old drunk upstairs did—which may be the only trait he and I share." He laughed harshly.

"Shouldn't talk that way. You ought to show a little respect for your dad. After all, he's helpless now."

"I remember when you and I were helpless. Can you ever forget the way he loved to quirt us?"

"No," he said. "That's not the sort of thing a man forgets."

Haynes straightened in his chair and examined his visitor. He said deliberately, "You're useful, T. J., but I don't like you, I never have. We've shared many an experience, and I guess you're the only one I've got to talk to. I need to get things out of my system every once in a while. But if I ever hear that you've told what you know about Macha's baby, I'll cut your throat." He paused, letting the ominous words take effect. "Do you believe me?"

T. J. put his drink to one side on the almost black table. It had been finished with soot and lampblack before being varnished. He had to make an effort to set the glass down without spilling it, for his hand shook. "Yes—I believe you."

They sat as the day deepened into darkness, each one lost in his own thoughts.

T. J. considered Macha to be the best-looking women he'd ever seen, half-breed or not. Her image obsessed him—he even dreamed about her—which puzzled him because, although he took great care never to admit this, women had always disgusted him. Sometimes the fury mounted and a pressure built that had to be released, and when that happened he'd drink until his face felt numb, and then he'd take the nearest prostitute to her room. But afterward, remembering, his body shook with revulsion.

He had come to the old Estévez ranch to warn Haynes about the letter concerning Tom English, but there had been another reason for the trip: he wanted to see Macha again.

He thought about her and felt a crackling like some inner lightning, a mixture of lust and self-hatred.

T. J.'s imagination had been inflamed ever since Haynes had told him about the first time Chato Verdugo brought Macha to his bedroom when she'd been around fourteen years old. He'd described the way she'd fought and how he finally had to hold a knife to her throat.

Haynes's voice broke into T. J.'s thoughts. "Tell me exactly what that letter from Santa Rita said."

"Dobbins wrote that a lot of cowboys from the Lazy E, that's the main Tom English ranch, you'll recall, are on a cattle drive with about seven thousand head. It seems that English sold them to J. B. Slaughter."

"The hell you say!"

"Thought that'd get your attention."

Julian Haynes sat upright. "Are they headed for Frisco?"

"Dobbins said the drive was going to the Arizona ranch. He wrote that English isn't with the herd. He's headed off to Tascosa by himself, selling more cattle to the XIT."

"If that's all there was in the letter, why'd you say he was on his way to get us?"

"I'm coming to that. Dobbins put in his letter that after he's made his deal in Tascosa, English plans to ride to the Slaughter headquarters ranch near Frisco to collect for the sale of his cattle. After that he intends to go to El Paso to settle some old business he has with you." He swallowed hard. "And, I guess, with me."

The two men sat for quite some time, drinking whiskey, not speaking. Finally, Haynes demanded, "How on earth could a livery hand know all of this?"

"That's the funny thing. The fat man, Calvin Laudermilk, and Tom English were in the livery stable while English saddled his horse, getting ready to head out for Tascosa. Dobbins heard them arguing. The fat man was trying to talk English out of going after revenge, but English told him he couldn't rest until he settled the score."

Speaking thoughtfully, Haynes said, "Slaughter's ranch house isn't but fifteen or twenty miles to the north of here."

"I know." A light came into T. J.'s face. Speaking slowly, he said, "You're thinking that you and me and that mean son of a bitch Chato could gun him on his way to it?"

"Of course not, T. J. That'd be foolish."

"You want to sit around until he comes after us?"

"T. J., use your head. We'll kill English *after* he's collected for the sale. God A'mighty, he'll be carrying a fortune."

Macha Cordero came to the big house three times a day to clean up the old man and feed him. She carried a bucket of water heated over the kitchen fire. The narrow winding back stairs creaked as she ascended from the kitchen to an open upstairs back porch, a place where the old *patrón* slept in the hot summertime.

Along the railing, drying in the wind, a set of worn blankets flapped along with the noon rags she'd used, frozen stiff but clean. She washed them at the well behind the house and brought them back to dry. Before using them, she'd thaw and dry them thoroughly at the fire she'd rekindle in the old man's bedroom.

She made several trips back and forth from the kitchen, and when not burdened by the weight of the heavy bucket she ran up and down the stairs, her muscular legs seemingly tireless.

Macha entered the bedroom off the upstairs porch again, this time carrying a tray with food: a glass of water, thin chicken soup with glistening yellow spots on its surface, and several squares of cornbread. She put this down on a square low table near the bed.

She'd already poked the blackened coals in the small stone fireplace, making bright sparks fly, had added kindling wood and two gnarled dry logs from the supply stacked in the corner.

Macha worked swiftly on first entering the room, speaking to the still form lying so quietly under his blankets, fighting against the involuntary ripples of nausea provoked by the smells of urine and human waste. No one could become truly accustomed to these.

She stripped the blankets back, rolled the slack naked form from side to side, washing him with the warm water, scouring the old withered body, drying it. His eggwhite eyes stayed open, unseeing. He never spoke. Then she pulled off the filthy blankets and put on the other set, after drying and warming them before the open fire. She wrapped these around the shivering man whose flesh, like wrinkled tissue paper, had the washed-out blue look of skim milk. The bones of his skeleton pressed against his fragile skin. An abundance of curling gray body hair remained as a vague reminder of his virile past.

She took a heavy flannel jacket from the foot of the bed and put it around his shoulders after she propped him up on the plumped-up pillows. She buttoned it to his neck, held him until he stopped shivering, then brushed her fingers through his hair, speaking all the time in Spanish to him.

"You are clean again. Don't you feel better?"

She expected no answer and got none. After crumbling a square of cornbread into the soup, she fed him, encouraging him to swallow when he'd try to turn his head away from the spoon. She talked and laughed and patted his bony shoulder occasionally, feeling sorry for someone so alone.

She did these things while thinking: *I tended to Pancho in this way when he was a baby—maybe only a woman can do these things.* Shrugging, she decided that at least Pancho had grown to love her, to show how much he cared. While her old father, even before he'd lost his sight, had never looked at her, never seen her—not as a person, certainly not as his child. She knew she'd never existed as far as he was concerned.

Why am I doing this? she wondered. *Because no one else will,* she decided. *And he is my father.* Her talkative mother left her in no doubt of this. She'd even been shyly proud that her daughter carried the blood of the old *patrón.*

He turned his head away, mouth closed tight against the soft pressure of the spoon with which she sought to tempt him. Reluctantly, she put it in the bowl and moved the tray to one side.

"You're tired," she said, always in Spanish. She knew some English, enough to get along, but rarely spoke it. Most people thought she didn't know the language at all.

Macha gently pulled one of the two fat pillows away and pulled him down in the bed, her arms around his bony frame. He must have less than half his former weight, she thought, marveling at his lightness. As she tugged she felt him go suddenly quite rigid, a spasm wrenched him and he arched his back. Choking noises came from his throat, sinews stood out around his face as it turned purple, and then a dry rattle sounded and the tension eased. She removed her arms and leaned over him.

His face looked awful, its color draining away. A rictus drew his mouth open, one corner lower than the other. His sightless clouded eyes stared at the ceiling, and he didn't breathe at all.

Macha, feeling her heart pound, sank into a chair beside the bed. She stared at the old *patrón,* felt the trembling in her body, then bowed her head automatically as she began to pray. Ending it at last, she crossed herself and started to rise, but her muscles didn't respond. Time passed, at least five minutes.

I must close his eyes, she thought. Rising, she leaned down and with her fingers touched his lids and pulled them down, but they popped open. A nerve or something caused that, she thought, forcing herself to raise fingers that shook like dry leaves in the wind. But as they touched him once more his face changed and she jumped back, startled almost out of her wits.

"*Agua,*" the old man croaked.

Hardly believing her ears, she took the glass of water and raised his head. Supporting him, she held it to his lips as he drank several swallows from it.

He coughed painfully and tried to speak. She leaned down to hear the words: "Who are you?"

"Macha. I'm your daughter Macha."

He didn't answer at first. Summoning up his strength, he asked, "Is it day or night?"

"Early night."

"It doesn't matter." The wind sounded on the porch, making the rags and blankets, now drying and freezing there, slap back and forth.

"Did you die?" the girl asked, watching him, spellbound, amazed and wondering if her prayers had brought him back to life. She thought: *He wasn't breathing.*

He ignored the question. He seemed to have more energy now than she'd seen in months. And for the first time in all this time he spoke to her.

"I know who you are. How old is your boy?"

"Five. Pancho's five." She added, although he hadn't asked, "And I'm nineteen, an age when others are still girls. But I feel old."

"I guess Julian still sends for you."

She didn't answer.

"Why don't you run away?"

"I have the boy—where would we go? How could we live?" She didn't tell him that she thought constantly of flight.

The old man's face creased from sudden pain. He gasped and said, "My left arm feels like someone hit it with a rock." Moments went by as he opened his mouth wide until the agony passed.

Then he said, "Go over to the far wall, to the top drawer of my chifforobe. Under the shirts you'll find a box. Bring it to me."

She rose, pulling her long shawl around her. Even with the fire, the night's cold made gooseflesh ripple on her arms. She kept saying to herself: *"He was dead. Since he came back to life, for the first time he's talking to me. I can't imagine why."*

She pawed about in the open drawer and her fingers came across a smooth hardness and closed about it. She took the heavy leather box and went back to the bedside, placing it in his hands.

In a hoarse whisper the old man said, "I married the only daughter of old Joaquín Estévez. When he died, I found this in his things. It might be of use to you." He groaned again. "My arm hurts." Then he murmured, "You've been good to me. You're the only one."

Fumbling with the box, he opened it and let a stream of gold coins trickle through his fingers, clinking down into a little pile, making ringing noises. Then he touched a sharpness and flinched. "I'd forgotten this was in here." He picked up a small stiletto, the blade sharp and gleaming. The firelight glowed along its length as he held it up.

"You might as well have this too."

Macha held the short dagger carefully. She moved closer to the firelight and saw reflections glancing from it. She looked carefully at its ivory handle, with shades of yellow blending into cream and white, with wispy cracks from age. Dark brass rivets bound the handle to the dagger.

"Old Joaquín told me that's Toledo steel," she heard him say.

Suddenly he demanded, "Water. Bring me some water."

She hurried to his side, reached for the glass on the tray, and then she heard a sound so soft she hardly noticed it, like a passing sigh. Looking over her shoulder, she saw that his eyes had closed.

Macha sat beside the body for a long, long time, wondering if he would come back to life again. Then she put the dagger in the leather box with the gold coins, wrapped her shawl around her, and went out into the frozen darkness on her way downstairs.

"Now we can run away," she whispered to herself.

Three

TOM ENGLISH rode his nervous horse, the wild-eyed dun he called Deuce, down the trail. He had the sheepskin collar of his heavy coat turned up around his ears and kept his head down, hiding as best he could from the north wind that whistled into the Texas Panhandle. He was finally on his way back to Tascosa after spending seven days, counting riding time, at the XIT headquarters in the little town of Channing up on the northern breaks of the Canadian River.

He had stayed at the Hotel Rivers during his time in Channing, a frame building that looked like a large house. It had front and side steps, a wide verandah on the first two floors, and some gabled rooms on the third. Behind the hotel stood a sturdy wooden windmill. While there he'd struck a bargain with W. S. Mabry to sell three thousand cows, calves, and steers to the XIT for early spring delivery.

He had the contract folded in his saddlebags and felt a touch of seller's remorse, wondering if he'd received as good a price as he should. Tom knew that Mabry was a much better trader than he was, and he felt annoyed that he had given in on a bargaining point. Tom hadn't intended to sell more than two thousand head, but Mabry had insisted on buying the thousand spotted Mexican steers his buyer had inspected when visiting the Lazy E. Tom had been wintering these cattle on his west range and felt they'd fatten up in a year; he said he preferred to keep them. Mabry had drawled that without them he wouldn't make the deal, and Tom finally agreed with some reluctance.

"Well, hell," Tom said out loud as he rode Deuce's smooth trot, "I guess it was the thing to do." But he knew he'd been out-traded.

He reached Tascosa at twilight with the day rapidly tailing into night. Jouncing down the dirt street, he heard the rhythmic creak of saddle leather as Deuce trotted past seven saloons. Only a few horses stood hitched at the rails before them. He pulled up on reaching the Russell Hotel, wearily dragged his saddlebags from his mount, and dropped them on the porch before riding to the livery stable run by a former gambler named Mickey McCormick.

"I see you made it back all right," McCormick said by way of greeting.

Tom nodded.

"No trouble with our mountains?"

Tom grinned, thinking of the awesome flatness of the panhandle country. "Deuce and I managed to clamber over the highest ones in the Canadian Valley," he answered.

"You lose your saddlebags?"

"No, I dropped them on the hotel porch so I wouldn't have to haul them over from here."

"Mighty trustin' to do that. Tascosa has some light-fingered fellas in it."

"Too cold a night for thievery," Tom said uneasily, thinking of the contract in his gear along with his travel money.

"The weather's never too brisk for a hard-workin' robber," McCormick commented, adding, "although most of 'em are more interested in rustlin' cattle. Some of the ranchers around here are gittin' right upset about that." He shook out the newspaper he'd been reading and held it under the lantern. After smoothing the pages, he pointed with a blunt forefinger to a notice printed with bold type:

Any person caught monkeying with any of my cattle without permission will catch h———l!

Yours in Christ,
Grizzley Calleen

Tom laughed as he read these words. "I've met a few Christians like Mr. Calleen, and you'd think a sensible rustler would steal from someone other than him."

McCormick agreed, then led Deuce to a stall as Tom took his leave, anxious to rescue his saddlebags.

After retrieving them he checked into the hotel, went to the room he'd had a week before, pulled off his boots, and collapsed on the bed. Half an hour later he found his way down the hall to a room with a great galvanized iron tub, and allowed a plump Mexican woman named Tita to wheedle fifty cents from him in exchange for filling the tub with hot water which she would haul in repeated trips from the kitchen downstairs.

Tom closed the door to the hall when Tita finally left the low-ceilinged bathroom. Steam billowed into the air all around him, wisps of mist rose past his face. He put his fresh clothes on a chair against the wall, stripped, and stepped tentatively into the tub. He drew in his breath and stood upright in the shockingly hot water. "Damn!"

He decided to try to cool it a little by swishing a foot back and forth, thinking that in a moment he'd ease himself down little by little so his body could gradually get accustomed to the hotness. Suddenly the door opened. Tom instinctively jerked an arm out awkwardly, grabbed a washcloth, and placed it protectively. Tita stood beside the tub as nonchalantly as if he'd been fully clothed. Her right shoulder tilted far down owing to the weight of another gallon of heated water in a large rusted pail with a heavy wooden handle. Tom jackknifed into the tub, lost his footing, and splashed into scalding waves which washed back and forth, making slapping noises on the galvanized rim.

Stung by the hot water as if caught by innumerable tiny fishhooks, Tom let out a great breath. Then he looked up and saw the amused round face watching him. He summoned what dignity he had left and sat up.

Overcome by embarrassment, he said emphatically, "You shouldn't be in here."

"Want me to wash your back?" She couldn't contain her amusement.

"No, that's fine, Tita, I can manage that myself. You better leave."

She poured a heated stream all around his upraised knees and into the water beside him, raising the container high as its load lightened, playing a game. With a farewell chuckle she departed with a wag of her well-rounded hips, darting a dark-eyed teasing look at him as she pulled the door behind her.

Warmth soaked into his aching bones, and slowly Tom relaxed, sinking down in the long tub. He washed his hair, scrubbed all over, then simply lay there until the soapy water cooled. When he climbed out of the tub he felt invigorated, the travel soreness washed away. Still enjoying the luxury of the long-delayed bath, he dried himself with a scratchy thin towel.

Tom dressed in the fresh clothes he'd brought from his saddlebags: long underwear, a clean gray flannel shirt, and woolen pants. He padded on bare feet to his hotel room and pulled on socks and boots. Then he strapped a gunbelt around his waist. He wore only one gun, the Colt .45 given him long years before by Jason Field.

In the area downstairs which served as a bar and also a dining room a man sat in a darkened corner, away from the light. At first Tom thought he must be asleep, but at Tom's entry he pulled his head up awkwardly from the table before allowing it to fall back where it had been.

A bartender stood motionless behind the bar, leaning against some shelves. In a straight chair in the middle of the room under the light of a suspended glass lantern with a tin shade, a tall man sat with his back straight as a ramrod, his knees apart, both boots planted firmly upon the floor. He wore a black wide-brimmed hat with the crown dented as if by accident. He'd buttoned a white shirt to his neck and over it he wore a dark vest but no coat or tie. His black pants hung down above old brown boots. A Winchester rifle lay across the seat of an unoccupied chair at his right side.

The tall man had a sun-wrinkled, walnut-brown face and a black mustache. Rising from his chair, he took off the hat and put it next to his rifle on the chair beside him. "You look familiar," he said to Tom, peering curiously at him. "Do we know each other?"

"I don't believe so."

"For a minute there I'd 'a sworn you were Tom English. You bear an uncanny resemblance to the pictures of him I've seen. But then I noticed you're only wearing one gun."

"I'm a rancher—been up here trying to sell a few cows to the XIT."

"They buy any?"

Tom nodded. The tall man sank to his seat, looking up at Tom. He was obviously curious about his identity, but many men kept this fact to themselves. He said, "You might as well sit down and have a drink with me. My name's Joe Ross—deputy sheriff from Socorro in New Mexico."

"You're a long way from home."

"That's true. A bounty hunter—a filthy son of a bitch, by the way —caught a man wanted in New Mexico for attempted train robbery along with attempted murder. I came here and paid him his two-hundred-dollar reward and now I've got to take Dick Lewis yonder,"

he pointed to the man in the corner with his head on the table, "all the
way back to Socorro for trial."

"That's your prisoner?"

"Yep. Got his hands cuffed to the crosspiece between the table legs.
That's why he's all hunkered over."

Ross poured a drink for Tom and replenished the whiskey in his
own glass. He said, "Dick Lewis and I've been friends for years, and I
don't think of him as being all that dangerous. But he's been acting
strange ever since he started reading all those dime novels. That's how
he came up with the idea for the train robbery."

Ross pushed his chair back a little and crossed his legs. He said,
"The Atchison, Topeka, and Santa Fe runs, as you no doubt are aware,
from Chicago to San Francisco. The main line enters New Mexico
near Raton, goes southwest to Albuquerque and then on west through
Arizona." He paused before saying, "If we didn't have all this progress,
Dick Lewis wouldn't have got in trouble with the law. Wouldn't have
been tempted."

Deputy Sheriff Ross reached into a vest pocket and withdrew a
small sack of tobacco and a straight-stemmed pipe. He tamped the
tobacco down, fumbled in a shirt pocket for a kitchen match, and
struck it on the bottom of the table. Like most pipe smokers, he had
great patience and he seemed to lose himself in this task. The match
flared yellow. With downcast eyes Ross lit his pipe, inhaled, and
puffed out a small blue cloud of smoke. Clenching the stem of the
pipe in his teeth, he looked up.

"They ran a southward extension of the Santa Fe Railway down
through Socorro a while back, and now it hooks up with the Southern
Pacific at El Paso. Another branch taps into the same line at Deming."

Changing the subject abruptly, he asked, "Are you hungry?" Tom
nodded, and Ross ordered steaks along with fried potatoes and frijoles
for the two of them and the same for his prisoner.

"Now," he said with a slight smile, "I'll get back to the story of Dick
Lewis and the Socorro train robbery. The steam engine pulled to a
stop just to the south of our town. There's a windmill there with an
elevated tank. Anyway, while they were taking on water, Dick Lewis
crawled up in the train's cab and stuck a handgun in the engineer's
ribs. Naturally he raised his hands, and Dick demanded to be taken to
the mail car, except they didn't have one. So Dick said he'd rob the
passengers, but they didn't have any of them either since the train was

hauling nothing more than a load of rocks and gravel for work on the railroad bed. This disgusted Dick since he had no particular need for rocks or gravel." A faint smile crossed Ross's face at these words. "He stole the engineer's watch and went back to his horse. This is when things went from bad to worse. The engineer for some damn reason kept an old carbine in the cab of the train, and he commenced to blast away at Dick, for he was furious about the loss of his watch. Dick yanked out his pistol and shot back, which so alarmed the engineer that he fell off the train and broke his collarbone."

Ross puffed on his pipe. "By the time the folks running the railroad heard about it, of course, the story had been blown out of all proportion. There were quite a few outraged telegrams sent to me from the Santa Fe Railway—all those companies have reached the point where they're real sensitive about such matters—and after this they posted a reward for the capture of Dick Lewis, dead or alive. As you can see, he's alive and at the moment is real sorry he ever read those glamorous stories about train robbers."

The deputy sheriff went to his prisoner's table, knelt on the floor, and unlocked the handcuffs. Tom watched the prisoner straighten in his chair, rubbing first one wrist, then the other, and heard him say, "Joe, you and me've been friends for years. No need to treat me like this." He sounded as though his feelings were gravely hurt. Then he lowered his voice and spoke earnestly to the deputy sheriff, but Tom couldn't hear him.

As their meals were served, Ross sat once again with Tom. His prisoner ate at the other side of the room by himself. Joe Ross said, "He told me that if I let him go he sure won't rob any more trains, but of course, I can't do that. I'm going to have to take poor Dick Lewis back to Socorro for trial."

"Did you get the watch?"

Ross shook his head. "Nope. Dick sold the engineer's Elgin watch for two dollars and spent it. So he has nothing left to show for the stunt he pulled."

When they'd finished their meals, Tita, the round-faced Mexican woman, brought them coffee. Tom avoided her laughing eyes as she set his cup before him and filled it.

They sat in the silence of the room, listening to the howls the brass weather stripping made in the upstairs windows as the wind pressed its force against them. A coffee cup, hot to Tom's touch, rested in

both hands. He raised it to his lips, and on putting it down saw Ross
examining him.

"You *are* Tom English, aren't you?"

"Yes."

"I thought so. Guess you're only wearing one gun so as not to call
attention to yourself—which seems to me to be a good idea." He had
his pipe in his hands and scraped the blackened bowl with the blade of
a small penknife. "Goin' back to your ranch from here?"

"No, I've business in Frisco."

"You can ride most of the way with my prisoner and me, although
we might hold you up a little. My horse threw a shoe and I've got to
get him shod proper tomorrow before we leave."

"I probably should head on out."

"Suit yourself." Ross added, "I'd be careful in that town."

"What do you mean by that?"

"There's no law in Frisco, and they've seen quite a bit of trouble
lately. If I didn't have this foolishness with Dick Lewis to tend to, I'd
be over there right now."

"What kind of trouble?"

"Frisco's close to the Slaughter headquarters ranch, and that outfit
must have eighty to a hundred cowboys. When you've got that many
men with nowhere else to go to let off steam you can expect a certain
amount of hell raisin'. But from what I've heard lately, they've gone
beyond that."

Macha woke with a start. *Someone's in the room,* she thought, eyes
wide with terror. She listened carefully to the silence but heard at first
only slight night noises outside the tiny shack. When she worked late
she slept here by herself while Pancho, her five-year-old, stayed with
her mother and the rest of the family on the other side of the hill.

The intruder made no sound but she knew he stood near her—she
could smell faint odors of tobacco and sweat. Her trembling fingers
slipped under the thin pillow, pried the lid from the leather box, and
her right hand closed on an ivory handle.

When she sat up, the heavy blanket trapped her for a heart-stop-
ping moment. She yanked at it—pulling it away, freeing her legs.
Then, muscles taut, she balanced upon her knees—waiting.

Then she heard his ragged breathing going in and out rapidly.

"What do you want?" Macha asked furiously. The sound of her own voice startled her in the silence. "I told you—no more. I won't go to him again." She almost sobbed the short Spanish phrases.

She couldn't bear it any longer. "Is that you, Chato?"

A man said, "No."

She trembled. Macha whispered, "Go away, *patrón.* Don't come any closer. When your father died two weeks ago, I told you I was leaving as soon as Pancho gets better. He has had a fever." Her voice rose as she babbled, trying to make human contact. "Please, *patrón,* don't hurt me—just leave."

He'd never done this before. Chato had always taken her to him. Fear gave her courage. She felt cornered, and she shuddered as she drew back her arm and waited.

A hand abruptly grasped her hair and yanked violently, throwing her back upon the narrow bed. She gasped as a heavy knee forced down on her stomach, and then rough hands tore at her nightclothes. Gathering all her strength, she jammed the dagger into the man's stomach. He screamed, fell forward, and hot slickness flooded across her chest and neck. His hand tightened in her hair and she pushed with all her strength, throwing him off her against the wall. Feeling his hands clutching at her, she fastened her fingers tightly around the dagger's handle and with an effort pulled it free. Then she stabbed him again, this time higher, just underneath the ribs, straining to force the sharp point upward into his heart.

She felt him arch back away from her, heard a slight sucking sound as the blade pulled free and then a choking howl as he toppled sideways and fell heavily off the bed.

Macha held the stiletto in a death grip. Shaking in every fiber, she raised it, ready to strike again as she cautiously stepped upon the dirt floor. She pressed herself close to the wall, fearing that at any moment he'd grab her legs and pull her down. But nothing happened. She didn't hear anything at first but then high moans started. It took a moment before she realized they came from her.

She moved to the rough pine box that served as a table, found a match, and struck it. The sulphur popped and flared as she held the match shakily over a slumped, face-down figure. She put the flame to the coal oil lamp's wick, put the glass chimney back, then turned the light up until she could make out the body clearly. She moved forward, leaning over, holding the blade ready, and touched him with her left hand. No movement. She tugged and managed to roll him on his back.

At first she only saw the man's shirt—a white collar and sleeves, but the entire sodden front gleamed scarlet in the lamplight. Her eyes moved up and looked at the distorted face with its open mouth and eyes. Astounded, she sank to her knees beside the corpse of T. J. Hoskins.

"You!" she hissed. Stunned, she kneeled beside a man she'd known all her life. She'd seen him staring at her for years, but he'd hardly ever spoken to her. Bewildered, she pushed her hair back from her face with the backs of her hands, but felt the wetness smear her forehead.

Revolted, she stood bolt upright. "I've got to get out of here," she said to herself. She jerked off the blood-soaked coarse cotton nightgown, rapidly pulled on her undergarments and the long skirt, then put on her blouse and tucked it in. She grasped her coat and then turned to a basin of water on the table where she washed her hands over and over. Then she washed her face and tried to smooth her hair.

She scrubbed the dagger, dried it on a blanket, and put it back in the leather box with the golden coins. She slipped soft deerskin moccasins upon her feet and packed hurriedly. After putting the box the old *patrón* had given her into a long blue woven bag with some clothing, she stood, indecisively, staring around the room. Moving to one side abruptly, she dragged the mattress off the bed and put it over the body, hoping for a delay in the discovery that would send men after her. Then she left.

Outside she found her way through the moonless night along the rocky path that led around the hill to her mother's place. She had to find Pancho and leave. *We'll go to Frisco first,* she decided, *to my cousin's house. He'll hide us until I can find a way to take Pancho away from here.*

She didn't have to wonder what would happen if she were caught. Julian Haynes, the *patrón,* hanged horse thieves and rustlers. He'd never shown mercy, but at least they died quickly. She wouldn't be that lucky if he found her, not after what had happened to the man who'd been his closest companion for thirty years. He would never give her a chance to explain, she knew that.

Macha's breath caught in her throat. She began to run.

Four

TOM ENGLISH rode into Frisco on the western side of the New Mexico territory early the next Saturday afternoon. The weak sun made an effort to warm the washed-out blue day, and as he entered the town he unbuttoned his coat. He felt a mild breeze on his face as Deuce trotted on hard ground past scattered small shacks with dark flecks of smoke coming from their chimneys.

The wind bore the rattling sound of horses' hooves on the main street, and Tom saw five cowboys race into town, leaning into a careening turn, hatbrims blown flat. The horses, wildly excited, showed the whites of their eyes as they clattered by not fifty feet in front of him with their manes and tails tossing. The men reined their mounts to sliding stops in front of a large saloon, flapping their arms, showing off. They dismounted in clouds of dust, and in that instant their grace ended. Bowlegged, two of them limping, they moved about stiff-legged. After looping their reins over the long hitching rail, the loud-voiced men entered the saloon.

Some twenty to thirty horses stood side by side, tails whipping automatically, heads lowered, some with a hind foot hung limply—a hoof barely touching the ground—as they rested in front of the weather-beaten frame bar that had a simple sign on it that read *Milligen's*. A dry goods store with a square false front lay just down from it, connected by a raised board sidewalk. Beyond it sat a hardware sign with a display of coiled ropes in its front window.

Tom examined the little town apprehensively, not knowing what to expect after the warnings he'd received from Joe Ross, the deputy sheriff from Socorro he'd met at the hotel in Tascosa. He held the reins in his left hand and involuntarily his right hand moved back, clearing his long coat away so as to free the butt of his six-shooter.

It looked like many other cowtowns that he'd seen. So far he hadn't noticed anything out of the ordinary. He turned his head and across some four hundred yards of sand and brush and cactus, he saw a solitary shack of the kind built with upright stakes driven into the ground, a *jacal*. Four posts stood in front of it which supported the flat roof that shedded out over the uneven rectangle of the door. Behind it lay a desert flatness with the low blue shape of a long hill in the distance off to the right.

Tom nudged the rowels of his spurs into Deuce's dusty sides and moved down the broad sandy trail that served as the town's main street. He saw on his left a little building with one office on the corner that said *Justice of the Peace*. The space beside it seemed to be vacant, and beyond it lay a small saddle shop. Slapping his reins, he moved into a brisk trot as he passed the saloon, and angled out through this irregular "town square" past a long-unused flagpole, riding toward three people he saw a few hundred yards away. They stood beside a small adobe house with a clay oven which had white smoke coming from a flue in its top.

When he saw the corn shucks and smelled the tamales, a smile crossed his lips. He tied Deuce to a leafless ragged cottonwood tree and walked around the house, putting both hands on his lower back. "I've been on the trail from Tascosa in the Texas Panhandle for a little more than five days," he said to himself, "but I feel like I've been horseback a month. Must be getting old."

An elderly Mexican with strands of white hair under a crumpled greasy sombrero looked up at his approach. A rough gray stubble covered his infrequently shaven cheeks. He wore a faded blue denim jacket with a homemade quilted lining, and his loose pants, held up by a short piece of cotton rope tied around his waist, dragged the ground beside his sandaled feet. Beyond him two adolescent Mexicans backed away. A dog that looked like a skeleton covered with clinging hide crouched next to the house, watchful for any dropped scrap.

The old Mexican said in slurred Spanish, "My name is Rafael Hernández and I've been selling tamales at this very place for forty years, except when I left during the drought and the other time when I almost died." Without pausing after giving this background information, he proceeded to the matter of business. "The price has gone up. Twenty cents a dozen."

"Sounds fair to me," Tom replied. He bought a dozen spicy tamales, each wrapped in a corn shuck. The Mexican cook wrapped his purchase in a newspaper that was soon stained dark with the shiny yellow oil of the tamales. Tom picked up the crumpled warm bundle and carried it a few yards off to one side where he sat on a slab of limestone that lay near the adobe back wall of the house. A youngster brought him a tin cup with cold water in it, and Tom thanked him courteously.

He shared his food with the two boys and the eager dog. After he had eaten he spoke in Spanish to the cook, expressing his appreciation for the fine meal. Then he said, "I'm on my way to the J. B. Slaughter ranch and would appreciate your advice on how to find the place."

The old man answered awkwardly, apparently deciding to put on display his mastery of English. "You crazy to get mix up with them people."

Tom smiled. "I don't intend to get mixed up with any of 'em; I've just got some cow business to talk."

"Bunch of Texans work out there. Shoot up the town," the old man grumbled. He excused himself for a moment and went into the house, returning with a clear bottle and two dusty glasses.

The white-haired man said, "It would be an honor if you would join me." He waited, looking hesitantly at Tom. When he saw him nod, he sloshed tequila into the two glasses.

The old man spoke again in Spanish. "About this time of day I get thirsty. Not safe in the saloon for Mexicans, so I drink here alone. Usually alone."

Surprised at the offer, Tom took the proffered glass and swallowed the cloudy liquor, feeling it burn its way down his throat to his stomach. After breathing out hard he said, "I appreciate your hospitality. Thank you, Señor Hernández."

"Call me Rafa," the old man said. He took his own drink in his hand and sat on a rickety stool. He looked sharply at Tom. "You from Texas?"

Sensing hostility, Tom admitted that he was, almost apologizing.

Rafa listened stolidly, but after another drink, he began to smile. He said, "I've been making tamales for forty years; selling them out here in the yard. In all that time you're the first gringo to sit down and eat a

meal with me. Not only that, you're the only one who has joined me
for a drink of tequila."

Uncomfortably, Tom said, "I'm surprised to hear that." Then he
praised the tamales and saw the old man's face flush with pleasure at
the compliments. Tom thought, *They* are *good tamales, as good as I've
eaten.*

"The Slaughter ranch," Rafa said, "lies to the west on the main trail.
You can ride there in around two or three hours. But men who work
there told one of my nephews that the big boss left yesterday for
Arizona and won't be back for a while. You planning to see him?"

"Yes."

"Well, amigo, you'll just have to wait a few days."

"They got a hotel in town?"

The eyes of Rafa Hernández crinkled in amusement and his laugh
ended in a wheezing cough. After catching his breath, he said, "The
only hotel you'll find in Frisco is my nephew Francisco's livery stable.
He rents out a few rooms there that he added to the back of the
stables. It's not really like a hotel—just four walls, a dirt floor and a
roof. No heat."

"Guess that'll have to do," Tom said. "It's bound to be warmer than
the mountainside where I spent last night." He accepted another short
drink of tequila from the cook, and asked, "Did you say your nephew
owns it?"

Rafa chuckled dryly. "I am related to nearly everyone in the town of
Frisco. Francisco's more like a son than a nephew—he and his family
live in that house next to mine," he said, wagging his head toward the
adobe house beyond his.

Rafa stood up and stared at the big saloon on the other side of the
square. More horsemen could be seen riding toward it, urging their
horses forward.

He said, uneasily, "I've got to close soon. On Saturdays they come,
almost all of them. Soon the trouble will begin."

Tom's eyes narrowed. He looked at the old man, wondering what he
meant.

Tom made arrangements at the livery stable with Francisco
Naranjo, the nephew of Rafa Hernández, to take care of Deuce and
rented a room for himself. He unsaddled his horse, took a rusted curry
comb which hung from a nail on the splintered wall, and scraped

dried lather from Deuce's back. When he turned him into the pen out back, Tom watched Deuce go through his end-of-the-day ritual: he walked deliberately in the corral, lay down in powdery dust, and rolled over on his back. The most graceful horse always looks awkward doing this, Tom observed. Deuce raised himself to his front hooves after the dust bath, and his powerful hindquarters rippled as he surged to a standing position. Then he ambled to a rack where slanted pine boards held a bale of hay that had been broken up for him.

Tom leaned down and picked up his saddle with his right hand and hauled it toward the tiny room he'd rented. He tilted sideways from the effort, for the forty-pound saddle also had the added weight of his bedroll and saddlebags. The girth and stirrups dragged along the ground and the dangling buckles made jingling silvery sounds. He went back for his bridle, saddle blanket, and Winchester rifle in its saddle scabbard which he'd pulled loose earlier. After storing his belongings, he left the stables and walked outside into the fading light of the short winter day.

Rafa Hernández had told him something about the town of Frisco, how it huddled in three irregular areas. The portion of town he'd first seen was called the Upper Plaza. That took in the big saloon he'd seen as well as most of the town's buildings. The next area down the slope was the Middle Plaza. This was merely another sparse collection of shacks and one sturdy frame house with various pens and chutes out behind it.

Facing this house from across the trail rested an old Catholic church built of stone with some raw cedar shingles where the roof had been patched. The church had a neat rectangular courtyard before it with neat walkways of white gravel. Behind it lay a simple cemetery.

This was a quiet Mexican town in the middle of ranching country, Tom thought, *a peaceful place. But now that's changing.* He knew the local people blamed the *Americanos* for this and he supposed they were right.

Following the slant of the land, Tom walked past the Middle Plaza down a long grade which ran toward a rocky creek with about a foot of water splashing through it. The shanty town near the river was what Rafa Hernández had described as the Lower Plaza. Some women hauled water in earthen jugs from the creek, and on large sharp rocks he could see clothing that had been washed and left out to dry.

At that moment he heard a crackling noise, like fire through pine trees but with occasionally a loud booming sound. Tom turned from the river and retraced his footsteps through the three distinct parts of the unusual little village. The closer he came to the Upper Plaza, the more noise he heard.

As he stopped to catch his breath at the church, he saw men on horseback riding in circles, firing their pistols at chickens and dogs. One horse, not accustomed to the explosions, began to buck and a rider cartwheeled off him into some gray bushes.

Tom walked past the church until he came to the livery stable. From this vantage point he could see that more than fifty horses now stood in a very long line before the saloon, and seven or eight men on horseback swirled around several hundred yards away. The crashes from the riders' six-guns echoed in the late afternoon. One cowboy leaned back in his saddle and discharged a shotgun into the wall of a wretched little shack. At the thunderous explosion all the nearby horses shied away, and Tom saw an obviously terrified woman with a small child in her arms run from the dwelling. The riders, finding a new game, rode in circles around her, waving their arms and whooping as if they were driving cattle.

Tom walked rapidly across the road and stepped up on the raised board sidewalk. He strode down it and entered the saloon.

He moved to one side of the large room, waiting for his eyes to get accustomed to the shadows. The lamps had been lit although it wasn't yet night. Looking down at his feet, he saw any number of old playing cards littering the floor. Layers of tobacco smoke hung just over the heads of the carousing cowboys. Men sat at tables throughout the room, drinking, waving their arms, calling to friends. Some of them played poker, but most were drinking steadily. Other cowboys stood at the bar in a ragged line, laughing and watching a tall angular man with a prominent chin, high cheekbones, and almost oriental-looking eyes who held a terrified Mexican boy by the scruff of his neck.

Tom edged his way to the end of the bar and ordered a drink. He heard a cowboy next to him chuckle and say, "McCarty's goin' to give us another show."

The tall man spoke. He had a deep, hollow-sounding voice, one that reverberated as he said, "I caught this kid out back—sneaking around —up to no good. What do you think we ought to do with him?"

"Teach him a thing or two, Mac," one man replied.

The cowboys who sat slouched at the tables and those who stood at the bar looked at the tall bony man with the dark mustache, willing to be entertained.

"You're right, we need to give him a lesson," McCarty agreed. "Let's have some music," he called out, his voice resonating from the rafters.

An older cowboy pulled a French harp from his shirt pocket, coaxed a few whining, mournful notes from it, but after these were greeted by a chorus of complaints, he began to bob his head as he struck up a livelier tune. Several men began to clap their hands in time with the music, encouraging him.

McCarty said, "Now, I'm goin' to git this here boy to dance for us. I *guess* this is a boy, but he's got long hair, maybe I got a girl here. I'm goin' to have to pull off his pants to find out."

"I'll help ye," a man said, lurching to his feet from a nearby table. He stood up ponderously and his large stomach sagged over his belt.

Tom felt his face freeze into a mask as a jolt of rage ran through him.

Roaring with laughter, the crowd surged forward to watch the fun. Over their heads the boy's thin screams wavered. Tom struggled through the packed men who elbowed for space. Looking past them, he saw the two men strip the Mexican boy—who sank down on his haunches, terrified, tears running down his face. Tom paused a second, looking at him. He couldn't have been more than thirteen.

McCarty's eyes gleamed and his thin lips pulled back in a wolfish grin. He rumbled, "I said *music.* This boy's goin' to do a dance for us." He pulled his six-gun and fired into the floor at the boy's bare feet. The sound of the detonation echoed sharply in the room, silencing the hum of conversations.

The naked boy jumped upright and looked down. Splinters from the torn floor had hit him, and a small trickle of blood ran down the calf of one leg. He held his hands instinctively down low in front of himself as he looked dumbly at his tormentor.

Tom shouldered past the jeering men who gathered about this scene. He swept the boy's clothing from the floor, pitched them to him, and said softly, "Get dressed." Then he turned toward the big man who loomed a full head taller than him.

McCarty, his pistol dangling menacingly from his hand, asked, "Just who the hell do you think you are, mister? We got fifty or sixty men here—you thinkin' about roustin' all of us?"

"No, just you."

The six-gun appeared as if by magic. All conversation and movement stopped as time stood still. The men, dumbfounded, fixed their
eyes upon it.

McCarty's eyes widened as he looked into the barrel of a Colt .45.
Those around him shrank back. The blue steel muzzle pointed for an
instant at McCarty's face and then whipped down, slamming against
his wrist, knocking McCarty's pistol flying. It clattered across the floor
as it dropped from nerveless fingers.

The panic-stricken boy took advantage of the confusion to grab his
clothes and sprint for safety. Several men tried to seize him as he ran
by, but he squirmed from their grasp and made it out the door.

Strong arms pinned Tom from behind. An arm went around his
neck, two men twisted his hands back, and one of them pulled his six-
gun from him.

Excitement exploded in the room. Voices filled it to overflowing.
The tall man, McCarty, eyes blazing, roared, "Quiet!" His bellow rumbled through the cavernous saloon. *"Quiet!"* he boomed out once
more.

In the silence that fell, McCarty stood, face white from pain. He
massaged his wrist as he glared at Tom. He said, "Ever'one just sit
down while I decide what ought to be done."

The cowboys holding Tom pulled him into a chair and held him
with strong, work-hardened hands. One man made a quick trip outside and returned holding a coiled rope in his hands. He whipped the
hard-woven fibers around Tom's body and feet, tying him to the chair.
Even after he'd been bound so tightly he couldn't move, the half-
drunk cowboy kept working, staggering around the chair, wrapping
Tom up like a mummy until at last he ran out of rope.

The tall, angular man stood high above his prisoner. Looking down
at Tom, he said, "We was goin' to teach that kid a lesson, but it seems
to me that this stranger needs to learn some manners first."

The laughter that had filled the room before was absent.

"Don't kill him, Mac. We're here to have a good time," one man said
nervously. Another echoed his concern. "That's right. Let's have some
fun with him—but nothin' serious. Or else there could be hell to pay
when Mr. Slaughter gets back from Arizona."

"I think you're right, boys. Take him outside while we still have a
little light and, like you say, let's have some fun."

The men grabbed their bottles and staggered from their tables, anxious not to miss the excitement.

Francisco Naranjo usually protected himself from the coldest days by sticking his head through a slit in a heavy Navajo blanket which he wore like an oversized serape. It kept the wind from biting. He wore a crumpled old sombrero on his head. The gringos had stopped riding drunkenly about the town, shooting at anything that moved, and he decided that it would be safe to cross the square and go to his home. But just as he began to leave his livery stable for the day he paused—hearing a threatening sound, a humming noise. It reminded him of the time he'd thrown a rock at a tree full of bees. A wild humming had started and then a fierce black cloud had surged out—and Francisco'd had to throw himself headlong into the shallow creek to escape their attack.

Instinctively he pulled back into the shadows of the livery stable, shrinking behind a corner and peeking around it. A large group of the *Tejanos* boiled out of the saloon, waving their arms, laughing, shouting.

"Mother of God," Francisco said emphatically even though he stood alone in the coldness, "what is happening?"

He saw two men dragging something—a chair—a chair with a man tied in it with a long rope. Wrapped up as tightly as if he were in a cocoon. No way at all for him to get loose. Now what? Francisco wondered.

A tall individual, the one with the big jaw he'd seen before, un-hitched his bay gelding from the rail and led him away from the other horses. He mounted, settled himself, then undid his rope. He pitched his loop down over the tied-up victim in the chair. A man on foot worked with the loop, made sure it was secure, and yanked on it. Meanwhile, the rider tied the end of the rope to his saddle horn and began to walk his horse away.

All this time, the cowboys kept up their ceaseless whooping. One of them pulled off his hat and with a cry, slapped it against the rear end of the big bay. The horse reared up a little and then bucked forward. The rope snapped as the rider moved off, cracking the chair off its feet. Then the chair hit and rolled and scraped and bounced wildly, pulled behind through clouds of dust and sand, flying now through air, plowing through cactus, bounding along, revolving, spinning.

Horrified, Francisco ran from the shadows. "You're killing him," he
screamed.

The rider leaned forward, quirting his horse with his reins. Two
hundred yards from the saloon, he angled left of the *jacal,* making a
big circle. His grotesque bundle—some thirty feet behind his bounding horse—scraped and banged on the hard ground. His horse
plunged into a dry arroyo and up the other side, and the dark burden
at the end of the rope smashed through dry brush, over rocks. Then
something happened. The loop slid off and the man tied so tightly in
the chair came loose. The chair had lost its form, broken now in
pieces, and from it rolled a sodden form.

Francisco watched the now silent men run toward it.

From across the square he saw them form into a crescent, leaning
over, looking down. Then they walked thoughtfully away, heading
back to Milligen's Saloon.

Francisco looked out over the mesa in the distance. He saw a new
moon in the darkening sky.

He felt his heart hammering in his chest. Francisco pulled the stiff,
heavy blanket around him as he hurried across the rocky ground toward his home. He saw movement in the doorway: his wife and children huddled there with yellow lamplight behind them. The slender
figure of his cousin Macha came from the lean-to out back where she
and her boy had been hiding. She walked out to meet him, both of
them walking fearfully toward the strange huddled shape with the
loose rope still around it.

Francisco had been brought up to pray. It came to him as naturally
as breathing. Automatically he said, "Forgive them, Father." But a
tremor ran through him as he thought: *I cannot.*

Five

FRANCISCO NARANJO sat slumped forward in the cowhide chair near the welcome heat of the fireplace. His wife and two children slept in the other room along with his cousin's child. In a corner not far from the fire, the gringo lay on his back without moving. Macha and Francisco had carried the unconscious man into the living room of the adobe house after pulling the wiry rope from around him. They had put some hay on the dirt floor and over this had made a thin pallet out of blankets.

Next to the living room was the kitchen, a narrow room with barely enough space for storage cupboards and a clay oven used for baking. Macha and her young son had been spending the nights there. A door led from the kitchen to the bedroom shared by Francisco and his wife Marta and their two small children. Smooth plaster with a fresh coat of whitewash covered all of the interior surfaces of the simple, thick-walled structure. The dirt floors were packed hard and immaculately swept. A hard-woven Indian rug with bright jagged stripes of red and blue, the house's only decoration, hung on the wall across from the smoking flame-filled fireplace.

Macha knelt beside the stranger's limp form with a bucket of water she'd heated over the fire. Patiently she dipped a rag in it and cleaned grit and blood from the abrasions on the gringo's arms and legs. Occasionally she would pause and with her fingernails patiently remove tiny cactus spines which had embedded themselves in her patient's flesh. Then, taking her rag once more, she washed caked blood from his face and touched the great lump on his forehead which was already turning blue.

She cut his shirt with a sharp kitchen knife and pulled its tatters away, noting an angry rope burn across his chest and upper arms. She examined him in the wavering light from the fire, touching his head carefully, wondering if his skull might be cracked. On a pine table beside her a long white candle burned dimly. She reached for it and held it over the man's face. He looked as if he were a figure carved from stone. She leaned close beside him, her hair hanging down on his face as she satisfied herself that he was breathing. Replacing the candle on the table, she began to wash more cuts.

Rafa Hernández entered the house, and the wind whipped dust and sand against the door as he forced it shut. The old man shuffled slowly through the room, nodded to his nephew, Francisco, and said, "Those animals are still drinking at the saloon."

"*Malcriados,*" Francisco snarled.

Rafa turned to Macha. "Has he opened his eyes?"

"No—he's hardly breathing. I think he may be dying."

Francisco, Rafa, and Macha spoke to one another in soft Spanish phrases, discussing the gringo. They felt, all of a sudden, responsible for him.

Rafa sank upon one knee, grunting from the effort. He placed both hands on the man's head and moved it back and forth experimentally. Then he rolled him heavily to one side and pressed his fingers along the spinal column. Apparently satisfied, he released his hold and allowed the gringo's weight to roll him over as he'd been. "I don't think his neck or his back are broken. They had him tied in a chair and that's what saved him. The chair protected his back, and when the wood broke, the rope that was pulling him came loose. That place on his head looks bad. Nothing we can do about it."

He continued checking, touching Tom's inert form with expert hands. His face darkened and he swore softly as his fingers probed along the body's side. "Got some broken ribs." Rafa moved the unconscious man's arms and legs. He noticed something wrong with the right arm and put it carefully by his side. "This arm's hurt—or maybe it's the shoulder. Something's wrong. The legs are bruised and cut, but I don't think either one is broken."

"This has got to stop," Francisco Naranjo said in an abrupt angry tone to his uncle. "Those cowboys from the Slaughter ranch and the other Texans have ruined our town. Did you see them shooting their guns everywhere? One of them even fired a shotgun into María Alpizar's house!"

"I saw," Rafa answered. "And I watched them circling around her on their big horses, scaring her to death when she ran with her children, trying to get away from them."

Francisco's dark eyes glowed with anger. "For a long time we told ourselves that the cowboys acted this way because of high spirits. But they've gone beyond having a good time. You can't tell me that they'd behave like this around their own people. They're treating Mexicans the way they would coyotes—as if we weren't human. Every weekend it's worse."

Rafa Hernández knitted his white eyebrows in a brooding scowl. "It is a great disgrace," he said at last.

"Tomorrow I'm going to Socorro," the younger man said. "We've got to get help."

"Who will come? We've sent word to the sheriff, but there's no answer."

"The sheriff is a white man; we can't expect anything from him. I've got to find some Mexicans to join us. Two weeks ago, when Elfego came to Frisco, we talked about it. His father was town marshal in Belén once, and Elfego's always been interested in the law. He's my best friend, he'll help."

"Elfego Baca is a boy—only nineteen years old," old Rafa Hernández said roughly. But then he changed his tone, trying to reason with his nephew. "Besides, Slaughter has over eighty men. They're well mounted, all of them have guns. What can you do to fight them? How many Mexicans will come from Socorro to help us? Five? Ten? It's hopeless."

"We have to do *something*," Francisco insisted furiously. He rose to his feet and paced back and forth. Then he said, "I'll leave before dawn tomorrow."

"When you get there," Rafa Hernández said, "tell them to get a doctor here quick to see this man."

"Uncle, he's just another gringo."

"Have you forgotten that the *Tejanos* punished him because he defended one of our people? Young Chico Caldera has not forgotten. One of those vaqueros was shooting at his feet!"

Old Rafa breathed heavily, his face showing his indignation. "Besides, he ate tamales with me at my house, and we shared a drink of tequila. No other gringo has done that. And we talked. He's a stranger, has some business with Slaughter himself, but he's not like the others. He's different."

"I suppose that's true," Francisco answered. "They treated him the way they might one of us." His voice sank as he recalled what had happened. "I've heard of those cowboys dragging a man to death. Maybe that's what they intended to do." Disgust filled his face as he added, "It was a terrible sight." He seemed to reach a decision. "I'll send a doctor from Socorro."

At first he felt only a terrible nausea which made him curl up on the hard blanket, wracked by involuntary dry heaving. A cool hand supported his forehead and when he fell back he looked up at a blur above him. Someone bathed his fever, gently swabbing the dry hotness of his face with a cool moist rag.

Hours passed. Tom opened his eyes and gradually a woman's form above him came into focus. The soft light of a candle made a pale halo hover faintly behind her head; he couldn't make out her features.

"Thank you," he managed to say.

"You're conscious again. Maybe this time you can stay awake."

"Where am I?"

"This is the house of my cousin, Francisco Naranjo. We brought you here two days ago, and Francisco has ridden to Socorro for a doctor."

She spoke to him in heavily accented but good English. He felt her hands on his face again.

"How do you feel?"

He couldn't answer.

He felt a pressure at his lips, and then the moisture, the coolness of water in a glass.

She held this for him. "Can you drink?" She supported his neck with her other hand, helping him as he took a few sips and then closed his eyes.

"Do you remember what happened?"

"No, nothing."

"What's your name?"

"My head . . ." he said weakly.

"That's all right," she said. "Don't try to talk yet."

Later Tom realized he must have been dozing, for when he opened his eyes he saw that the tall candle he'd seen earlier behind the woman was guttering in its holder. He lay very still, conscious of the woman's eyes upon his. Although the dark of night clung to the windows, a rooster crowed in the distance from the direction of the Middle Plaza. She lit another candle, smoothed her hair back, then rose and went to the fireplace. She put a short log in it and stirred the bright orange coals. Then she poured water into a coffee pot and hung it from an iron hook above the smoldering fire.

"When the water boils, I'll put in some coffee."

He didn't answer.

"Does your head hurt?"

"Yes."

"Marta, Francisco's wife, has been keeping the children quiet. They're asleep in the other room. I'll wait until they wake up, and then I'll cook breakfast for you. You have to eat something."

He took a deep breath and felt a stabbing pain in his side. Instinctively he tried to reach it with his right hand, but this caused an equally sharp clawing in his shoulder.

"Don't try to move," she said. "Rafa checked you very carefully the first night, and then again last evening. Rafa's very old—he must be sixty, maybe more—and he knows about these things. He says you have some broken ribs, and at first he thought your arm was broken too, but now he thinks it could be something wrong with your shoulder."

"Anything else?"

"That's all he found except, of course, for the place on your head. He worked with you yesterday, when you first came to. You talked to him a little—don't you remember?"

"No, I don't. The last thing I recall was being in the saloon when all the men caught my arms."

"We heard what happened. They were tormenting the boy and you tried to make them stop."

"How long did you say I'd been here?"

"This is almost Tuesday morning, and we brought you here Saturday night."

They could hear sounds from the other room, and in a moment several small faces appeared at the door, peering at him curiously. A little boy of five ran into the room and came to the woman sitting with him.

"This is my son, Pancho," she said. "And my name is Macha Cordero." She made a vague gesture and for some reason felt the need to add, "Cordero is my mother's name." She lowered her eyes, then said, "She and Francisco's mother were sisters."

"So you're related to Rafa Hernández too."

She laughed. "Almost everyone in Frisco is related to Rafael Hernández."

Suddenly Tom stiffened. He put his left hand at his waist, then looked up. "I was wearing a gunbelt."

"It's on that peg in the kitchen. There wasn't a gun in it."

Tom felt his pulse pound in his ears. He wet his lips and said, "I've had that gun since I was seventeen. It means a lot to me. And besides, I don't like being unarmed." He tried to smile, but his headache had come back.

"I don't know what we can do, but maybe Rafa can ask around. Or I might try."

"I can't stand feeling helpless," he muttered, turning to the wall. "Damn! Excuse the language."

Macha laughed softly. "You are the first gringo who has ever said he was sorry to me about anything."

Tom looked at the exceptionally pretty young woman beside him, noticing her appearance for the first time. She wore a long dress, had a well-proportioned body, and luminous dark eyes. He said, "I have a funny feeling, like little pinpricks at the back of my neck. In the past this has served as a warning. I know that probably sounds crazy to you, but I've learned to pay attention to it."

"It doesn't sound crazy to me," Macha said. The Jicarilla Indians who lived on the ranch where she'd spent all of her life had told her much stranger stories.

He tried to sit up but a pain from his ribs took his breath away. "Anyway, I've got these feelings of danger—and I know I'll need that gun."

"We'll try to help you," Macha said.

"Well, you're a mighty pretty little thing," the bartender said, looking at the slender Mexican girl with the great dark eyes.

"My uncle said you have the gun they took from that cowboy Saturday night."

"What on earth is all the interest in that Colt? The old-timer who sells tamales was in here tryin' to talk me out of it just this morning. I bought that gun for ten dollars from the man who picked it up off the floor. Looks to be in good condition, though far from new."

"Will you sell it to me?"

"Where would a girl like you git any money? What do you want with a gun in the first place? Besides that, I don't know that it's a good idea to sell it to a Meskin."

"Don't worry, I'm not going to rob you." She laughed, showing the whiteness of her even teeth. "It's just that my uncle told me that he thinks that's a lucky gun."

The bartender looked incredulously at her, thinking at first that she must be teasing him. Then he snorted. "Lucky? Guess you don't know what happened to the man that owned it. I suppose he's off dead in an arroya somewhere. The coyotes probably ate what's left of him."

The bartender wore a filthy derby on his head and a soiled apron around his ample waist. He had long sideburns and a full mustache that drooped past his chin on either side. He watched with interest as the girl dropped the blanket which she had over her shoulders. Her long dress had the top four buttons open, giving a hint of the firmness of her breasts. His eyes fixed on them. Stealthily he looked around, satisfying himself that no one else was in Milligen's Saloon.

"My uncle gave me these for my birthday," she said, holding out two twenty-dollar gold pieces. "There's nothing to spend money on in Frisco, so I thought I'd offer them to you for the lucky gun. What do you say?"

"Forty dollars for a used gun? Well, I'll admit that's tempting, but . . ."

He began to cough and had to bend over until the fit passed. Then he picked up a mug of beer and drank from it. Speaking in a crafty manner, he said, "Now, if I thought that you and I could get to know each other better I might just sacrifice and sell this Colt to you."

Macha stood before him, her level gaze upon his flushed face. Gradually her smooth lips parted into an inviting smile. "Not too many good-looking men in this town. What's your name?"

"Buster," the bartender said feverishly. "The name is Buster."

He fumbled beneath the bar and brought out a blue steel Colt .45 with a wooden grip made smooth by use. With a wide, toothy grin beneath his great bush of a mustache, he shoved it to her in exchange for the two gold coins.

Macha picked it up and put it in a cloth bag hanging from her shoulder. Then she wrapped the blanket about her, preparing to leave.

Perhaps to show that he was no fool, the bartender bit each coin, squinching up his face, testing them. Then he nodded sagely. "Don't rush, darlin'—what's your name?"

"Lucky," Macha said. "Call me Lucky."

The bartender burst out laughing as she moved toward the door. "Sounds like as good a name as any," he called after her. "There'll be no business on a weekday night, so I'll be closin' early. Why not come by around ten tonight and we can get acquainted?" He leaned forward expectantly, but she didn't look behind her as she left the saloon.

Feelings of excitement swept through Macha as she burst into her cousin's house. She hurried to the pallet where the gringo lay and she sat on the dirt floor beside him. "Look what I've got!" she said, taking the revolver from the cloth bag which hung from her shoulder.

Tom's eyes showed his relief even before he spoke. "I can't thank you enough," he said in a weak voice.

"Let me tell you all about it," Macha began. With a rush the words poured out. She played her part and then, imitating the bartender, played his. With pleased laughter she ended, "And so I walked out with your gun."

She felt his forehead. "I think the fever has come back." Rising abruptly, she found a cotton rag and moistened it in a large earthen jar filled with water from the well out back. She placed the rag on his head.

"Close your eyes and be still," she said as her patient struggled to sit up. "These things take time. The doctor from Socorro should be here soon—he'll have medicine to make you feel better." Searching for something to encourage him, she said, "That swelling on your head has gone down. The bruise has turned dark purple—but these things go away. You're really lucky—those people could have killed you."

He didn't speak.

"There's a special reason that this was an adventure for me. I've only been here a few times, so I'm a stranger here just like you are." She looked down at him. "I've lived all my life on the ranch once owned by the Estévez family. The old *patrón* married the daughter of Joaquín Estévez years ago." She fell silent after mentioning her father in this indirect way. Then, her voice hardening, she said, "His son, the new *patrón,* will be hunting for me." She didn't touch on the strange relationship that existed between them.

"I'm hiding," she said. "My cousin Francisco is helping me get away. He has written to a friend who has a good job on a place called Ghost Ranch on the Chama River northwest of Santa Fe. It's near a little town called Abiqui. Francisco wrote that he hoped his friend might make room for me and my son—for we are running away. Francisco says when he makes sure his friend is still there—and that he can take me in—then he'll help me get a horse and a buggy so I can travel that far with my little boy."

She saw the stranger looking at her, listening with interest to every word she spoke. This flattered her. He had, she saw, the strangest-looking eyes she'd ever seen. The color, she thought, of the sky at midday, a shining pale blue. "Since I arrived, I've been in hiding and have stayed inside almost all the time. Occasionally I go around to the lean-to behind the house along with Pancho, trying to get out of Francisco's house so he and Marta and their kids can have some time together. I feel in the way sometimes. Can you understand that? But I haven't really left the house. So I had the sense today of going on a great adventure. I'd never been near that saloon before—never dreamed of actually walking into it."

"That took nerve," the gringo said, a faint smile on his face.

"It *did,"* Macha agreed, delighted with herself.

"Can you tell me why the man you call the *patrón* is hunting you?"

"It's an ugly story." She hesitated, then went on. "I heard someone in my room late at night—he caught my hair, pulled at me—and I had a knife." Her voice fell. "I killed him. An old friend of the *patrón,* and he won't be satisfied until he makes me pay for that."

"Who is this *patrón?"*

"A gringo," she said, her voice trembling. "Or, really, a half-gringo; his mother was an Estévez, his father was named Haynes."

The white man on the pallet looked startled. He stared at her with his strange eyes. "Is it possible that the man after you is Julian Haynes?"

She looked perplexed as she slowly nodded. "How did you know his name?"

Tom English allowed his head to drop to the pallet, but his eyes never left her face.

"I thought Julian Haynes was in El Paso."

"Not now. He's at his ranch—what's left of it—about fourteen miles from here."

At last he spoke: "You and I have something in common, Macha."

"What is that?"

"We have the same enemy."

"You're in no condition to fight anyone now, especially not someone like Julian Haynes."

Tom English closed his eyes. "Leave the gun by my side," he said.

When she put it by him, his fingers closed around it.

Six

EARLY THURSDAY MORNING Macha and Francisco's wife Marta helped Tom prop up on some pillows. The headache had left him, and with their help he could walk, but he was terribly dizzy and at times he suffered from a terrible ringing in his ears. Tom's right shoulder only hurt if he moved his arm, so Macha had put this in a sturdy sling she'd made out of a torn denim skirt of Marta's.

He leaned back on clean pillows as the first rays of sunrise came through the window upon him. Macha kneeled by his pallet, efficiently bathing him with a coarse rag which she dipped into the bucket beside her. Then she toweled him off with dry cloths.

"You're a good nurse."

"I had lots of practice taking care of the old *patrón* before he died."

She pulled the blanket down to Tom's waist and looked at the scars on his arms and body. Earlier, when she cleaned his back she'd noticed the clear signs of gunshot wounds as well as a terrible series of long discolored welts crisscrossing it.

"I never saw anyone as scarred as you." Her fingers touched ridges on his arms, slipped as light as a feather over red and bluish puckered signs of old punctures on his right arm and on his chest and shoulder. *"Madre de Dios,"* she breathed out. "These are horrible. How could anyone live with such wounds?"

"Well," Tom said, feeling decidedly uncomfortable at this close scrutiny, "those are just brands that folks put on me at different times." He grinned at her.

"How can you joke about such things?" Her full lips tightened and she frowned at him. "What kind of life have you led?" she asked.

"When I asked you this yesterday you told me your name, as if that explained everything. But I never heard of you."

"I sure wish no one else had either."

The front door opened and Francisco Naranjo entered his home followed by a young man. Marta and the children swarmed from the back of the house to greet Francisco while the person with him smiled at the cries of pleasure.

Flurries of Spanish with occasional English words mixed in went back and forth, all of them speaking at once.

Francisco said, "Macha, I want you to meet Elfego Baca, my best friend. He rode with me from Socorro. We got in last night after midnight and stayed at the livery stables. I didn't want to wake everybody up."

While his wife wailed her protests, he grinned and they argued, then he hugged her and the children.

"You stayed at the *livery stable* instead of coming home to your own bed? I knew when you opened that business a few years ago that it might give you too many excuses to stay away from home." Marta, a plump, round-faced woman, pushed playfully at her husband, obviously thrilled to see him again. "Are you sure that you didn't have some sweetheart with you?"

"I swear it," Francisco said, laughing along with the others.

Marta and Macha spoke for a few minutes to the new arrivals, then both of them hurried to the kitchen to prepare tortillas and frijoles for a welcome breakfast.

Tom had not been introduced to the young Mexican with Francisco. The wiry boy, around eighteen or nineteen years old, had spurs on his boots. When he unbuttoned a bulky jacket it revealed a six-gun holstered on his right hip. He had unblinking steady black eyes and a big nose above the wispy beginnings of a mustache. He held his unusually large hands hooked in his gunbelt while he observed the domestic scene before him.

Francisco came over to the pallet where Tom lay. "I tried to get the doctor to come with me from Socorro, but he refused—said he wasn't about to get in the middle of some trouble between Mexicans and whites. I told him the man who was hurt was white, but he said our conversation was over and closed the door in my face."

Francisco pulled up a chair near Tom and sat down. "You look a lot

better than you did early Sunday morning when I left. We thought you
were about to die."

Macha said, "Rafa helped us look after him. He's been conscious a
couple of days now and seems better, but I think a doctor should see
him."

Francisco shrugged. "This man looks pretty tough to me."

Old Rafa opened the door and shuffled in, the frayed cuffs of his
pants still dragging on the ground about his sandals. He greeted his
nephew with an enthusiastic embrace and then put his arm about
Elfego Baca's shoulders. "So you're the only one with the nerve to
come help us, eh? Well, we got to have more than you. The best thing
for everyone will be to lie low and wait for this trouble to pass."

Later, after breakfast, Francisco talked of his trip. He and Elfego
had begun their journey on the banks of the meandering Rio Grande
River where Socorro lay. They rode their horses uphill, following the
rocky trail through the hills on the way to Magdalena. They stopped
for a noon meal on the first day there, then filled their canteens and
rode across the dry plains of San Augustine until after nightfall, finally
finding a place to camp near Horse Mountain. On Wednesday they
broke camp early, expecting to arrive in Frisco that afternoon with no
trouble, but Francisco's horse pulled up lame, favoring his right fore-
foot, so he had to lead the limping mount the last ten miles or so.

Francisco said, "We had reached the headwaters of the Tularosa
River, where the river's clear and only five or six feet wide. All we had
to do was follow the creek downstream to Frisco, and I was in a hurry.
So I told Elfego that we'd make better time riding double on his horse.
But God, what a mean little animal that mustang turned out to be.

"His name is Calvo because he's got a big white blaze on his face
that goes right up on top of his head. Makes him look like a baldy.
Elfego told me that Calvo wouldn't carry double, but I said, 'Well, he'll
just have to.' So while Elfego was complaining and muttering that this
wasn't going to work, I climbed a little boulder and jumped up behind
him. The second I put my weight on his back, Calvo's ears went back
flat and he put his head down between his legs. I had a death grip
around Elfego's waist, but the bucking caught me off guard. Calvo
landed stiff-legged and I felt myself coming loose, and on the second
jump I fell off—hit in some rocks, flipped over, and skidded down a
little slope with the wind knocked half out of me. I looked around and
saw that the saddle had slipped clear around on the horse's side, and

Elfego looked like he was spurring the horse's back and his belly before he flew off on his head. He hit some bushes and a dead tree and crashed right through them."

Francisco laughed until tears came to his eyes at the recollection. "So there we were, with one lame horse and one that had run off. Took us four hours to catch him. And when we finally did, Elfego, my good friend, looked at me without smiling and said, 'I told you Calvo didn't carry double.' "

Francisco shook with amusement while his friend grinned, showing a line of white strong teeth which stood out in contrast to his dark face.

Elfego spoke for the first time. "I was over here a month ago—and I knew then that it was only a matter of time before something would have to be done. That's why I came when all the others refused to help." He seemed to have absolute confidence in himself. Standing before the family of his friend and the stranger on the pallet, he had the attitude of a man with a mission in spite of his youthful appearance. His unlined face looked earnest as he talked to them.

"It is my opinion that it is in men's nature to respect the law." He said the last word with reverence. "The problem is simply that we haven't had anyone in Frisco to enforce this." With complete composure he added, "Until now."

"Muchacho," Rafa said in a patronizing tone, "with all respect for your opinion, the vaqueros who ride for J. B. Slaughter have no regard for the law."

"I'm going to prove you wrong, old man."

"How do you plan to do that?"

"When they begin to shoot up the town this Saturday, I'm going to maintain order. I'm going to jerk a knot in this place." With that he opened his coat and showed a bright shiny tin star pinned on his shirt. "What do you think of this?"

Rafa shambled toward him like an aging old bear and leaned forward, peering at the metal emblem. "That's not the badge of a sheriff or deputy sheriff of Socorro County—or of any other county."

Elfego said with a touch of arrogance, "It is the star of a lawman."

"Hijo de puta." Old Rafa wheezed out the obscenity in a slur as his eyes crinkled almost shut. He whooped with laughter, not caring at all that the teenaged friend of his nephew looked mortally offended. "Boy, if you wear that out in the street they'll drag you at the end of a

rope like they did this man." He pointed to Tom English lying on his back. *"Madre de Dios,* where did you get that badge?"

"It's true that they didn't give this to me in Socorro—they don't have any Mexican sheriffs that I've heard of in the New Mexico Territory, although my father served as town marshal for a while in Belén."

"There can't be more than twenty people in Belén, Elfego," old Rafa stormed at him, "and all of them are Mexicans. Of *course* they could have a Mexican town marshal there. Stop dodging my question —who gave you that star?"

"I earned it," Elfego said uncertainly, a little of the bravado going out of him. "This came in the mail from Chicago especially for me after I'd finished the entire correspondence course from the Certified Western Detective School."

"The *Certified Western Detective School?* May Joseph and Mary protect you. May saints from the heavens surround you until you come to your senses. Is that some mail-order correspondence school they advertise in a magazine?"

Francisco broke in. "Don't tease Elfego, Uncle. He's the only one who came from Socorro—and I talked to around fifty of our people there. We met at the church for hours."

"The men from Socorro showed uncommon sense, it seems to me," Rafa growled as he held out his cup for more coffee.

Tom shoved his pillows into a pile against the adobe wall, struggled into a sitting position, and then leaned back on them. He fixed his penetrating pale blue eyes upon the young man from Socorro.

Elfego Baca looked ill at ease as he pretended to ignore the way the stranger looked at him. He swaggered back and forth, both thumbs hooked in his wide gunbelt, and with his back arched.

"Why you starin' at me?" the youngster finally demanded in exasperation. He stopped his pacing and took a position at the foot of Tom's pallet, feet apart, challenging the older man.

The others had left the house; only the two of them remained inside.

Tom ignored the question. He wondered what there was about the kid that irritated him so. He despised people who postured, who bragged—they put his teeth on edge. He had never been able to stand arrogance. But it went deeper than that. Fear had something to do with it, perhaps. He couldn't help remembering other young men—

ones entering that dangerous young bull stage when they felt they had
to prove their manhood by going up against the one they saw as the
herd bull. And he had been the one who, all too often, they considered
their rival. He recalled so many of them—the cocky young punks and
the brash kids on the prod, the ones who had tried to provoke him
into a gunfight in the simpleminded notion that in one fell swoop
they'd build a fearsome reputation. They'd become known as the one
who'd downed "the meanest man in West Texas."

A bitter taste came into Tom's mouth and an old rage at the helpless
fear that was always so close at hand made him strike out at the
puzzled kid nearby. Although he spoke softly, the words had edges to
them as sharp as razors. "Do I understand that your intention is to
tame the town of Frisco?"

"That's exactly what I have in mind," Elfego retorted, his feelings
hurt, stung by the other's obvious disapproval of him.

"Well, I admire your spirit if not your judgment." The words were
cold, they were not warmed by a smile or sympathetic gesture.

Elfego, his face reddening, replied, "I'm not like other men."

"That may be true, but you're a good bit like a lot of boys I've seen."

Elfego spun on his heels and without another word strode from the
room.

The cowboys began to arrive just after noon on Saturday. Some
spurred into a high lope, making a flamboyant entry, but most sat their
saddles as their horses trotted, jolting down the rutted broad road
from the west and then rounding the corner between the livery stable
and Milligen's big barn of a saloon. All wore wide-brimmed hats with
no two having the crowns creased alike. All wore sidearms and most
had saddle guns. Coiled ropes rested on their right legs, tied by saddle
strings just in front of the swell sloping down from the horn. They
came in twos and threes and a few rode alone. But all proceeded as if
to an appointment, riding with purpose to the front of the saloon.

Tom had asked Francisco to bring his gear from the little room he'd
rented from him earlier at the livery stable. His saddle and bedroll had
been piled in the lean-to behind the adobe house, but his saddlebags
and his Winchester in its long leather saddle scabbard lay in a corner
of the main room.

Tom sat in a wooden rocking chair by a low window. With a growing sense of apprehension, he watched the cowboys ride into Frisco.

He had a clear view from here of the saloon and, closer at hand, the small shack owned by María Alpizar which sat at the western edge of the Upper Plaza. This solitary, crude dwelling crouched all by itself about a hundred yards from the cluster of adobe houses which included Francisco's and as well that of Rafa Hernández. A chicken pecked at the ground near the Alpizar place and two children played a game with sticks out behind it near a water well.

Elfego Baca stood next door at Rafa's house, standing with the old man and Francisco and the local justice of the peace. The wind blew by them and carried their words.

"Do you have a jail in town?" Elfego asked Guillermo Jones, the justice of the peace. In spite of having a gringo father, Guillermo spoke very little English and he frequently admitted that his Spanish wasn't very good either.

Guillermo Jones, a small man, even smaller than Elfego, said in his tortured accent, "No. We've never had the need to lock people up."

"Don't start talking about jails, in the name of God," Rafa blustered, poking a long stick into the bowels of the smoke-stained large outdoor oven, prodding the fire. "Who knows what might happen if you provoke these men. If you try to arrest one of them, his friends will take this town apart. We've had enough trouble without that."

The smell of smoke mixed with the rich odor of the tamales cooking in the oven. A chill wind from the northwest made the men pull up their coat collars.

Rafa leaned forward and spoke with heavy emphasis. "Elfego, it's crazy for you to try to stand up against all those white cowboys. In the first place, they're not going to listen to anyone—I don't care who's talking to them. And in the second place, they're going to get *enojado,* truly enraged, amigo, if a Mexican tries to tell them what they can and can't do."

Elfego finished the tamale he was eating and wiped his hands on his pants leg. "I'm not going to do anything foolish, *Don* Rafael," he said respectfully. "But there's no harm in my going to talk to the bartender. I spoke with him yesterday and we agreed that it's not good for the town to get shot up every week. He admitted that whiskey plays a big part in the trouble, so I told him that the people of Frisco were going to expect him not to sell liquor to anyone who has had too much to drink."

Elfego Baca added, "I may have to make an example out of one of

these men, and show the others that no one is above the law. If that
happens, I'll take him to your office, Guillermo. So I want you to go
there and wait for me *por si acaso*—just in case. You hold the only
official position in Frisco except for the *alcalde,* and Francisco says that
the *alcalde* stays with his chickens and goats down in the Middle Plaza
most of the time."

Elfego started across the open space, walking on worn-down
bootheels, his spurs clinking with every step. When he was more than
halfway there, Tom saw him stop and move the tin star from his shirt
to the lapel of his shabby sheepskin coat where it could be seen more
readily. Then he began walking again.

A tall cowboy came from Milligen's Saloon. He untied his horse and
backed him away from the others at the long hitching rail. Then he
put his left foot in the stirrup and swung up into the saddle. With a
flourish, he reined the horse around and put him into a rocking slow
gallop. He circled far out, heading directly toward Elfego, then
swerved at the last moment and clattered through white soft caliche
rocks and through dry brush as he made his first circle. His right hand
came up with a six-shooter as he neared the shack of María Alpizar
and he thumbed back the hammer. Then it kicked and exploded, with
a bullet kicking dust from the earth by a scrawny chicken which
squawked and fled, head down, as another bullet struck a flat rock
next to it and ricocheted off with a wild whining buzz.

María rushed from her shack, mouth open in horror. She stood
stock-still on the barren grassless hard dirt before bolting to the rear of
her home and shepherding her two children inside.

Tom English gripped the arm of his rocking chair with his left hand
as he looked at the receding form of the cowboy who swayed in his
saddle—obviously he'd been drinking heavily. He recognized the troublemaker: McCarty—the man who had dragged him at the end of a
rope. Cursing his helplessness, he gazed out of his window.

The man cantered around the town, taking careful aim at a sign in
front of the saddle shop and at another sign hanging before the office
of the justice of the peace. He circled once again by the saloon, past
about twenty cowboys who'd come out from it to watch. He shot at a
yellow dog and this time struck his target. The animal doubled up and
jumped high in the air, and as he did the cowboy fired a second time,
hitting the animal squarely. The dog crumpled in a dusty heap and all
movement stopped except for its dying spasms.

The men who had come from the saloon cheered these lucky shots. McCarty leaned back in his saddle, holstered his gun, and pulled back on the reins, slowing his horse to a walk. He took off his hat and bowed from the waist ceremoniously, accepting the raucous applause from his friends as he approached. He didn't notice the furious expression on the short thin Mexican boy who strode toward him.

McCarty dismounted and staggered ever so slightly. He rose to his full height, which must have been six feet five, and thrust out his lantern jaw belligerently as the boy hurried toward him, the clink of his spurs sounding with every step.

The tall man looked at his friends, a growing grin on his face. He turned around and this vanished instantly. Elfego Baca pushed a large single-action Colt .44 against the point of his prominent nose. With his left hand, Elfego fished out McCarty's six-gun and stuck it in his belt. Then he pressed the muzzle of his Colt into McCarty's ear and began to march the bewildered drunk across the broad rutted road.

The cowboys before the saloon swept out toward him, but Elfego said calmly, "If you come any closer, I'll blow his head off."

One of them, a sandy-haired waddy named J. H. Cook, later became friends with Tom English, and told him how astonished all of the Slaughter cowboys felt at that instant. In trying to piece together all the quick events that took place, Tom afterward was heard to say that it was hard to remember what he saw, what Cook told him, and what he heard from Elfego Baca and from Guillermo Jones, the justice of the peace.

Guillermo Jones sat in his wood slat-backed chair behind his rickety desk as the door of his office creaked open and the youngster he'd met only that morning entered with a bewildered-looking tall cowboy. To make sure that McCarty knew he couldn't get away, Elfego had pulled his head over to one side with one hand while keeping his pistol stuck in the prisoner's ear with the other.

"I'm arresting this man for disturbing the peace," Elfego announced with finality. He pushed his man down into the only other chair in the room and stood behind him.

Guillermo Jones sat without saying a word, slack-jawed, horrified at this turn of events.

Outside the window, the cowboys could be seen milling about. Dozens of men boiled from the saloon and circled about one of their number who could be seen giving orders.

McCarty opened his mouth and said in his hollow, deep voice, "That there is Mr. Perham who just happens to be the foreman for the Slaughter outfit. I'm sorry to say this," he said to Guillermo and Elfego, "but you have just riled a man who has a terrible temper."

Perham wore a sweat-stained white hat with a wide brim shading his face. He took the reins of a sturdy dun horse with a black mane and tail, backed him away from the hitching rail, then stepped into the saddle. Riding toward the frame one-story building, he slid a rifle from his slanted saddle holster and, with a quick cocking action, he levered a shell into the firing chamber. Holding the rifle in one hand, muzzle up, he roared out, "Let's go, boys."

A host of cowboys on foot drew their handguns or took rifles from their saddles and followed their mounted leader. They began calling encouragement to one another as they scuffed deliberately forward, a small dust cloud forming about their booted feet.

Elfego threw open the door, pointed his Colt for an instant at his prisoner who remained seated in a chair behind him, and said to McCarty in clearly understandable English, "If you try to get up, you son of a bitch, I'll put a bullet right between your eyes."

Directing his attention to the swarm of men, he called out in ringing tones, speaking English again, "I'm a lawman. You can see that by my badge. Anybody who tries to interfere with my official duties will go right straight to jail or maybe to hell. It don't bother me which one you choose."

The armed men made rumbling noises as they advanced. Elfego held his pistol out at them and called out, "I said that I represent law and order in Frisco—and you're going to get only one warning. That's all. I'm going to count to three and then start shooting to kill if you men don't back down."

Perham pulled on his reins and his excited dun half reared, kicking out with his forefeet. "Come on, boys, follow me," he called again.

Elfego didn't waste time. He didn't count slowly or deliberately, he didn't ask them to listen to reason. In a loud voice he cried, "One, two, three." At the very second that he called out the last word his Colt bucked in his hand as he fired five quick shots. The explosions echoed wildly through the air.

Perham's big horse reared straight up and fell backward on his rider. Another man pitched forward on the ground, holding his knee, screaming with fear and pain at a sudden wrenching agony.

"Jesus," McCarty blurted out, standing up in spite of the warning from Elfego not to move. "You shot Boots Allen through the knee, you Meskin butcher. You done that deliberately—you *crippled* him." Then he saw the dun horse roll over and rise uncertainly to his feet.

The cowboys fell back with great confusion, but one of their number returned across the street, waving his hands to show he wasn't armed. "In the name of God, don't shoot," he hollered. He knelt beside the foreman and then looked back at the other men, who had retreated to the front of Milligen's Saloon. His voice croaked as if his throat had suddenly gone dry. "The foreman's dead. He's been *crushed* —damn near ever' bone in his body is broke. Perham's dead."

He looked down at their fallen leader, aghast at the sight. Nearby the cowboy named Boots Allen shrieked as he rolled back and forth upon his back, bright blood spurting from his shattered knee.

Silence had fallen like a great blanket over the town, torn only by the hoarse screams of the wounded man. Elfego retreated inside the office and slammed the door behind him.

An ominous rush of voices from the mob across the way turned into a roar. The cowboys surged forward then, all caution thrown to the wind. They began to fire their weapons into the office, glass splinters crashing as the windows flew into pieces.

Elfego asked, "This place got a back door, Guillermo?"

The justice of the peace nodded, snapping out of his trance. He leaped from his chair and dashed out the rear of the building. The two men took their prisoner with them down through the dry arroyo, across empty lots, hidden by the building from the attacking mob which rained bullets into the abandoned office.

Elfego and Guillermo and their drunken prisoner stumbled down into the Middle Plaza to the *alcalde*'s big ramshackle house located across from the church. They pulled him inside, then Elfego got some rope and tied him securely. He used piggin' string from a saddle and secured McCarty's hands, and found a length of mecate which he used to secure his feet.

The local mayor, a widower named Luís Herrero, lived alone now that his children had grown up and moved away. Alone, that is, except for the chickens and goats that roamed through the large dirt-floored house. Feathers and white chicken droppings littered the unkempt interior of the place. A short-haired brown Spanish goat nosed near their prisoner until Herrero kicked at him, uttering harsh imprecations

but smiling fondly at the animal. Then he looked at the spectacle of
the giant cowboy, tied up and lying on his floor. He hadn't been fully
aware of what was happening, having just awakened from one of his
frequent naps. Now, eyes rolling in his head, Luís Herrero took stock
of the situation. He announced finally, "They'll burn Frisco tonight
unless we turn this man loose." He moved toward McCarty, pulling at
his bonds.

"Leave him alone," Elfego commanded. He didn't seem to think it
strange at all that he, not even a resident of the town, was at the age of
nineteen giving orders to the *alcalde* and the justice of the peace.
"We've got to try the prisoner," he said with some satisfaction, "in
accordance with the law."

Luis Herrero and Guillermo Jones looked at one another with disbelief.

An hour later Rafa Hernández ventured from his house and came
next door to Francisco Naranjo's. He slipped through the door and
came up to Tom, who still sat at the window.

Rafa asked, "Did you see what happened?"

"Most of it."

"That Elfego, I don't know what has gotten into him." He raised his
eyes to the heavens.

"I saw some men leave town, riding hell-bent for election off toward
the Slaughter ranch."

"They're going for reinforcements. What is going to happen now?"

"Trouble," Tom English said. He turned to Francisco. "The horse I
left in the pen behind your livery stable is part thoroughbred. He's in
good condition and is well rested now. If you could find someone in
town who's a good rider, I'd like to send a message to a man I know in
Socorro."

"My cousin José Lara has ridden all his life, and he knows the way
as well as I do. But I don't think anyone there will help us. We've tried
before."

Tom asked for paper and a pencil. When he had these he wrote a
brief note, then said, "Tell José to saddle my horse, Deuce, and take
this to a deputy sheriff named Joe Ross in Socorro. He knows me, and
if José can find him, I think he'll give us a hand."

"Even if José does manage to locate Ross, they couldn't possibly get back here before Monday afternoon or maybe Tuesday morning. They'll be too late," Rafa said.

"I hope not," Tom replied, staring out the window. Pain shot through his shoulder as he sat there, feeling useless. Trying to make the best of it, he drawled, "Well, as we say in Texas, the fat's in the fire."

Seven

ON SUNDAY, the dangerous light of early dawn seeped slowly along the rooftops of Frisco. A momentary wash of gold tinged with white brushed across signs and false fronts and the stone chimney above Milligen's Saloon. In the brittle tension that cloaked the town, even the roosters remained silent.

Few of the Mexicans who cowered in their homes had slept well, and the cowboys who remained inside the saloon, nervously checking their weapons and, worrying about their dwindling supply of ammunition, probably hadn't slept at all.

On the afternoon before, Tom English had watched seven riders lashing at their horses, careening out of town. This happened after the charge upon the office of Guillermo Jones, the justice of the peace, and after McCarty had been hauled off to the *alcalde*'s house which served as a temporary jail. Booted men had bolted out of the double doors of Milligen's Saloon, jerked their mounts from the hitching rail, and leaped upon them. One made a spectacular departure, holding to his saddle horn with both hands, hanging at the side of his horse until it hit a high run, and then he lowered his feet, bounced them off the hard dirt of the trail, and flipped up with practiced balance, landing astride his saddle. With a plume of dust whipping behind, he leaned low over the flapping mane of his straining horse, howling an excited "heeyah" squall.

The Mexicans, making up virtually all of the town's population, kept out of sight while these urgent pale-skinned messengers raced away from Frisco.

Rafa had come into Francisco's house once again and pulled up a chair beside Tom's rocker. They stared silently through the window at the absolutely vacant Upper Plaza, remembering the astonishing sights they'd seen there the day before.

Rafa rolled a cigarette with thick nicotine-stained fingers. His white mustache also had a yellowish tinge. A rain of tobacco flakes fell unnoticed on his sagging belly as he wrapped the thin paper into a crumpled tube, licked, and sealed it. After twisting the end shut, he lit the cigarette with satisfaction. Drawing smoke deep into his lungs, he hacked out a morning cough, cleared his throat, then squinted his eyes at Tom through the cloud he expelled. As he talked, bits of smoke came from his mouth in curls.

"Lupe Moreno found herself in the middle of all that trouble yesterday afternoon. Scared her half to death. All those cowboys went crazy when their foreman, a man named Perham, got crushed by his horse. And then Elfego shot another cowboy in the knee." He looked over his shoulder at the wooden crucifix on the wall and recited a rapid incantation. After crossing himself, he said, "I *told* Elfego not to start anything. Young people don't listen to their elders anymore," he groused.

With a sigh Rafa shifted his weight in the uncomfortable chair, causing it to creak and groan. "Lupe told me that right after the gunfire, the cowboys almost fell over each other running for safety. They poured into the saloon and were so relieved to get there that at first they slumped down in chairs or just leaned on the bar. Lupe said that after a while they began to grab for bottles, acting like men who've come in off the desert—crazy with thirst. When they seemed to have enough whiskey to pick up their nerve, several of them began talking at once. Before long they decided that it was an uprising, that the Mexicans had decided to kill every gringo in the town. Lupe said that three or four began hollering that Mexicans would come in the night and cut their throats, that they'd be massacred without mercy. So they posted guards at the doors and windows and most of them sank down on the floor for safety in case of attack. *Dios mío,* as if any of us would do such a thing! Those cowboys, according to Lupe, acted as if Elfego had fired the first shots in some kind of race war."

"Who's Lupe Moreno?" Tom asked.

"Lupe's one of the whores who works the saloon. Takes her customers to what looks like a horse stall out back," Rafa said, aware that people have to accept whatever employment they can find in this hard life.

Rafa mused, "In a little town there are no secrets. Everyone knows within an hour what has happened in Frisco. They know when a man is mad at his woman, what they're having for supper, and if she's running around on him." Old Rafa rattled along, seeking out a familiar topic. "So it's not surprising that we know exactly what went on in the saloon yesterday." A deep belly laugh rumbled out as he added, "We got our spies everywhere."

"You said the cowboys are worked up about what they consider a race war?" Tom asked incredulously.

"That's why the riders went out. They're going to the Slaughter headquarters and to all the other gringo ranches. Lupe heard the instructions they got—to spread the alarm that the Mexicans have gone on the warpath—that they plan to wipe out all the *Americanos* living near this settlement."

"The cowpunchers have all the firepower. I haven't seen hide nor hair of a Mexican since mid-afternoon yesterday; they're the ones who have reason to be terrified."

Rafa commented thoughtfully. "We've gotten along together for years, but now the whites are herded together in the saloon, afraid to stick their noses outside. And all the Mexicans are hiding in their houses."

When mid-morning came, the bells at the church rang out their summons, but for the first time in living memory none of the parishioners appeared. A priest in a black habit so old that it had a faint shiny green cast to it stood in the door of the church, looking about the Middle Plaza. Then he went back inside.

For an hour the American cowboys had been appearing, coming into Frisco in tightly bunched groups. The riders bristled with weapons, and many wore extra cartridge belts across their chests. Two wagons appeared, loaded with heavy wooden cases full of ammunition. All of the new arrivals joined the men who congregated in the Upper Plaza at the saloon. After a time, the cowboys came outside, heartened by their strength of numbers and by the absence of any Mexicans.

Three men under a white flag of truce walked past the livery stable and by the church at the Middle Plaza and came to a halt in front of the *alcalde*'s house. He and Guillermo Jones came out to meet the delegation.

J. H. Cook, Clement Hightower, and Jerome Martin had been selected by the cowboys to act as their spokesmen.

When the two groups stood face to face, with several of the men
shifting their weight uneasily from one foot to the other, Clement
Hightower spoke up. "We've come for McCarty. You've no call to hold
him."

"With respect, *señor,*" Guillermo Jones replied, "this man was
drunk, he shot his pistol all over the town—not only in the air but into
the houses of our people." His face clinched up like a fist. "And he
shot the sign in front of my office."

"Well," Hightower replied. He turned and conferred in whispers
with his fellow delegates.

Elfego Baca walked from the house, his tin star shining on his
sheepskin coat. He had this coat unbuttoned and pushed behind his
six-gun.

"McCarty broke the law," Elfego said simply.

The whites looked at him coldly. Hightower pointed to Elfego and
said to his companions, "That's the youngster who killed Perham and
shot Boots Allen in the knee."

He said gruffly to the *alcalde,* "Mayor, McCarty may have shot at
your sign, and maybe let off a few shots in the air while having some
fun, but he meant no harm. If anyone is to be held, it ought to be this
kid. He's guilty of murder and we plan to take him to justice."

Elfego put his hand on the butt of his Colt. "Don't call me a kid. *I'm
a lawman.* We've gone too long in Frisco without one. From now on,
there's going to be law and order here, and to prove that, we're going
to put your man on trial."

J. H. Cook sidled up to the *alcalde.* They'd known each other for
years. The two men walked some twenty yards away and spoke briefly
in private. The *alcalde* made a hand signal and Guillermo Jones, the
justice of the peace, joined them for a few minutes while Elfego
watched this turn of events suspiciously. Then Cook returned to the
spot where his friends stood and said, "That sounds all right to me."

Hightower and Jerome Martin both glared, but Cook took them
aside and spoke rapidly to them. Then he turned about and said,
"Let's get this over. If McCarty's to be tried, let's select a jury and get
it over."

Elfego said, "We'll use our own system. We have Spanish law here,
and the judge makes his decisions without a jury."

"Fine," Cook said.

For the past hour the cowboys congregated around Milligen's Saloon had been passing the time by watering their horses at the long wooden troughs that lay close to the hitching posts before the dry goods store. They'd broken out hay for them from the stacks behind the livery stable. When these men saw their three-man delegation returning with McCarty and three Mexicans, some of them started to cheer. But when the seven men turned and went to the office of the justice of the peace, the cowboys observing them looked at one another questioningly. Some of them mounted and rode about aimlessly while others clustered in the road, milling about on foot.

Clement Hightower stood on the board sidewalk before the office of the justice of the peace and called out, "There's to be a trial right now, boys. We've been assured that McCarty will be treated fair." A suggestion of a smile touched his lips. "Maybe if you men stand right over here, we can make sure that comes about."

The trial itself, the subject of so much tension, proved to be an anticlimax. In fact it took less than ten minutes. Guillermo Jones listened without expression to Elfego Baca who acted as McCarty's prosecutor. Then he said, "The man is guilty. No question about it. So I hereby impose a fine of five dollars for disturbing the peace." With that, he stood up.

"Five dollars!" Elfego protested in outrage. "What kind of sentence is that? At least send him to jail in Socorro—or let me chain him to a tree right here in Frisco for a few days. You have to do something to make it clear to the rest of them that they can't act this way."

"No," Guillermo said, "that's where you're wrong, Elfego. You talk about the law, but you've taken it into your own hands and yesterday you scared the wits out of the *alcalde* and me. As far as we're concerned, what we want most of all is to keep those cowboys from destroying our town. So, five dollars is the fine—and we're turning him loose before things get out of hand."

Clement Hightower slapped the five dollars down on Guillermo's desk, took McCarty by the arm, and then the four *Americanos* strode out to the street where they were greeted by a great roar from the waiting cowboys.

McCarty jutted out his lantern jaw and bared his teeth in a wide grin, waving his arms victoriously over his head.

At that moment Elfego came out of the office to the covered sidewalk, and an angry buzz of conversation began.

"Let's hang that little Meskin for killin' the foreman," a man cried out.

Several men dismounted and one took his coiled rope from the front of his saddle.

Elfego slid his Colt from its scabbard, checked its cylinder, then carefully holstered it. The crowd fell silent.

He walked out before them and took a position all by himself in the center of the broad road. He asked, "Which man wants to be the first?"

His words rang in the still cold air of the Upper Plaza. "I'll fight you one by one. There's plenty of time and I'm not running. If I have to, we'll keep this up till I've gunned down every man here."

Elfego rose to his full height of five feet six and squared his shoulders. He made sure his unbuttoned coat rested behind the butt of his six-gun, and hooked the thumbs of his large hands in his cartridge belt. The bluff seemed to be working.

Again, heavily accented English words hung in the electric silence. "Who will be the first to die?"

The eighty armed men in front of him edged their horses forward a few steps, and Elfego wisely began to back away.

A Texan who'd arrived a week before at the Slaughter ranch, a man named Jim Herne, moved to the front of the hesitating gringos.

The other cowboys looked at one another uncertainly. Clearly, none considered himself a gunfighter, and the idea of accepting the challenge of a duel to the death with six-guns was not greeted with enthusiasm.

Herne dismounted and walked toward Elfego while his companions raised their rifles. Elfego examined them with expressionless dark eyes, then turned about and began to walk rapidly away. A single weapon fired and dirt kicked away almost at Elfego's feet. He dropped all pretense then and fled as fast as he could with the tail of his coat flapping behind him.

The cowboys, roaring with relieved laughter, shot over his head and spattered bullets into the ground near him as he raced across the open ground of the Upper Plaza. Elfego reached the far end of the small town and threw himself into the *jacal* owned by María Alpizar. Seconds later she fled from it, holding her youngest child in her arms and pulling the other by the hand. The mother and her children disappeared in the direction of the Middle Plaza.

Jim Herne headed the mob that pursued Elfego. He'd been leading his horse, but he stopped now and handed the reins to a man behind him. Herne dragged his rifle out of its saddle boot and said, "I'll git this dirty little Meskin." The men within earshot cheered him on.

The rifleman moved closer to the rickety dwelling. It stood not over six feet high, for inside it had been dug out to a depth of a foot and a half below ground level. Long years before, men had begun the construction of the *jacal* by driving long stakes into the ground. Mud had been chinked between the upright poles and plaster had been slathered over the walls inside and out. But this had long since largely flaked away. It had a flat roof with some dirt on it. Twisting, weathered boards had been nailed to an uneven timber supported by four thick posts, forming a shed roof over the lopsided door of the tiny one-roomed house. The shack stood alone at the edge of the plaza with rolling prairie behind it. In the blue distance off to the right, a low hill with a flat mesa on top could be seen.

"Come out'a there," Herne bellowed. "Be quick about it."

A hush fell over the large crowd. Some of the more cautious among them held back, standing on the sidewalk before the saloon. Then it happened: they saw small blue spurts of flame at the bottom of the *jacal*'s front wall before they heard the echoing crashes of two sharp explosions. Jim Herne jerked back and spun sideways as heavy lead slugs struck his upper belly and his chest, and then he dropped backward, his arms widespread. His head bounced as it struck the ground, but Jim Herne never knew it. All the watching cowboys could see that he'd been killed instantly.

Tom English, as if in a front-row-center seat, sat at his window and stared out before him at the sight: a crumpled body lay in a widening small dark pool some thirty yards away from the shack where Elfego Baca had gone to ground.

Tom said to Rafa, "Elfego must be lying on the dug-out floor. You can see the barrel of a pistol poking from between the stakes just at the level of the dirt outside."

They looked out at the scene before them where a nineteen-year-old Mexican boy lay at bay. Francisco Naranjo and the women had been standing behind Tom and old Rafa for some time now, gazing at the spectacle. It was three o'clock, Sunday afternoon.

"Elfego decided to bring law and order to Frisco by force, and look what's happened," Rafa said. "Do you see any law out there? Do you see order?"

The cowboys, caught up by some deep-seated blood lust, turned into a mob. They became a pack with a pack's fury.

A cannonade of shots slammed into the rough shelter as eighty men took what cover they could find and began firing as fast as they could pull their triggers. A hail of bullets kicked dry pieces of wood from the walls of the *jacal.*

Helpless, Tom could only sit and watch. He called out to Rafa, "Where's Francisco?"

"He left," Rafa said. "He's circling out of range on his way to the Middle Plaza. Our people are going to have to figure a way to get Elfego some ammunition. He'll run out real quick. And he'll have to get his hands on a rifle. No question about that."

In his excitement he almost babbled as he spoke. "I guess María had some food in her house. And there's no problem with water." The old man jumped up and paced back and forth, his sandaled feet scuffing upon the packed earth of the floor. "The well is not far from the back door. Elfego can slip outside on his stomach when it's dark, but he'll have to watch himself. The gringos are sure to surround the place and try to take him when he goes to sleep."

During the ensuing hours, incessant volleys crashed full into the shack. The crackling sounded something like a wind-whipped prairie fire at first, and then like the repetitive beat of drums with heavier bass notes as a buffalo rifle thundered among the rattling from pistols and Winchesters. A few times a shotgun bellowed uselessly, far beyond its range.

Francisco's wife Marta sobbed, "God in heaven, they're killing him."

The children began to cry, and she shepherded them into the tiny bedroom, speaking soothingly as she drew them to her.

The day passed slowly, with eruptions of gunfire sporadically mixed with silence as men crept cautiously toward the primitive fortress where their prey lay. Several got close to some cottonwood trees and strung a blanket there to shield them from view. A cowboy kneeled behind the flapping blanket as if it were a bulwark and removed his hat. He put it on a stick and pushed it out.

Others watched him. No bullet whirred through the air into it. The cowboy stood up and pushed the blanket down a little, looking at the silent shot-and-shell-blasted poles and timbers where Elfego stubbornly lay. The cowpuncher stepped around the edge of the cottonwood tree and out into the open, bending over, holding his rifle. He fired it from the hip, pumping the lever down and up. The terrible risk he ran must have frightened him for he threw himself facedown into a hollow and curled there for a moment, all balled up, his knees against his chest. Yet as the minutes passed with no returning fire from the strange little shack, he raised his head cautiously, got to his feet, and prepared to advance once more. At that moment a single well-aimed shot cracked out.

The cowboy's mouth spread out into an astonished "O" and he whirled down with a bullet in his upper leg. He lay without screaming on his back, writhing on the ground, digging his fingers into the dry rocky soil.

His friends behind the blanket no longer treated the dangling wool fabric as an impenetrable barrier. They leaped away from it and scurried behind the skinny cottonwood trees, cowering behind them.

"Damn it," the downed man cried out, "I'm bleedin' to death."

One of his friends tied a bandana on his rifle barrel and poked it out. He cautiously started forward toward his companion, but a slug cut a furrow through the fleshy part of his arm. He immediately howled with shock and pain as he tumbled down upon the ground.

The two wounded men lay within pistolshot of the *jacal*. They looked fearfully at the barrel that pushed between the stakes of the wall, and then both of them began shouting to their friends. The other cowboys held their fire, and in the sudden stillness they could hear a curious mixture of curses and demands for help.

Twelve men crept forward to rescue their comrades, but they froze as Elfego's voice rang out: "Get away—or I'll kill both of 'em."

The cowboys started to back away, but then Elfego called out again, "I'll tell you what. If you retreat about two hundred yards, I'll get help for these two men. That wagon over there will carry them to you."

He had seen Francisco Naranjo on a knock-kneed wagon, its wheels wobbling over the rocky land as it emerged from the dry arroyo. As the cowboys withdrew, Francisco lashed his long reins on the back of a dusty burro which showed his resentment by laying his unnaturally long shaggy ears back against his head. Circling near the *jacal*, Francisco pulled the burro to a stop and hurriedly shoved a rifle and a wooden crate off the back of the wagon. Then he slapped the reins on the burro's back and creaked toward the two wounded men.

The wagon groaned to a stop another thirty yards into the plaza, and Francisco hauled the man with the bullet in his leg up upon the wagonbed. Next, he pulled the man who'd been shot through the arm to his feet and helped him into the driver's seat. Francisco ran for cover as the second cowboy slapped the reins on the burro's back and leaned sideways in his seat. The wagon rolled toward safety, bumping drunkenly over rocks and clumps of cactus.

While this took place, Elfego squirmed from the front of the *jacal* and pulled the rifle and the heavy ammunition box back to his shelter.

A number of the cowboys who had fallen back saw this and began muttering. They raised their rifles but others cautioned them that if provoked, the damn Meskin would shoot their wounded companions.

Some attackers heeded these warnings. Others held their fire because the wagon with the two Texans in it shielded Elfego Baca.

Francisco ran behind the *jacal* and back toward the Middle Plaza, disappearing into the rocky arroyo. He apparently didn't want the cowboys to see him go into his house for fear that the attack on Elfego might broaden to include one on his own home.

In the remaining hours until dark fell, the cowboys kept a safe distance. They'd seen or heard from friends that the wagon had dropped off ammunition to their enemy, and when several men on horseback ventured out to test this information, a bullet had dropped the lead horse in his tracks. The rider had tumbled off hard, breaking his arm. So now, the furious men fell back into Milligen's Saloon.

At dusk a few riders set out, but the shooting had lessened. However, with the fall of night, skirmishers crept out and the crackling of rifle fire began again.

Francisco slipped in the back door. "It took me hours to get here," he said, sinking into a chair and breathing heavily. His wife and children surrounded him, then left as he waved them off. He sat by Rafa Hernández and Tom and opened a bottle of tequila.

Swallowing the first taste of liquor since being dragged at the end of a rope, Tom felt his headache start instantly, as though tiny flares of lightning had gone off in his head. "No more for me," he said faintly, leaning back. "Lord, I feel weak."

Tom wondered if he had fever. Odd thrills spun in his stomach and his head throbbed with every heartbeat. At each breath the broken ribs sent ripples of sick pain clear up into his throat.

While Macha helped him back to his pallet, Rafa and Francisco sat staring at the yellow windows in the distant saloon. Night had fallen quickly and the moon had not yet risen. They looked at the darkness of the *jacal.*

"There's not a sound coming from it," Francisco said at last. "Do you think Elfego's alive?"

"I smell something," Rafa said instead of answering. He opened the window a crack. A harsh wind whistled past it as he leaned forward, sniffing the air. "It's smoke," he announced as he heaved the window shut.

Francisco began to laugh. "What a man," he exclaimed. "He's not only alive, he's decided to do some cooking. I guess María left a fire in her stove, and she'd have what he'd need to fix himself some frijoles and tortillas. God," he added fervently, "I hope it isn't his last supper."

Rafa bent down below the window frame, out of sight, and struck a match. It threw a flare across his grizzled face as he lit the cigarette he'd been rolling in the darkness. Then he began to cough as he sat up straight again.

Rafa strained forward, looking into the blackness. He said, "Look, do you see some little lights over there, creeping along close to the ground?"

"Where?"

"There," Rafa barked in alarm, "moving fast toward the side of María's house."

The two men saw the small lights turn into a white sputtering, a thin stream of jetting sparks, and then a silvery streak hissed in a bright arc through the velvet sky and thumped to the flat roof of the *jacal* concealing Elfego.

"Madre Santísima," Francisco cried. *"It's dynamite!"*

Eight

THE DYNAMITE blew an orange hole in the blackness, flaring high above the wretched shack, tearing a piece of the roof away, but most of its force flew upward. Shock waves cracked against the windows of Francisco Naranjo's small adobe house a hundred yards away and rippled toward the excited cowboys who clustered under the dark cloak of night. A roar surged from them and then a torch appeared, wavering across the plaza, held by an invisible hand.

As it neared, the witnesses who clustered at their vantage point in Francisco's house could see a long-haired hatless man raising the fire-streaming torch above his head. He ran holding it slanted forward as though it were a battle flag, and scores of men could be seen in the tattered streaks of its flared light, brandishing rifles and pistols, surging forward to drag their bloodied prey from his ruined lair.

There was an instant of paralyzed silence shattered by a sharp detonation sounded from the *jacal,* an explosion that quivered through the air. After that the single rifle cracked shot after shot in rapid fire. The runner with the torch dove headlong to the ground, seeking protection. Some of the cowboys following him sprawled into the dirt while others fanned out in two flanking movements, calling encouragement to one another as they ran bent over. Looking toward the *jacal,* all they could see were the repeated spurts of orange from a rifle's muzzle. Everything else looked as dark as if they held their eyes shut tight.

Behind them every window in Milligen's Saloon was ablaze and the light from it flowed out upon the square. The yellowed illumination backlit the bending, rushing men who thought that they were charging invisibly under the total cover of the moonless night.

Elfego's rifle kept barking frantically. Over and over its muzzle flashed, propped at ground level at the bottom of the *jacal*'s front wall. The attackers cowered as the bullets whined overhead, but took heart when none came near them. Those who had taken cover gradually rose to their knees and then stood, crouching over fearfully. The defending flood of rifle fire sounded as if two or three men might have been shooting. But the whizzing slugs flew harmlessly wide of their targets, making cracking noises as they whipped by.

In Francisco Naranjo's adobe house, all of the occupants watched the one-sided battle helplessly. "He doesn't have a chance," Marta moaned. Francisco pulled her close to him as they stood at the window.

"The gringos are starting to edge closer," old Rafa grunted. "They've got more dynamite—they'll kill him this time. If he could only hit some of them . . ." The words dwindled into a pained pool of silent frustration. Then he added, "Looks to me like that boy's a pretty good pistol shot, but he can't hit the broad side of a barn with a rifle."

Francisco defended his friend. "Elfego doesn't own a rifle. Even if he did, how would he ever have enough money to afford cartridges for practice?"

Rafa growled, *"Basta, sobrino.* I'm just stating facts."

Tom had struggled from the pallet on the floor at the shuddering blast of the dynamite's explosion, and he stood at the other window watching the violence which erupted across the Upper Plaza.

Macha pressed against him, hypnotized by the view. She put her hand upon his left arm and gripped it fiercely, as if holding on for dear life.

Finally he spoke. "He's got more than his share of nerve—but that's not going to save his life." Turning to her, he said, "I need my saddle-bags."

Without questioning him, she went to get them. She hurried to the small alcove containing her cot and the oven. Returning with the leather saddlebags drooping in her hands, she commented, "They're heavy."

He didn't reply. Sitting in a chair, holding his cartridge belt, he removed the holster from its right side. Leaning forward, he picked up the Colt .45 that Macha had retrieved for him from the saloon and slid this in the holster, then carefully put it away. After this he fished through the saddlebags and pulled from them another holster and a matching Colt. With practiced hands he put this on the cartridge belt's left side. The holster, like its mate, had a long leather loop.

"A second gun?" Macha's curiosity showed in her tone of voice.

A momentary lull must have occurred, for the sounds of gunfire died away outside. Tom's eyes met those of the young woman for an instant. She looked confused and afraid.

"A matched pair," he answered. "Not exactly the same, but close. Took me a long time to find this one." He didn't explain himself further.

Francisco turned from his vantage point at the window and watched as Tom stood up and awkwardly adjusted the sling which supported his right arm. He wore only the left gun now, and loosened it in his holster. "I'm a little sore," he said, "but I can walk all right."

Outside now, standing near Francisco's house, he felt the sharp sting of the winter night upon his face but was hardly conscious of it. Moving stiffly at first, he made his way toward the back of María Alpizar's *jacal*. When he reached the well he called out.

"Elfego! I've come to help you."

In answer, a pistol blasted from the nearby shack, and a bullet slashed past Tom's ear, hitting a rusty iron wheel that held the rope leading down to a wooden bucket in the well. The ricochet howled off, warbling wildly into the night.

"You don't have a chance by yourself. They've got dynamite—hold your fire and open the door."

"It's a trick." Elfego's muffled voice came from his dark shelter. "Who are you? Why would you help me?"

Tom lay behind the well. He called out, "I'm the beat-up gringo who was on the pallet in Francisco's house. Damn it—let me in!"

Rifle fire picked up, rattling sharply into the front of the shack.

Elfego grudgingly threw open the small back door, and Tom rushed through it, stumbling when he did, almost losing his balance, for he had to step down about a foot and a half onto the dug-out floor of the *jacal*.

Breathing heavily, Tom took the rifle from Elfego's hands. His fingers moved up the barrel, feeling the smooth steel's hotness. Looking through the spaces between the upright poles and sticks that made up the wall, he could make out fleeting shadows of the men approaching. Without taking his eyes from them he asked, "How much ammunition do you have?"

"A lot—I don't know exactly. There's a big box of shells that Francisco brought me."

"I had you wrong, Elfego. You're a real man—even if you don't have a grain of sense. But you may be the worst rifle shot I've ever seen."

He crouched and rested the Winchester on the ledge of dirt formed by the base of the wall. At this point, where Elfego had been making his stand, the dried wood of a few of the sticks and narrow poles of the wall had been broken off at the bottom which made it possible for the muzzle to swing from one side to the other, covering the entire field of fire before the *jacal.*

He sank down, winced as he withdrew his right arm from the sling, then, supporting the weight of the Winchester with his left hand, he pulled the combination lever and trigger guard down and then clicked it back in place, hearing the greased-steel sounds of the cartridge sliding into the firing chamber. The movement hurt his shoulder a little but not much. With care he extended his left arm a little, pushed the barrel forward while at the same time he forced the butt plate against his right shoulder. Ordinarily he raised his right elbow parallel to the ground when taking aim, but a twinge caused him to experiment aiming with the elbow low. He'd just have to adjust to the inconvenience, he decided. As his finger touched the slender curved trigger, sensing its tension, a deadly calm came over him as he stared over the sights at men who rose from their crouches. They charged, yelling with excitement, holding their handguns and their rifles low as they came.

He heard questions within his mind: *This isn't my fight—how'd I get mixed up in it?* He didn't have any answers. He had no time for this— all reasoning faded away. His heart beat rapidly as combat instincts took control.

A match flared, surprising him. Tom looked to his right and saw young Elfego Baca holding it as he lit a cigarette. He grinned and said in rippling Spanish, "To tell the truth, I was getting lonely. It's good to have some company."

A hail of bullets swept into the *jacal,* knocking wood and dust and dirt down on them. And then the side walls and the back wall began to rip. It was as though they found themselves within a giant snare drum with a dozen frantic drummers pounding on it. Elfego threw himself across the floor and began firing with his pistol at the muzzle flashes in back of them. Tom stared over his sights, waiting.

The man who'd had the torch suddenly grasped it again as the cowboys surged up behind him. Holding the flowing stream of flame above his head, he sprinted forward once more, shrieking out a rebel yell just as he reached the cottonwood trees. The hatless man ducked behind a protective trunk and stopped, bending over, catching his breath. He pushed the flaring torch out and began to run as fast as he could toward the savaged *jacal*.

A single rifle shot split the fabric of darkness, making a ripping noise. The man holding the torch pitched forward on his face without a sound. The host of attackers following him divided as though a great wedge had been driven into their midst. Some dove to the right, others left, and all fell sprawling upon the sheltering dirt, hugging as close to it as they could, their fierce enthusiasm replaced by terror.

"That Meskin bastard!" someone yelled.

The cowboys summoned their courage again and crawled forward, inching across the crusted bare earth. From Francisco's adobe house it looked as though the plaza's floor had taken life, for they could see it move. Around both sides of the *jacal* the shadowed waves crept on, washing ever closer to the ruined shack. Then, deciding they were out of the line of fire, a few lit more torches. These whirled, throwing off sparks as they spun through the darkness. Some hit the staked walls and fell away harmlessly, but a few landed on the flat roof. They smoldered there in the dirt and sputtered out.

The attackers began to fire their weapons, and once again the beleaguered shelter felt the leaden axes. At this closer distance, the force of the bullets tore away a two-foot hole high on the front wall. But after a time the onslaught died down, and the shooting, which had been a continuous roar, dwindled into sporadic, separated jolts of vibrating sound.

The moon appeared at the horizon, a smooth luminous rim which rose gradually, appearing enormous at the edge of the earth.

Perhaps it was this sudden light, turning the blackness into an eerie gray mirror, which caused the cowboys to pause. Whatever the reason, a silence fell. Moments later a rifle shot cracked out, followed by a curdled shriek. The rifle fired twice more, with each shot causing a howl of agony.

Confusion fell upon the cowboys. Cries and calls and curses echoed on the small battleground, for in their very midst they found men shot down, bleeding, and possibly dying.

"Where is the son of a bitch?" yelled one man.

"Careful, boys," another cried in confused alarm.

A fourth rifle shot hammered out, and instantly a hoarse voice screamed in pain.

Three men rose from a hollow about a hundred and fifty yards in front of the *jacal* and began running as fast as they could to their right. The rifle cracked three times and each man went down, tumbling, rolling, and shrieking with horrified surprise.

A cowboy rose up on his knees and yelled a strident warning. "Jesus Christ, watch out!" But as the last syllable sounded, a slug pickaxed into his arm and spun him up and onto his back, throwing him as violently as if he'd been a rag doll.

The attacking force fell back from the two sides of the *jacal,* firing wildly left and right with rifles and six-guns.

"Hold your fire, goddamnit, you're goin' to shoot each other," a voice raged. The explosions dwindled and then stopped altogether.

The moon hung higher, and Rafa stood at one side of the window in the darkened room of Francisco Naranjo's house, a spectator of the night battle. "Who in the name of God *is* that man?" he said, awestruck. "Have you ever seen anything like that in all your life?"

He didn't really expect Francisco to answer. Then he blurted out in alarm, "Men are coming this way." With that he sank back as close to the plastered wall as his bulk would allow.

Francisco and Rafa, deciding that in the unlit room they couldn't be seen through the window, drew up to it again. They looked out as a cluster of barely discernible silhouettes approached.

The moon shaded its glow upon four men as they came by the adobe house, bending over awkwardly, carrying two limp forms. One stumbled and swore angrily. Another said, "The Meskin's bound to have been hit, what with all the gunfire."

"You're right," another voice replied. "And surely that dynamite would have wounded him, goin' off right over his head."

"I hope to hell that's the case," a cowboy drawled. "He's one dangerous son of a bitch. Once he'd got the range, he was like nothin' I've ever seen with that rifle."

"The bastard has to be bleedin' to death as we talk," the first man said, sounding hopeful that his prophecy might be true. "We'll likely be able to come back in the mornin' to find his body," he added.

The voices dwindled as the men carried their moaning comrades on their line of retreat along the edge of the broad plaza and back toward the saloon.

Francisco stood close to the window, staring at the dim shape of the *jacal.* "I better go check on Elfego. He may be hurt."

But Rafa grasped his arm. "Do you want to die too? They've got gunmen all around that place. Besides, the gringo's with him."

"I think I can get through to him."

"Don't chance it. After all, you've got a family."

"I guess you're right," Francisco muttered.

The men waited in the darkness. Then Rafa said, "I was an old man when all this began, and I've aged twenty years tonight. You're going to have to carry me home. I'm too weak and feeble to make it by myself."

"You'll outlive us all, *Tío,*" Francisco replied to him.

"How many of the cowboys has the gringo killed by now?"

"*¿Quién sabe?*" Francisco answered his uncle automatically.

"This is a dangerous night. The Slaughter cowboys will be wild with anger and they'll be afraid—a bad combination. It looks to me as if most of them have pulled back, so I'm going to my house next door and try to sleep if I can. But I'll probably just lie there, like last night."

"You'll sleep, Uncle. Do you want to stay here with us?"

"There's no room. Besides, I want to get in my own bed."

An hour had passed since old Rafa left. Francisco and Marta had taken the children with them to the other room of their tiny home. Macha lay upon her cot beside the oven.

Sporadically a rifle bullet whined through the night outside, but gradually all sounds stopped except for an occasional creaking in the poles and dried-out boards that made up the roof of the adobe house.

The door opened and Tom came through it. He closed the door and leaned back against the roughness of the wood. His head felt as though it might explode. When he'd been in the *jacal* with Elfego, after the cowboys had drawn back, he'd felt the odd thrills, the quivering shivers that ran up from the pit of his stomach as the fever returned and took control of his body. He'd fallen to one side, dropping the rifle. He remembered Elfego's voice saying, "You've got to get out

of here." And then he'd had the vague recollection of the coldness of
the winter night upon his face. He had turned to Elfego and told him
to make a run for it, but Elfego had said the cowboys would have their
guards posted—and besides, he wasn't going to give them the satisfaction of scaring him off. "What the hell," the boy had said, "I might
even win this fight."

The pain blinded him then, he couldn't really hear or think. Allowing himself to be guided, he stumbled toward Francisco's adobe
house, heard Elfego whisper a hurried farewell—and then Tom had
found his way across what had become a battleground. By the grace of
God, and perhaps because of clouds across the moon, he'd not been
seen.

Macha came from her alcove. She rushed to his side and helped
him as he slid down toward his pallet.

She watched him as he unbuckled his gunbelt, then fumbled with
the leather thongs which held the holster to his left thigh. Dragging all
this from his body, he shoved it to one side of the coarse mattress.

The young Mexican woman wore a loose-fitting thin cotton nightgown of Marta's. Her long hair hung down as she bent over. In a low
voice, not wanting to wake the others, she asked, "Where is Elfego?"

"In the *jacal.*"

"Why didn't he run away?"

The night's activities had drained his strength. He managed to say
only, "I don't know."

"How do you feel?"

Tom tried to still the involuntary twitches in his arms and legs as he
turned back and forth upon the pallet. Fighting against a surge of
nausea, he mumbled, "I'm fine. I feel all right."

She sat on the pallet beside him, pulling the blanket over him.

"I'm freezing, to tell the truth." He spoke with an effort, his teeth
chattering.

"It's the fever." She went on bare feet across the dirt floor to her cot
and took a blanket from it, then returned and spread it on top of the
blanket already covering Tom. Leaning down, she felt his face again,
then quietly slipped under the two blankets, folding her supple form
against him. Gently she held him, saying over and over, *"Pobrecito."*

Tom felt the warmth, the incredible comfort. It seemed as if a small
furnace spread life-giving heat which sank all the way through his

flesh to his aching bones. Not even thinking of the strangeness, he accepted this gift from the angular young woman whose soft breasts pressed upon his side and chest. Her long hair fell across his face as she held him closer, making soothing sounds.

Nine

A FULL MOON hung heavily above the great mansion, gilding the dull red tiles of the roof with silver. The white boulders on the hill nearby, the one called Pico Blanco, mirrored the chill moonglow.

Chato Verdugo took his duties as main bodyguard to the *patrón* seriously. He led the three new arrivals from the corral to the massive front door of Julian Haynes's ranch house and opened it for them. The four men took their hard, dirty sombreros from their heads as they entered the great hall. The three riders all wore large-roweled Spanish spurs with wicked points. These clanked as they followed Chato down the length of the hall. Hanging lanterns threw yellow patterns upon the plank floor that led to the room where the *patrón* stood waiting.

The four men entered, holding their sombreros before them. Julian Haynes moved to the wide-mouthed crackling fireplace, then turned about to face them. Fire shadows danced upon the floor and glinting reddish lights reflected from crystal glasses on a credenza off to one side.

"What news?" he demanded of them harshly.

"Macha is still in Frisco," Chato said. "Rigo can tell you about it." He moved away from the three men he'd escorted into Julian Haynes's presence, and leaned against a wall with his arms crossed on his chest.

The man named Rigo took a step forward to give his report. The first thing strangers noticed about him was the fact that a mottled purple birthmark covered the right side of his face. His jet-black hair, slanted dark eyes, and high cheekbones gave token of his part-Indian heritage.

Rigo said, "The one you want us to bring to you is in a house in the

Upper Plaza. She's staying with her cousin, a man named Francisco
Naranjo. We got to Frisco Saturday, talked to the people, and it didn't
take us long to locate her. But then we ran into problems."

"What kind of problems?"

"Well, one thing we didn't expect is that some Texan is in the house
with her, along with Naranjo's family."

"A Texan?" The questioner's tone showed his disbelief.

"A troublemaker who came through—a drifter, I suppose. The
Slaughter cowboys dragged him at the end of a rope. We heard he's
torn up some."

"I'm surprised to hear that Mexicans would take in a white man.
Some riders came through here a few days ago, men who work for
Slaughter, and warned me of big trouble—saying that the Mexicans
are after all the whites in Frisco. Of course, those cowboys will never
understand how things really are in the New Mexico Territory."

The men smiled. They knew that the *patrón,* in spite of his name,
was descended from the Estévez line on his mother's side of the
family, and they considered him one of their own.

"I don't suppose," Haynes said, "that a beat-up cowboy could have
slowed you down much."

"That's true," Rigo said with a half smile. "But then the real problems came up."

Haynes walked to the heavy sideboard at the end of the room and
poured brandy from a decanter into a pear-shaped glass. He made no
motion to offer anything to the four men who stood before him, and
they obviously expected nothing from him.

Rigo, whose full name was Rigoberto López Cantarana, waited for
his employer to give him a sign to continue speaking. He was a small
man, a little older than the others, and they showed him signs of
respect, for he had earned a sinister reputation. Men around El Paso
mentioned his name in hushed tones. It was well known that his gun
had cut down seven victims.

When Rigo saw Haynes swallow the sip of brandy and nod curtly to
him, he said, "A youngster named Elfego Baca came into town wearing
a badge, trying to say he was the law. Anyway, all hell broke loose, and
now the cowboys have Baca pinned down in a little shack."

"Is that why you didn't bring her to me?" Julian glared through
slitted eyes at the three men. "Didn't I tell you to bring that bitch out
here when you found her?"

"No way to do that, *patrón,*" Rigo replied. "Macha's hiding out in the closest house in Frisco to the one where Elfego Baca's cornered. There's a war going on in that part of town. Until those cowboys capture Baca, you won't be able to get within half a mile of the house where Macha's hiding. There are men all over the Upper Plaza, shooting at anything that moves."

"Are you sure she can't get away from us while all of that's going on?"

"Not a chance," Rigo declared.

Haynes went to a heavy carved chair and sat down in it. "I want all of you to get a good night's sleep. Tomorrow this gunplay you've told me about will be over. There's no way one man can hold out against so many. So the five of us will go to Frisco, get hold of Macha, and bring her out here."

"Her cousin Francisco might cause trouble," one of the younger men advised.

"Well, that's true," Chato agreed. "He might slow us down by ten seconds or so."

Rigo smiled, but this faded as Julian Haynes fixed him with his stone-faced stare.

At last Haynes said, "All of you know what that *puta* did. She enticed my oldest friend into her bed and then knifed him in the gut."

A cruel light shone in the eyes of Chato Verdugo. He asked, "What will you do when we've captured her?"

"I'll have to think about that," Haynes replied. "She'll have to die in a way that will be remembered for a long, long time. I plan to make an example of her."

Tom awakened in the darkness of early dawn. For a moment he recalled the horror of the night before: the sight of men attacking. He relived the sudden heat of rage he'd felt, the blind compulsion to avenge himself against the men who'd laughed as they tied him in that chair, the ones who'd been a party to his being dragged at the end of a rope. They'd meant to kill him. He'd fired those shots at running shadows, trying as much as anything to hit back at the memory of his fear. He'd been driven by dark impulses, the unspoken instincts that have controlled those who've fought for survival through the ages.

Lying on his back, he was conscious of a dull ache from his ribs.

When he moved his right arm, the sharp pain in his shoulder made him stop instantly.

Had he dreamed that Macha slept beside him on the pallet? He saw her approaching him. The same brown dress she'd worn before had replaced the flimsy nightgown, and she wore Francisco's serape around her shoulders. A too long belt had been knotted around her narrow waist.

She sank down beside him and felt his forehead with an experienced hand. Apparently pleased, she smiled. "The fever's gone. How do you feel?"

"Better. A lot better."

She left and then returned, holding out to him a cup of freshly made coffee. Her feet made whispering sounds upon the earthen floor when she moved. She put one arm about his shoulders, helping him as he struggled to a sitting position, then backed away and sat on a stool nearby, smoothing her skirt across her knees. Her eyes were shining.

He examined her through the steam that rose past his face, smelling the rich aroma, feeling the heat of the cup he held with both hands in his lap. After sipping it appreciatively, he said, "Thank you for taking care of me last night." He averted his eyes, feeling unaccountably embarrassed.

She answered with the traditional phrase, "It was nothing," but her face colored with pleasure.

"All the men I've ever known have been," she hesitated, searching for the word, "rough—they've been cruel to me. You're different."

Tom didn't know how to answer. He remained silent.

"Do you have a woman?" A direct question.

"Yes," he answered.

She stood up, moving to the window. Without looking back she said, "I thought you would."

In the growing light of early dawn, Tom admired her stark loveliness. Their troubled eyes met, but then sounds came from Francisco's room. Macha turned away and fled to the alcove that served as a kitchen. With guilty haste she made up her cot and shoved it against the wall.

Sharpshooters poured their fire into the shattered opening in the wall of the *jacal,* the hole torn by bullets earlier. A line of men advanced under their covering barrage, and a dozen or more threw themselves into the slight depressions in the bare ground behind the cottonwood trees. Others crept around the far edge of the Upper Plaza and took cover behind Rafa's and Francisco's houses. Their words sounded clearly through the crisp bright chill of the early morning air.

"God A'mighty, I think I'm froze," a man with a deep voice complained. "That wind's colder than a witch's tit."

A second man said, "He hasn't returned our fire. Probably dead, is my guess." And the one with the deep voice replied gruffly, "Playin' possum sounds more likely to me."

A third man, evidently lying behind the house, called out to them, "Is somethin' burnin'? Do you smell fire?"

"Well I'll be dad-blamed," another said as he began to chuckle. "There's smoke all right—it's comin' from the stovepipe sticking out the edge of that hut. And there's other smells—like coffee and bacon and tortillas. That Meskin son of a bitch is cookin' hisself some breakfast while we're crawlin' on our bellies out here tryin' to see if he's still alive." The man cackled with laughter and then he said with reluctant admiration, "If that don't beat the Dutch!"

Gradually the rest of the more than eighty men realized what was happening and with a rage born of frustration, they hurled themselves forward and began firing their rifles with abandon. The ensuing hailstorm which flailed against the fragile stakes of the *jacal* eclipsed all previous attacks. It lasted a full thirty minutes without ceasing. As it dwindled, Francisco rose to one knee and peered out the window.

"Look!" he said.

The others in the adobe house crowded near, taking care to hold their heads low. They saw a lone man crawling forward. He held a heavy shield before himself protectively with both hands. The careful attacker advanced with great difficulty, shoving his burden ahead as he wormed forward on his belly. Looking carefully, they could see that it was the cast-iron front of what had once been a stove. Behind this armor, the stealthy figure squirmed along the crusted rocky floor of the plaza, edging nearer and nearer to Elfego Baca's shelter.

Rifle and then pistol fire from the *jacal* erupted, spitting gravel when bullets struck short of the advancing threat. Several times a loud clang rang out when a shell hit the cast-iron shield. The man stopped each time this happened, but after a moment he would go forward once again, pushing gravel to one side in a shallow furrow.

The observers in Francisco's house heard someone outside shout a question. "Ain't that Harmon?"

Another said, "It sure is," before yelling as loud as he could, *"Go git him, Harmon."*

These voices so close at hand startled the people inside the house. Tom and the others stood at the windows and watched the cowboys run off to one side and take cover in a shallow ditch.

Tom walked to the alcove and pulled his Winchester from its saddle scabbard. He flicked the lever quickly, then went back to the door. With it opened, he sank to one knee, holding the rifle in readiness. Once he sighted down the barrel but lowered it when no clear shot presented itself.

"What are you doing?" Francisco protested. "They'll see you— they'll attack my house if you fire."

"Everyone's watching that cowboy crawling toward Elfego—they won't be expecting anything from here. The thing is, he wouldn't be taking this risk unless he had a chance to end the standoff, so my bet is that he's going to try to blow up the *jacal.*"

Marta retreated from her vantage point as though she couldn't bear to watch what might happen. She held the back of one hand to her mouth and began to tremble. Francisco started to go to his wife's side but couldn't make himself move. He remained in his crouch, fingers on the dusty sill, a captive of the events unfolding on the plaza. Macha stood at one side of the other window, peering through it, but with her eyes flicking to one side at Tom, who was kneeling at the doorway with the rifle.

Silently, they watched the attacker's snaking progress. Moments later they saw him pause, reach down, and pull a single foot-long stick of dynamite from his belt. The man crouched behind his cast-iron buckler as he neared Elfego's flimsy shelter. He took off his hat with great care, placing it beside him, then fished a match from his shirt pocket. Very cautiously, he began to lift his head to look over the rusted edge of his homemade shield. But before his eyes reached the top of it, a rifle fired from the door of Francisco's adobe house, and a bullet ripped a scarlet furrow along the exposed surface of the cowboy's head. The force of the perfectly aimed shot flipped him to his back. Moments later he rolled over and held both hands to his bloody wound.

Horrified by this turn of events, the other cowboys waited helplessly and then they saw their wounded comrade struggle to his hands and knees and, with his bleeding head held down, begin to crawl back toward them, leaving the front of the old stove behind where it had fallen.

For the rest of the long day, desultory shots whacked into the front door and into the riddled poles which made up the walls of the shack, but whenever curious attackers ventured within two hundred yards, they'd be driven back by the threatening sounds of Elfego Baca's erratic rifle shots which whipped over their heads.

Most of the Slaughter cowboys who had huddled in the ditches and the low spots on the Upper Plaza drew back and after a time the majority of the gringos regrouped in front of Milligen's Saloon, out of range of Baca's rifle. They could be seen talking, gesturing, apparently arguing about their next course of action.

While all of this went on, a buckboard pulled by a rawboned gray horse entered Frisco on the far side of town, swung around a corner, and jounced over deep ruts in the road. It swerved into the open space and came to a rocking stop in front of the cowboys clustered before the saloon. The stranger driving the buckboard could be seen talking to them.

Tom stared at the distant sight, making out a broad-shouldered man wearing a wide-brimmed black hat. A sun dazzle glinted off something on his chest, and he held a rifle cradled in the crook of one elbow.

"It's about time," Tom English said, gazing out the window with the others.

"Who is that man?" asked old Rafa Hernández who had come from his home to join them as soon as the snipers had fallen back.

"It has to be Joe Ross, the deputy sheriff from Socorro."

"The one you sent the message to last Saturday," Francisco said. "I never thought he would come."

Francisco moved to the door. "I'm going to check on Elfego, and then I need to see Guillermo Jones and the *alcalde.*" He didn't explain himself further, but simply went out the front door and strode into the plaza, walking briskly. Those who remained behind saw him approach the *jacal,* calling out to Elfego, then stopping near it. Elfego cracked the door open a few inches and the two talked for a few minutes.

Some of the cowboys who had stayed behind in the depressions close to the cottonwood trees came to their knees, pointing their rifles at Francisco, but they didn't fire.

A moment later, Francisco backed away from the *jacal* and moved off toward the Middle Plaza of the town of Frisco.

Tom saw that Joe Ross had pulled the big gray around and was slapping his reins on the horse's back. As the buckboard started across the plaza toward them, he said to Macha, "Would you help me get my boots on?"

A few minutes later, with Rafa standing on one side and Macha on the other, Tom limped from the house.

The lawman sat on the buckboard's wooden seat, waiting for them to approach. His walnut-brown, sun-wrinkled face creased in a smile, and with an automatic gesture he rubbed his fingers on his heavy black mustache. "Howdy, Tom. You look like death warmed over." He nodded to the others, then wrapped his reins around the brake handle and stepped down stiffly to the ground.

"I got your message and came as fast as I could. Looks like I arrived just in time."

Tom shook hands with Joe Ross and, turning about, introduced him to his new friends.

"The boy you sent to Socorro on that fine horse of yours told me a little about what was going on," Ross said.

Before he could say anything else, they heard the sound of a great many people. Looking about, they saw what appeared to be the entire population of Frisco tumbling up from the Middle and Lower Plazas. Mexican men, women, and children streamed from the mean little crooked alleys and rough streets out to the dry arroyo. Dust rose over their heads as they moved down it and then climbed up, trudging side by side at an angle until they neared María Alpizar's *jacal* where Elfego Baca remained at bay. A number of the men carried rifles while others, including many women and young people, carried a variety of weapons ranging from pitchforks to clubs.

The local population had stayed out of sight for the last three days but now they appeared in force. Observing them, the badly outnumbered cowboys nervously put their hands on their pistols as some three or four hundred Mexicans took up a position in the Upper Plaza.

Francisco Naranjo walked rapidly across the open ground until he joined Tom and Rafa. On being introduced to the deputy sheriff, he shook his hand.

Francisco said, "We sent many times to Socorro for help but none came. Finally Elfego Baca tried to bring law to Frisco, and you can see what happened."

At first Joe Ross didn't know how to reply. He hesitated before saying, "You've got good cause to be upset—I'll be the first to admit that—and we need to talk about it later. But right now we've got to get matters settled down."

Ross started to say something else, but Francisco interrupted him. "The *alcalde* and our justice of the peace have been meeting with the citizens of Frisco. Everyone had decided they couldn't stand by any longer, so when you came, they knew this was the right time to let the gringos know we are going to get even with them for shooting up our town."

The deputy sheriff said dryly, "We're not going back to vigilante justice. The Territory of New Mexico will take care of legal matters. I've told the Slaughter cowboys that they've got to get the hell out of Frisco, which ought to satisfy you and your *alcalde*. But the facts have to be faced: Elfego Baca has killed and wounded a good many men. Regardless of how all this began, he's got to go to trial. I told the cowboys that would happen, and they said they'd leave if I took Elfego in as my prisoner."

"No," Rafa said abruptly. "The people won't stand for that. The cowboys started this trouble."

"There's no other way to defuse the situation," Joe Ross insisted.

"You might be able to talk us into that," old Rafa said reluctantly, "but you can just forget it when it comes to Elfego. He'll never give up or agree to trial in one of your courts."

The wall of Mexicans moved closer. Tom glanced about and saw Macha's face suddenly turn pale. She ducked her head and walked quickly back to Francisco's house where Marta stood with the three children. Taking Pancho by the hand, Macha led her five-year-old boy inside.

Ross addressed Tom gruffly. "I've already given my word to the cowboys that Elfego Baca is to go with me to be tried for murder. Those men are naturally right upset. In fact, they're mad as hell, and it took a good bit of talking to get them to agree to leave this matter up to the law to handle. Now I've got to convince Baca—so I need one of you to help me assure him that he'll get a fair trial. I've heard the story told by the Slaughter cowboys, and it ties in with what you've said. So it's my opinion that he acted in self-defense."

"Let's talk to him," Francisco said, leading the way toward the *jacal*.

While Francisco spoke earnestly to Elfego, Tom drew Ross to one side. "I guess you heard that I got dragged at the end of a rope—and that these folks helped me."

Ross nodded, and then Tom continued. "The Slaughter men had dynamite, and they were swarming all over the place. You never saw such a sight. The boy was on the point of being killed—and all because he tried to bring some order to this town." Tom's eyes grew cold. "I couldn't stand off to one side."

Ross looked at him curiously. "After what those waddies did to you, I guess it was too much to ask for you to stay out of it. Did you get involved?"

Tom nodded.

"When I visited with the cowboys they told me that earlier the rifle bullets had gone wide of the mark—but all of a sudden it looked as if they couldn't miss."

Tom didn't speak.

"So—that was *you* handlin' that Winchester. No wonder things turned out the way they did."

Francisco led Elfego from the *jacal* and they joined Tom and Joe Ross. Elfego reached out with his large hands, taking Tom's right in both of his. "You saved my life last night—and again this morning. There's no way I can find the words to thank you. And I don't even know your name," he faltered.

The deputy sheriff examined him a moment, and then said, "This is Tom English, son. You were mighty lucky to have him pitch in last night."

"Tom English?" Elfego stepped back. "I had no idea," he murmured in confusion. "I've read so much about you . . ." Again he fell silent when he couldn't find the words he sought. Finally, speaking simply, he said, "I am very grateful."

Tom looked embarrassed. "You were doin' fine, it looked to me. But I'm glad I could be of some help." Turning to Ross, he said, "I can't let Elfego stand trial for those men I shot. I'll go with you and turn myself in."

"I know how these things work, and it'll be best if he goes alone. The judges who hold court in these parts are well acquainted with me,

not that there are that many of them. None would bend the law as a
favor," Ross added with a faint smile, "but they'll heed my advice. The
main thing is that we've got to restore order. We'll need to have a trial
to satisfy all sides, and this will allow a little time to pass so all the hot
blood can cool down. After that, I'm going to advise the court that if
he finds against Elfego he's liable to start some kind of civil war. The
people of Frisco have been pushed as far as they're going to allow." He
glanced out at the host of Mexicans who milled about nearby. Then he
added, "That's going to be the main thing he'll have in mind when he
makes his judgment, Tom—so I don't think you'll be needed. No use
complicating things."

"You'll send for me if Elfego might get into trouble?"

"Yes, but I don't expect that. If it's necessary, I'll testify as to what
I've found out. As I said before, in my view it's a clear-cut case of self-
defense."

"Sheriff," Elfego said, "you said I was lucky, but I think that something more than luck sent this man to help me. I'd like to ask you
people to come over here—I've got something to show you. It's in
here," he said, gesturing toward María Alpizar's shack, "where I spent
the last day and a half."

He stood by the door, waiting for them, and said, "I can't believe
that I've fought side by side with Tom English."

Moments later he welcomed Rafa Hernandez and Francisco and all
the others as they crowded into the tiny one-roomed shack. "Watch
your step," he warned as they stepped down. When all of them stood
on the dugout floor, Elfego closed the splintered door. "Look at that,"
he said.

The men stared at the daylight streaming through shivered, gaping
holes. "I've had lots of time to study that door," Elfego said. "And I've
counted three hundred and sixty-seven bullet holes. At least that
many. And look over here," he said.

The young man with the tin mail-order star pinned proudly on his
jacket pointed to a broom with a badly shivered handle. "This is the
strangest thing you'll ever see," he said proudly.

"*Dios mío,*" Rafa declared, examining it. The others huddled about
as Elfego showed them that the narrow handle had been hit or grazed
by eight bullets.

"How could a man live in here?" Francisco said in a wondering tone.
"The walls must have been hit by thousands of bullets. The roof is

half torn off by dynamite." He embraced Elfego, almost picking the small young man off his feet.

Flushed, Elfego said, "I lay down on the floor. It was God's will that I should survive. Splinters and dust fell all over me. Bullets went through this house like sand through the air in a windstorm. The saint protected me," he said, pointing to a plaster of Paris statuette about ten inches in height which lay at an angle in one corner of the lowered dirt floor next to an earthenware pot with a supply of water. "I found her in here, and I prayed to her. When she would say, 'Elfego, you better look out,' I'd raise up. That's when I'd shoot—and drive them off."

He leaned over and pointed at the spaces between the poles that made up the walls. He showed how he had knelt on the excavated floor and propped his rifle and his pistol so their barrels would be at ground level outside.

"*La Señora de Santa Ana,*" he said simply, nodding to the little statue, "called for me to take cover here. By the grace of God I found myself in a perfect fortress. You'll never make me believe that it was only luck that sent Tom English to help me last night—I think it was due to the Virgin's looking after me."

Behind him, a small rusted iron stove smoked slightly, its sides pocked and slashed by ricocheting bullets. Elfego showed them these things and also the well behind the house.

Then he looked at Tom. "Your right arm is hurt."

"It'll be all right."

"But you can't use a gun. You'll need someone to help you till you get better."

"My left hand works fine," Tom said. He observed the boy curiously, then said, "The sheriff has made a deal with the cowboys. They'll pull out of Frisco if he's able to take you to trial."

"Do you think I should go?"

Tom hesitated a moment before saying, "Yes, I do."

Joe Ross broke in, "It'll be a fair trial. I promise you that."

"Where will it be?" Elfego asked stiffly.

"One of this importance can't really take place around here, or even in Socorro. I would say that the best town would be Albuquerque."

"I'll not go unless I can wear my Colt and carry this rifle."

"No," Joe Ross said, his face tightening. "We don't have prisoners carrying weapons in this territory."

"That's the point I'll make. I'm going with you to clear my name and not as a prisoner. After all, I'm a man of the law myself."

Joe Ross smiled. "All right, son, that's fine by me. We'll ride to Albuquerque in the buckboard, and you can keep your weapons."

Looking pleased with himself, Elfego Baca agreed.

Francisco rushed off to seek the help of the *alcalde* and Guillermo Jones in explaining matters to the milling body of Mexicans. Before leaving he said to Joe Ross, "The people of Frisco are here to protect their town—and they look on Elfego as a hero. They're not going to want him taken prisoner—so I better try to explain to them what's happening."

The explanations took almost an hour, but at last the crowd of men and women and children began to disperse.

Joe Ross glanced at Tom, looking vastly relieved. "Looks like it's time for me to move on out. This has been one hell of a strange day." And then his face broke into a broad smile, white teeth shining.

Ross and his captive climbed into the buckboard, and Elfego could be seen showing the deputy sheriff his badge.

After they had left, the cowboys kept their word. Obviously worn out, they tightened the cinches on their long-saddled mounts, then rode out of town together.

Tom watched the cowboys as they stopped at a ridge above the town where they stopped and looked back. He figured they were watching the buckboard pulled by the rawboned gray with Ross and Elfego in it. The buggy took the fork to the right and soon was out of sight. When he glanced back at the ridge he saw that the cowboys had also disappeared.

Tom limped slowly back to Francisco's house. Rafa walked beside him and asked, "What do you think will happen to Elfego?"

"I don't know. With luck, he'll get acquitted."

"And where will you go from here?"

"I've some business with Mr. Slaughter."

"You'll need to be careful going out there. You've made a lot of bad enemies."

"I'm aware of that," Tom said.

He stepped into Francisco's house and Macha came up to him, clutching his arm.

"You've got to help me," she whispered. Terror showed in her eyes.

"What is it?" Tom asked, taken by surprise.

"When all the people of Frisco came to the Upper Plaza—that big crowd with rifles and weapons—I saw four men with them who work for Julian Haynes. One was Chato Verdugo. They've been sent to take me back to the *patrón.*" Her voice shook. "I know him well—there's no doubt in my mind why these men are here. The *patrón* has sent them to capture me and bring me to him so he can punish me." Her voice broke. "He'll torture me before I die. It's because of what happened when I fought against his friend, the one I killed. But," her words seemed to wander as if she couldn't control herself, "I didn't have any choice."

"I'll help you," Tom English said.

Ten

WILEY CALLAN spoke with enthusiasm to the two draft horses that leaned into their traces, pulling the bizarre red wagon up a slight incline. His voice rang out cheerfully. "Creep in your petty pace from day to day, you shaggy oat eaters, bang me against every rock and bump you can find clean to the last syllable of recorded time. Far be it from me to complain. Out here with nary a soul to hear, I'll declaim at the top of my lungs whenever I feel like it with no critic to point the finger of scorn." A beatific smile wreathed his sunburned face as he jostled along upon the high board seat. Wiley managed to find happiness in the most unlikely places, and he welcomed its appearance with unreserved pleasure.

The metal rims of the yellow spoked wheels clattered through patches of shale, and the tall-bodied wagon swayed perilously. Wiley dropped his voice to a deeper baritone and pronounced sonorously in his Texas twang, unconscious of the exaggerated dramatic gestures that he made with his free hand, "And all our yesterdays have lighted fools the way to dusty death." Shaking his head with enormous satisfaction, he added, "God, if that ain't the truth."

The wagon had a roofed enclosure upon it, some twelve feet in length and seven feet high. A water barrel and a chuck box hung to its rear. Bright red originally, it had faded somewhat but remained garish. On both sides a craftsman had created the representation of an ornate oval frame and with painstaking care had painted within it the representation of ideal human health and beauty: a bare-chested muscular man who flexed his muscles for the admiration of a seated long-haired woman. While the paintings had also faded, the mottoes beneath them, in bold black curlicued script, had not.

"Doctor Callan's Magical Elixir," the top line read, and in slightly smaller letters beneath it, "A scientifically prepared potion which guarantees grand health, potency, and power beyond belief. It inspires love and admiration from the opposite sex, and regulates the bowels."

Wiley took off his derby hat and mopped his brow with a bandana. The fist which held it had large knuckles, lumpy with scar tissue. He dried his freckled face, touched his peeling reddened nose, and observed his surroundings with intently staring blue-green eyes, taking note of everything he saw with great interest.

A man in his early thirties, he had close-cropped orange hair which he cut himself. It grew in ragged patches to a height of half an inch here, three quarters of an inch there, but nowhere did it lie flat. The harsh treatment to which Wiley Callan subjected the hair of his head did not extend to his abundant mustache. Far from being clipped to a moderate length, it grew luxuriously. This flowing growth, of a somewhat darker shade of red than his hair, had ends which had been trained with a modest application of mustache wax into upturned points at the ends.

Wiley's nose had been broken many times and had irregular bumps and ridges. In addition, his face showed further insults: small white scars showed near both eyes and through his eyebrows. His ears were also scarred and slightly thickened.

When people first met Wiley Callan, they weren't conscious of his size. However, they did sense something different about him although they weren't able to put their finger upon it. For one thing, he had an abnormally thick neck, one which required seamstresses to make his shirts specially. He stood at least six feet one and carried two hundred and twenty pounds of solid muscle with no noticeable fat at all upon his big frame. He had a habit of leaning back, totally relaxed— slumped over inside his loose clothing, allowing his shoulders to droop —and he gave a first impression which was totally unthreatening.

A buckboard rattled along from the west, the direction toward which he headed. Wiley pulled to one side to permit it to draw alongside. His day brightening, he began to compose flowery sentences, perfectly delighted at the unexpected opportunity for some conversation out on the windswept prairie. Wiley did love being with other human beings. Expectantly, he swept his arm high in the air and exuberantly bellowed, "Howdy," as the buckboard swept past.

Disappointment etched itself upon his transparent features. He gazed after the buggy's dust as it moved rapidly away. His sun-faded light orange eyebrows went high in the center of his wrinkled forehead and sloped down to the corners of his eyes as he woefully registered the only reply to his sincere and open and terribly friendly smile: a mere handwave from the black-hatted driver. He got a quick impression of two men, each wearing a lawman's star and armed, hurrying along the road to Socorro. Shrugging as if it didn't matter, but with his feelings hurt, Wiley slapped the reins on the backs of the unwilling horses which had begun to search the barren earth for something to eat.

With a voice of sounding brass, Wiley began to sing a song as his wagon once again traveled westward, making up the melody as he went along, singing words written almost three hundred years before.

The tilting tall red wagon with yellow wheels caused a minor sensation as it entered the small community of Frisco. A trail of Mexican children fell in behind it and three skinny long-tailed dogs barked at the feathered fetlocks of the two lather-streaked workhorses. Wiley took a coiled bullwhip from behind his seat and with a practiced lunge of his right shoulder stung one dog which ran howling away, dragging its injured hindquarters. Two more skillful snaps from the frazzled tip of the bullwhip, and the other dogs fled, also filling the air with high-pitched, outraged yapping. The horses, weary heads working up and down as they walked, followed the ruts leading into the Upper Plaza. The Mexican children drew back, then ran toward the Middle Plaza, knowing the danger of approaching too close to Milligen's Saloon.

When he had reached this place, the driver leaned back in his seat. He made a great show of hauling on the reins and shouting, "Whoa," as though it were difficult to halt the weary horses. These had already ceased all forward motion and had lowered their heads until their muzzles sank gratefully into the mossy water in the wooden trough clear up to their flaring nostrils. But this was the way Wiley liked to come to a stop. He had a fine sense of style.

He went to the back of his wagon and came out with two nosebags full of oats, fastening these so his animals could have a reward that would hold their appetites until he could find them some hay. He spoke to them in low tones as he rubbed their backs and pounded his big-knuckled hands upon them, raising small clouds of dust. Having seen to their comfort, he elected to attend to his own and walked into the saloon.

The wind died down in late afternoon and weak sunlight strained to touch the Upper Plaza. A hint of relative warmth fell on the town of Frisco as Francisco Naranjo came home from reconnoitering.

"Everything is still quiet," he said on entering.

"Did all the gringos leave town?" his wife Marta asked.

"No. A handful of the Slaughter cowboys had already started drinking and they stayed behind. And so did some of the men who own small ranches out in the hills. I guess they're like hunters who see a deer get away from them. They feel cheated that they didn't get to shoot Elfego."

"What a thing to say, Francisco," Marta admonished.

He looked at her without comment before going outside with a mug of coffee. He pulled a rickety chair with one broken leg to the side of the house, then gingerly sat down in it, tilting back against the barely perceptible heat of the sun-warmed wall. He had put his Navajo blanket with the slit in its center over his head and it gave him good protection. His wife pushed the door open and left it ajar. She asked if he wasn't cold but he said no, that it felt good to be able to stay outside a little after the weather they'd been having.

"He sees something," Marta said to Tom and Macha. "That's why he didn't stay in here with us."

Tom moved to the door. "Are they still there?"

"Yes. One's in those rocks a few hundred yards behind the house. I guess his job is to make sure that Macha doesn't get out the back door. The others are in the arroyo."

"How many?"

"I can't tell. At least two, maybe three. A head comes up real slow every now and then."

"Come inside, Francisco," his wife called to him. "They might shoot you."

"I don't think so," he said stoically. "They don't know we've spotted them—and they're waiting to try to surprise us. That's their best chance of taking Macha alive, and she's convinced me that's what they mean to do. But I'll see them in hell first," he added fiercely.

"They probably saw me before I spotted them," Francisco said, "but they didn't shoot. Their plan must be to attack after nightfall."

Tom buckled his gunbelt about his waist, then swiftly tied the leather thongs from the bottom of his left holster around his thigh. The hurt shoulder was better, but he decided to use the sling. He put it around his neck and adjusted his right arm in it before addressing Francisco.

"I think you're right. As soon as it's dark I'll get her out of here."

"Where will you take her? Where can you hide?"

"This is your town, Francisco. What's your suggestion?"

"Well, maybe the *alcalde*'s house."

"Wouldn't they think of that?"

"I guess so," Francisco said, squinting his eyes out the window as he thought. "You know, there's one place they probably wouldn't look. The cemetery next to the church has a little shed where they keep some tools. A long time ago an old man who was caretaker for the church lived there but he died."

Tom looked toward the Middle Plaza. "Right now our problem is how to get Macha out of here with armed men on the lookout— expecting us to make a run for it."

He looked at the strange red wagon with yellow wheels and a roofed box on it with pictures and slogans painted on its sides. It sat across the rocky plaza in front of the saloon. "Francisco, did you get close enough to that peculiar-looking wagon to see what's printed on it?"

A long pause ensued. Then Francisco said, sounding embarrassed, "I can't read." Defensively, he added, "I can sign my name though."

"There aren't that many men out here who can read, Francisco. It doesn't matter. I was just curious about that wagon."

"I'm as confused about it as you are," Francisco replied. "Never saw anything like it."

"We've got a few hours until sundown," Tom said. "I think I'll test those fellas and see if their kindness in not putting a bullet in you, Francisco, will extend to me."

He walked tentatively through the door, stood outside a moment, then returned. "The weather's not as mild as it looks," he said, reaching for his heavy coat. Owing to the sling, he couldn't put his right arm in it, so he simply wore it as a cloak, fastening its buttons at his neck. This also served the purpose of leaving his left arm and his Colt free of any encumbrance.

With that, he walked slowly out of the house, feeling the familiar weight of the six-gun on his left leg, and began his four-hundred-yard walk toward Milligen's Saloon. It felt good to be moving about even though his legs felt weak. He'd left his spurs in the bags along with the Colt that he'd removed from his cartridge belt. He could almost feel the aim of unseen riflemen in the arroyo, and for a moment he braced himself. But nothing happened.

When he reached what had at a distance looked like a circus wagon, he paused to examine it. Then, shaking his head and smiling, he proceeded to enter the saloon.

Tom English stood inside the door, focusing his eyes. A thin Mexican girl in a tight blue dress walked up to him provocatively but he waved her off. He went to the bar and ordered a bottle.

The bartender examined him for a moment. "Ain't you the man McCarty dragged at the end of his rope?"

Several men nearby snickered. Beyond them, seven or eight stood at the bar, intent upon their drinking. Others sat at some tables, and at the far wall, six men at a large round table played poker. All had stopped what they were doing at his entrance, first staring at him with fixed expressions, then ignoring him.

He paid for the bottle and looked for a place to sit. The cowboys at the bar turned their backs on him. Sensing their hostility, wondering if there were something special about him that prompted it or if that was how they felt toward all strangers, he took the bottle in his good hand and headed toward a lone table at the back of the room. As he walked toward it a voice called out to him.

"Howdy," Wiley Callan said, his freckled face crinkling into a smile. An empty plate except for a knife and fork crossed upon it sat before him.

Tom paused, looking at the man, noting his spiky, bristly orange hair.

Wiley Callan appeared to be totally relaxed and as friendly as a puppy. "I've just finished my steak, mister, and I'd enjoy some company." He pushed a chair out with his foot. "Take a seat and join me."

Wiley rose with easy grace to his feet and started to shake hands but then noticed the sling. Discomfited, he sat back down in his chair.

"My name's Tom."

"Mine's Wiley Callan." He didn't question the fact that a last name had not been mentioned. He'd known many men who kept their own counsel, most of whom had left some form of trouble behind them.

"I saw your wagon. Almost the size of a boxcar."

"Ain't it a caution? I love that wagon. It has everything a man needs: a bed, storage for all my gear, and as much of a kitchen as I need in a box at the back. If I feel like using it, there's a table that folds down on one side with an awning I prop over it for shade. With that and Macbeth, I can spend many happy hours."

"Macbeth?"

"You won't understand unless I give you some background." He sighed with pleasure. "Would you like to hear the story of my life? I promise that you'll be fascinated."

"Well—"

Leaning back in his chair, completely at ease, Wiley began to speak, acting as if he intended to settle into the conversation for as long as it might take. "I love talking about myself. I was raised on a big ranch in South Texas. My daddy wasn't the best businessman maybe, or it might have been that lack of rain and tick fever amongst his cattle somehow kept following him about. He traded the big ranch for a smaller one, and that one for one still smaller yet, and finally he ended up with a farm."

Wiley looked at Tom and asked, "Have you ever tried farming? No glamour to it. You can't stand behind a plow and think to yourself: *My, but I'll bet I look picturesque.* Now, a cowboy on the other hand, in spite of building fence and working on windmills and doing all sorts of maintenance work like some kind of outdoor mechanic, can sit on his horse and admire the picture that he makes. And that takes much of the sting out of harsh reality." He felt the curled tips of his exuberant mustache with the fingers of his right hand, first one side and then the other. "Does that make any sense to you?"

"I never thought about it in quite that way," Tom started to say, but his host interrupted him.

"Of course you have. There's no cowboy alive who hasn't been proud as punch of bein' part of a grand tradition. One that's been dying since the day it started, and who knows, maybe by now it's dead as a doornail. Well, back to me"—he grinned as he said this—"back to the marvelous tale of the life of Wiley Algernon Callan, the cowboy who moved on."

He seemed to drift momentarily through a daydream before saying,

"Such wind as scatters young men through the world, to seek their fortunes further than at home where small experience grows."

"What?" Tom asked, mystified by the man.

"I often find Shakespeare's words surprisingly on the mark. They explain better than I ever could why I had to move on. I couldn't bear even the thought of farming so I tried cowboyin' for others. This proved to be very much like work, and in spite of the fine picture I cut —ridin' rank broncs, takin' the edge off 'em at first light every morning, and all the rest—it soon palled on me. So I decided to go east and find something that would suit a gentleman. Of course, I'm not one of those, but I've always felt a cut above my fellow man. That's a terrible thing to admit, but it's true. I've regularly indulged in the sin of pride."

"Wouldn't you join me in a drink?" Tom asked, pouring a second one for himself.

"I don't drink whiskey or smoke tobacco. This body is the only one the Lord has seen fit to give me, and I take the best care of it I can. In fact, I lift iron dumbbells to keep my arms and shoulders strong, and run every morning for several miles to keep my wind in good condition. Got started doing that when I was a box fighter, but I'm gettin' ahead of myself."

And with that he launched again into his narrative. He'd always thought of himself as being "different," laying great stress on this. On arriving in St. Louis, he'd fallen in with a group of traveling actors. He began by moving scenery for them, then playing bit parts in various melodramas. In a brief time he fell in love with one of the troupe, a girl named Mary Carol Harmly.

His wind-burned peeling face turned even redder as he mentioned her name. She had been, he emphasized, a classic actress, and she instilled in him the ambition to become an actor. And thus his lifelong passion had begun for the works of William Shakespeare and in particular for the dramatic tragedy of *Macbeth*.

"I carry that book around with me, and have memorized it from the first scene to the last. It's the only play I own, but I've decided it's the only one I need."

"Did you ever have a chance to act any of the parts?" Tom asked.

Wiley Callan's face molded itself into a mask of sadness. "Never. Not even once, although I've offered in more than one saloon to play out the entire drama, performing every character's part, including

Lady Macbeth and the witches, all by myself. But there have been no takers for my offer."

Wiley frowned at the memory of so much rejection. Then he said, "About this time Mary Carol left me for another man, which completely unnerved me. I was disconsolate. After that the thought of the stage saddened me—so I left it." He winked slowly before adding, "Besides, I realized I'd starve to death as an actor. Anyway, that's when I took up the art and craft of boxing. This worked pretty well, especially when I began to train and get myself in condition. Bareknuckle boxing is performed in the east for the most part in gentlemen's clubs and athletic arenas or even in stables. After a few years of trading blows with men my size or bigger, I began to have a constant headache, and it occurred to me that this profession might not be the one for me.

"During that period I'd worried about my health and had come up with a tonic that gave me pep. The stuff tastes terrible, but it does make a man or woman perky. I had a sudden inspiration one evening after drinking some of it: I'd find a way to sell it that permitted me to combine all I'd learned about acting and athletics. Besides, I love to travel, and by selling my wares from town to town, I hope to see the entire United States and all the territories. When I finish my grand tour of New Mexico, for example, I'm headed west, but not until after the spring thaws come, since some of the mountain passes would be difficult with a big wagon like mine."

Wiley Callan said wistfully, "I don't believe you've been paying attention. You've a far-off look to your eye."

Tom said he was sorry, and Wiley instantly accepted the apology. "That's all right. Most people don't listen to me as carefully as they should. And when I tell jokes, they hardly ever laugh. Well, you seem an awfully friendly fellow, and I'd like to sit here and spend the rest of the afternoon with more conversation, but I've got to earn my daily bread. This won't take long—and it might entertain you."

Wiley took a deep breath, then rose and walked to the bar. Taking a spoon, he clattered it against the side of a glass.

"Gentlemen," he said in his stage voice, one that had deep sonorous tones which vibrated richly, *"I can whip the bejeesus out of any man in the house."*

The friendly way he stood at the bar, slumped over and smiling timidly, did not match the belligerent message. The surprised cowboys began to laugh and drawl insults at him.

Wiley held his hand high and something in it winked a quick reflection. "I'm holding here a twenty-dollar gold piece—twenty days' wages, I suspect, for most of you. And it belongs to the man who can whip me in a fair fight, but only if I get to take some of my tonic first."

"What on earth is he talkin' about?" one man grumbled. Others made catcalls and gibes. A high voice rang out, "If you aren't careful we'll sic Lud Grossbach on you. He's our blacksmith out at the ranch. How about it, Lud, reckon you can handle this stranger for twenty dollars?"

The cowboys, delighted at the prospect of watching a fight, began to egg him on with considerable eagerness.

The man named Lud seemed the only one to be less than enthusiastic about the notion.

"This way," Wiley said as he walked out to the street, making beckoning motions with his hand.

Tom held back until all of them had left, even the bartender, but then curiosity got the better of him, and he went out on the sidewalk in front of the swinging doors. He looked across the plaza at Francisco's home and saw nothing happening. Glancing at the sun, he decided he had at least an hour or two before darkness fell.

Wiley proceeded to his tall red wagon and released several ropes so the tabletop that was fastened by hinges to one side of it could fall into place. Legs under it folded down for further support. Upon this Wiley set a large placard which proclaimed in bold letters, "Doctor Callan's Magical Elixir, Pure-dee Potency, Strength, and Power for only $1.00 a bottle. Amaze your wife or girl friend. Improve your Regularity. Also good for Aches and Pains."

Wiley worked rapidly, setting a dozen clear glass bottles full of a brownish green liquid out on the rough tabletop. He uncorked one of these and took a long pull from it. Shuddering, he wagged his head from one side to the other, peeled off his coat, stood up straight for the first time, and his chest swelled. He raised his shirt-sleeve-clad arms and in a great voice called out, "Let your challenger beware. I've just taken a swig of Doctor Callan's Magical Elixir, and this gives me a great advantage. In fact, now that I think of it, it seems unfair." He struck a pose as he stood before them, his orange eyebrows quizzically arched.

The sight of his actual stature had momentarily sobered the cowboys, but the foolish statement reinforced their original certainty that
their man would have no difficulty handling this bombastic, foolish
stranger.

"Whup him good, Lud," one man encouraged.

"Try not to kill him," another blustered. "We sure don't want the
law over at Socorro to have to come back over here."

Wiley proceeded to the opening behind his wagon. He wore heavy
brogans on his feet but walked lightly. He pulled on a pair of thin
leather gloves and smiled at the bulky man who approached.

Lud Grossbach stood a little over six feet and weighed at least thirty
pounds more than Wiley. In spite of the cold, he rolled up his sleeves,
revealing massive arms.

At this, the cowboys began cheering. They offered to bet on their
man, expecting no takers. But Wiley called out, "I'll cheerfully cover
all wagers. Who will hold the money and keep a tally?"

The bartender was pressed into service. He filled his pockets with
two- and three-dollar bets, making notes to himself as he did so. Then
he announced to Wiley Callan, "You'll need seventeen dollars to cover
this."

Wiley disappeared into his big wagon, then emerged from it with a
handful of money which he gave to the bartender. He returned to the
table and took another quick pull from the bottle of tonic and turned
about, invigorated.

"What's in that stuff?" one inquisitive cowboy asked.

Wiley faced him and one eyelid slowly closed as if it were a flesh-
colored eyepatch. "I will inform you of the ingredients," he said, concluding the gross wink and opening his twinkling eye. He looked as if
he were having the time of his life. "However, they are terrible to
contemplate. I begin with eye of newt and toe of frog, then add wool
of bat and tongue of dog."

With relish he began to sing, employing a melody that he himself
composed. The cowboys standing about gaped at him.

> Liver of blaspheming Jew,
> gall of goat, and slips of yew
> silvered in the moon's eclipse,
> nose of Turk and Tartar's lips,

finger of birth-strangled babe
ditch delivered by a drab.

The crowd had fallen silent. At last one man said, "God A'mighty, he's crazy as a bedbug. Git out there and whip his tail, Lud. Only an insane man could think up words like those. A lunatic like that is liable to be dangerous." A sincere chorus from the other men supported this conclusion.

The big German stood and stuck out his lantern jaw. "You first, and then it'll be my turn," he said in a reverberating voice that sounded as if it were coming out of a stone well.

"No, no, no," Wiley Callan protested, backing away. "We don't do it that way, Lud. That's old-fashioned. Nowadays you get to prance about and defend yourself. Just a regular old fight except you can only use your hands." He rolled his eyes heavenward, despairing of having to deal with provincials, then raised his arms, bending the elbows artfully. He had his knees flexed, his back slightly arched, and he began shuffling toward his opponent, bobbing his head slightly, keeping his left foot forward.

The bulky blacksmith advanced, ignored the annoyance of a solid left jab in the mouth, and wrapped his huge arms around Wiley. He began to squeeze with all his might, lifting his captive off his feet.

The mob of cowboys cheered raucously as Wiley's face turned beet red. Lud leaned backward and then flung Wiley to the ground and as he rolled over, kicked him right behind the ear, knocking the red-haired boxer head over heels.

Wiley scrambled to his feet, face flaming, eyes aglow, all rules canceled. Lud backed away to the side of the wagon and grasped a bottle of Doctor Callan's Elixir which he held up as he would a club. But by this time the doctor himself flew through the air and crashed with all his force into the bull-shouldered German. The two went down in a cloud of dust, rolled back and forth, kicking and punching and grunting, the bottle popping free and tumbling off to one side. And then, after more rolling and clawing, they made it to their feet. Each proceeded more cautiously now, hunched over, weaving, and aware that he faced a powerful adversary.

Lud attacked with a great bellow, his big legs churning and his head down low. This time Wiley was prepared. A powerful overhead right pounded the German on the ear, felling him. Lud rose and charged again. Wiley popped him under the chin with a carefully timed kick, then slammed a rapid left-right combination to the German's solar plexus. Lud's face went blank as he gasped for air, and at that instant Wiley gathered all his strength, wound up, and threw a right-hand roundhouse haymaker, following through with all his weight. His fist landed with a loud splat, sounding as if an army mule had kicked a ripe watermelon.

Wiley Callan backed away and waited, massaging his injured knuckles and staring with disbelief at the barrel-chested blacksmith who wavered but still stood upright, staring at the world with glazed eyes.

Tom came close and Wiley hissed to him, "If that one didn't stop him, I want you to run and get me a shotgun." But fortunately, Lud Grossbach's knees began to sag. His eyes rolled up in his head and he tumbled over like a tower in an earthquake, slamming nose first into the hard dirt, not even holding out his hands to break the fall.

"Lord," Wiley complained petulantly, addressing himself to Tom, "I surely do hate to fight amateurs. Things like this keep happening. There must be a less painful way to attract a crowd."

He peeled off his gloves, explaining that it was his opinion that their use helped him from breaking his knuckles, and then mounted the front of his wagon after stuffing the dollars he had won into his pockets.

"Friends," Wiley called out in his stage voice, "you've sent a worthy representative to test me, and I'll be the first to admit that no ordinary human could stand up to him. Has any man ever bested Lud Grossbach up till now?"

He waited for the expected response, which came first from shaking heads and a few comments which indicated that no one had come close to whipping the German before. Then he said, "I'm a man of peace, a healer, and the only reason that I've engaged in the sport of boxing was to show that even a mild fellow like me can be given the grandest gift—the bestowal of *potency and power*—if he takes two ounces a day of this elixir." He raised a bottle of the suspicious-looking liquid high.

"Only a dollar, boys, and it will give you strength you've never dreamed of. You'll be amazed at the way the ladies will look at you after three short days of use. And if by chance any of you suffer from aching joints, or piles from being on those hard saddles too long each day, Doctor Callan's elixir will cure them too. And make you regular as clockwork to boot. All for just a dollar. Can't beat that. You boys have shown that you're gamblers, how about chancing a single measly dollar against a lifetime of happiness? How about it?"

Tom watched with disbelief as the men queued up before Wiley's sales table, each one purchasing a bottle.

One said, "What the hell, might as well try it."

Another stated, "Maybe this'll help them stiff knees of mine," but a friend said, "Now, Jack, I know that what you really have in mind is to drink that bottle and then go hunt up that señorita in the saloon." The men in the line laughed good-naturedly.

When the last sale had been made, the cowboys left for Milligen's Saloon, supporting the groggy Lud Grossbach who had partially regained his senses.

Wiley Callan came up beside Tom. "You've had a preoccupied air about you since we first met. And even now, after the entertainment I promised, it hasn't left."

The two men hunkered down beside the wagon. For fifteen minutes Tom spoke earnestly, telling Wiley about the things that had been going on in Frisco. Then he said, "There are hunters out of sight over there," gesturing with his hand toward the arroyo, "and behind that adobe house."

"Hunters?"

"They're after the girl I've been telling you about, the one named Macha."

"Unnatural troubles," Wiley declared.

Tom looked at him through narrowed eyes. "There'll be trouble all right—and it will start, I expect, right after dark."

"It strikes me, my new friend, that you need some assistance."

Scattered clouds in the west hung above the horizon, turning brilliant red and orange colors. The sky in the huge inverted bowl over them shaded from pink into light blue and on toward the east it became a rich darkening violet.

"I'll be happy to accept any offers of help I can get," Tom said.

Eleven

THE GRAND PROCESSION started with Wiley Callan pulling hard on his reins, drawing his team of horses in a tight circle. He went past the saddle shop and the office of the justice of the peace, then proceeded into the Middle Plaza where children playing in the deepening twilight watched his approach. They stood stock-still at first, struck dumb by the marvelous sight of the gaily painted vehicle. When it drew by them, they frolicked behind it. As soon as he had gathered up this unlikely retinue, Wiley turned back to the Upper Plaza, going past the livery stables and the pens behind it.

The red wagon with yellow wheels bumped through the rough low spots where the dry arroyo was shallow and angled across the square. By this time eight Mexican children—boys and girls ranging from six to twelve years of age—chased behind him. The patent medicine seller's long, tall wagon lurched through the powdery wallows and depressions near the cottonwood trees, clattered on rocks past María Alpizar's ruined and empty *jacal,* and paused at the front door of Francisco Naranjo's adobe house. Only an instant's hesitation, but long enough for two dark figures, concealed by long shadows, to run from the house. They climbed past the driver, stepped beyond his high board seat into the open door which led to the interior of his rolling home on wheels, and closed it behind them.

As the door slammed, Wiley began lashing his long bullwhip before him. Each time he did this it sounded like a pistol shot cracking through the air. Although the bullwhip's fringed tip missed the horses' ears by at least a foot, the vicious snapping startled them, and they fell into a lumbering, rocking gallop, their big hooves pounding like kettledrums across the rock-hard ground. The wood of the wagon creaked and groaned along the way, and these sounds were punctuated by metallic clashing coming from pots and pans banging against each other and by the jingling of harness chains. The children, arms swinging as they scurried in a vain attempt to keep up, shrieked with laughter at the game. Then they stopped running as they watched the strange vehicle bound away.

A man standing in the rocks, almost out of sight in the approach of night, leveled his rifle, but he was confused and couldn't see his moving target well. Three other men, also clutching rifles, ran from the arroyo. They turned and scrambled over its side, plowing through dry scrub brush and cactus. A moment later they emerged on horseback and fell into pursuit.

The ponderous long wagon, leaning perilously off to the left, almost toppled over on its side as it made the turn by the office of the justice of the peace across from Milligen's Saloon. It teetered as it skidded around the corner, wheels jolting and throwing stones in a spray, before settling back and almost overturning on the other side.

By this time the bulky draft horses had the bits in their teeth. With thick necks outstretched, manes and tails flying, they blundered in a downhill course, blasting by the church and past the *alcalde's* house, exploding over a rocky hump in the road which caused the hurtling burden behind them to land with a hollow crash. Wiley no longer had to encourage his team but rather had seized the reins, pulling on them with all his might in an effort to regain control as he flew down the unfamiliar path past tiny shacks and hovels. With legs spread wide and broganed feet planted firmly on a brace-board, he leaned back and fought to keep his balance. Sheer excitement caused him to howl from time to time.

As they reached the Lower Plaza, the trail grew ever rockier and steeper. The horses, fighting for breath, tossing their heads and rolling their eyes, slowed into a gallop and as they came over a rise, began to jab their forefeet on the ground, jarring back into a trot. They surged over a final hump and headed steeply downhill with the weight of the wagon forcing them forward. Unable to stop, their momentum carried them into the shallow river. Obviously taken by surprise, the horses craned their heads around and looked back at their driver accusingly. Icy waves rippled past their hairy knees.

Wiley Callan, hooting with laughter, hollered at his team as he hauled on the long reins, urging them to wheel about and return to the sandy shore. The horses leaned into their traces and labored up the bank to a shuddering halt. They expressed their complaints with low fluttered nickering.

Wiley swiveled about and opened the door to the wagon. An instant later Macha came through the small door, followed by Tom. She wore Francisco's Navajo blanket as protection against the cold and she carried another heavy woolen blanket in her arms. Tom made sure the Colt on his left side was securely seated in its holster before buttoning his fleece-lined coat.

"You're a terrible wagon driver, Wiley," he said after he and Macha stepped to the ground.

"In Roman days, I'd 'a been one hell of a chariot racer," Wiley replied. "I hear horses—they'll be here any second."

Tom said, "I'll wait out of their sight in case there's trouble."

"I've always been able to talk my way out of tight spots. Don't even think of tarryin'—you get that gal to safety."

Tom and Macha turned away and ran toward the shacks up from the river.

Wiley heard the sounds made by hooves striking stones. In the gloom he saw their pursuers come to a stop on the slope above him: three black shadows against the surrounding grayness. One of them went into a shack and returned from it with a lighted coal oil lantern dangling by its suspension wire from his left hand. In his right he held a handgun. The other men dismounted also and they held pistols pointing up at Wiley as they all came closer.

"Baje lentamente," one of them ordered.

The words held no significance for Wiley, but the weapons wagging at him gave an indication of their meaning.

He became aware of a fourth man riding up nearby. In the wavering glow from the lantern he could see that the rider held a rifle pointed at him.

The mounted late arrival spoke to the other men in rapid Spanish. "Macha's not in that adobe house where she was staying. No one else was either—I guess they ran away."

"We'll deal with them later," one of the three men on foot said. He wore a long slicker over his coat and appeared to be their leader. Approaching the wagon, he said to Wiley in heavily accented English, "You don't hear so good? We said for you to get down from there."

"I'm merely resting my horses, gentlemen, after my traditional parade through town at close of day. Wherever I go to sell my wares, I make it a practice to be noticed. And you should certainly agree that I got the attention of the populace of Frisco this evening."

By the time he'd finished speaking he'd descended from the wagon seat and stood beside the three armed men. In a conversational way he said, "Allow me to introduce myself. I'm Doctor Wiley Algernon Callan, inventor of Doctor Callan's Magical Elixir."

The leader of the group ignored this. He raised his pistol and fired a shot high into the wagon and shouted, "Come on out of there. We know you're inside, Macha."

He shoved Wiley roughly to one side and crawled up to the driver's seat.

Wiley, eyes widening, muttered, "The devil damn thee black, thou cream-faced loon."

"What did he say?"

"Ignore him—he's loco."

The man wearing the slicker reached down and took the lantern from his companion, then cautiously opened the short door into the red wagon. Flattened off to one side of it, he thrust his arm out and banged the barrel of his pistol on the wall. "One last chance to come out, Macha."

But there was no answer. Summoning his courage, he ventured inside. A moment later he reappeared. *"No hay nadie,"* he announced tersely to his companions.

Wiley deciphered what that must have meant. "I could have told you that," he huffed. "I live and travel alone, going from one town to another, offering hope to suffering humanity. As I've said, this evening parade is a tradition with me. It's a way of letting the entire town know that the famous Doctor Callan has arrived. By tomorrow, the curious and those with aches and pains will seek me out. I'll spend my day treating the halt and the infirm, easing the way for all who may suffer from what in their innocence they call 'the misery,' a term that encompasses all the slings and arrows the flesh is heir to—ranging from mere chilblains to brain fever and humors of the blood."

The leader snorted with emphatic disgust, shouldering past Wiley.

As they made their way to their horses, they spoke to one another. One said, "Macha must have run out of the house in all the confusion." Another replied, "She can't have gone far. The weather's getting worse—she'll have to find shelter somewhere in town."

"We'll find her," the man in the slicker said. Reining his horse about, he said impatiently, "Come on. We'll start at the other end of town and go through every house in Frisco if it takes half the night. Haynes will have our hides if we don't find that whore of his."

Black boiling clouds, at times glowing with vivid interior flashes, blotted out the sight of stars. A spasm of light twitched across the sky a moment before a thunderclap resonated. Then quietness fell and the front of the storm bludgeoned in from the north, a stiff wind slashing in a clean sharp line, penetrating every dwelling in Frisco. Sleet as hard as pebbles stung across the roofs and chattered against windows. Then the snow began. Random flakes mingled with the sleet and hail, turning the air densely white, sealing off every house into a snow-bound island. It slanted at shallow gusting angles upon bare-armed defenseless trees. These in moments became transformed, along with the clusters of prickly pear and cholla cactus and ragged weeds which lined the harsh draws, changing strangely in occasional lightning flashes into glittering soft shadows, a dazzling canvas framed by the dark of night.

The church, with its weathered bare walls, also took on a strange beauty. Snow painted it white. The small bell tower with its lonely cross overlooked the adjoining cemetery where random fellow crosses stood over snow-clad humped graves and one ancient masonry crypt. The earth took refuge underneath a frozen cottony blanket. A marveling child stretched out a curious hand from the cracked-open door of a small hut but drew it back instantly after touching iciness.

A rustling of wind, like starched petticoats in motion, accompanied the fantastic swirls of powder. Hours passed, and still the feathered whiteness drifted slowly down. A full four inches concealed the naked rawness of the earth while three-foot drifts leaned heavily on walls.

Near midnight the blizzard ended. Brass church bells vibrated across crystal surfaces beneath air too cold to move, air which felt like frozen steel.

Next to the primitive cemetery by the church lay an abandoned hut where the old caretaker had once lived. It served now as a toolshed. The small front door pressed against the weight of snow, forcing it back.

Pain struck Tom English in the face as he looked through the opening, and harsh cold bit deep into his nose and throat. Shocked by the sensation, he shoved the small door closed. As he forced the rough boards against the crude lintel, white steam puffed from his mouth. Behind him, within a rock fireplace, flames leaped brightly but only cast their momentary warmth in a fragile, wavering semicircle before the stone chimney sucked all heat away. Macha huddled near the fire, holding herself within two blankets.

"Did you see anything?" she asked.

"No."

"You must be freezing; come closer."

Tom moved next to her and held his numbed hands out to the fire.

"Do you ever get tired of being so respectable?"

The question took him off guard. In confusion he looked into her dancing eyes and saw she was teasing him.

"Don't be so shy," Macha said, sliding next to him, throwing the blankets about the two of them.

The heat of their bodies, wrapped in rough, scratchy blankets, together with the flickering warmth from the fire gradually stilled his shivering.

"Your hands are like ice," she said, holding them in hers.

She wrapped her arms about him and they both leaned forward toward the flames.

Bright changing shapes and wavering shadows played upon the walls and low ceiling of the tiny shack, reflecting the firelight. Old tools—two shovels, a pick, and various rusted hoes and rakes—lay scattered about, leaning in corners. Dull cobwebs and the dirt of ages lay on every surface.

Gradually the feeling came back into Tom's hands. A splintered tingling began at his fingertips and spread. He rubbed both hands together roughly, then reached out from the protective blankets. He grasped hold of a dry branch and put it carefully upon the fire. Sparks flew out as a bottom log fell into ashes.

When they had first arrived, a short time after full dark had fallen, the priest had met them. "I've been waiting for you," he had said. Francisco had advised him they would be arriving.

The priest, an older man wearing a heavy overcoat and what looked like a woman's woolen scarf tied under his chin, protecting his ears, showed them to the toolshed. "It's much warmer in my quarters," he had said. "I have a little apartment in the back of the church. You'll be welcome."

But they had refused. "Men will be looking for me," Macha explained. The priest looked at her and then at Tom. Although obviously confused, he asked no questions.

"I've brought you a loaf of bread and this red wine." He seemed distressed that he hadn't anything else to offer them.

"Thank you, padre," Tom said as the priest left.

Then the full force of the storm had struck. Now, with the sound of the midnight bells still in their ears, the blazing fire gradually began to warm the shed. The knife blades of wind that had stabbed through the cracks in the walls had stopped probing. The whining from out-of-doors had disappeared and the only sound they heard was the crackling of the fire.

They sat on an old mattress stuffed with cornshucks and feathers, the two blankets draped around their shoulders. Freeing their arms, they broke thick chunks of bread from the long heavy loaf. They poured dark red wine in two small glasses which the priest had given them.

"I'm starving," Tom said. "This must be bread and wine for the mass."

Macha stopped eating and crossed herself. "I hadn't thought of that."

She began to cry then, and Tom tried to comfort her.

"Francisco says he'll have your son with him tomorrow, and that he'll take both of you to Ghost Ranch on the Chama River where his friend works. He never heard from him, but you can't wait around here any longer."

"Those men will find me," she said in a low voice. "I know what's going to happen."

"Macha, you'll be safe. No one will think to look here."

"There'll be smoke from our chimney when dawn comes. We'll die without the fire—it's colder than I ever remember in all my life."

"Well," Tom said uncertainly, "even if they do see it, there's no way I'll let them take you."

He leaned back slightly and examined her face in the firelight. She had large slightly slanted eyes of luminous deep brown and high cheekbones. Her lips were perhaps too full, but she was one of the loveliest women he'd ever seen.

"There are four of them. And Julian Haynes must be around somewhere. You can't really protect me."

"You're wrong," Tom English said.

Her tears had stopped. She put her head on his chest and said, "I'm so afraid—not just for myself. I'm worried about Pancho too."

"He's with Francisco and Marta. They'll look after him."

He talked to her then, told her about his family, about Sally and Rebecca and Ben, the baby. She pulled away slightly.

He said, "You're a fine nurse. As you saw, I've been hurt quite a few times. But I've never had better care."

She leaned against him again. "I like to take care of people. I've never had anyone to love except for Mama and Pancho. I guess I never will."

"Don't say things like that. Francisco is going to help you get away. You'll start a new life up on the Chama."

She didn't answer at first. Then she said, "Would you hold me again?"

They lay before the fire wrapped in blankets on the moldy, discolored mattress. The dark-haired head rested on his shoulder till break of day. Neither of them slept.

Twelve

THE CHARRED LOG crumbled into glowing coals, and Tom looked at it through strands of Macha's hair. Seeking warmth, she nuzzled even closer, arms and legs surrounding him. The strangeness of his situation struck him: *I'm in bed with a beautiful, warm-bodied Mexican girl—and armed men are wandering around outside intent on killing us.* Gently he began to pull free of her, but she put both arms around his neck. He paused, looking down a few inches into her solemn eyes.

"Don't leave," she whispered.

"I need to get the fire started," he began to explain but fell silent. Something broke in the distance followed by other cracking noises. A horse whinnied, another answered, and then he heard the sounds of hooves crunching through the snow's frozen crust. Voices speaking in Spanish sounded clearly through the Arctic air of early dawn.

"No tracks around this shed."

"She could have hidden in it before the snow fell. Look inside it."

Leather groaned as a man dismounted. "Rigo, no smoke's coming from the chimney. If she's in there she must be frozen."

"Look anyway."

Tom rose and stood behind the door. Macha huddled on the old mattress that had been their cocoon that night, holding the blankets about her, eyes wild with fear.

Tom pulled out his Colt and ratcheted the hammer back with his thumb, the oiled metal clicking out a small deadly sound. Macha's eyes went to the upright barrel and then shifted to his face.

Someone pushed the door partially open and thrust his head inside. He only saw the other side of the dark, dingy shed—the few rusted tools resting in a corner. Hurriedly he moved away, leaving the door ajar.

"No hay nada más que basura adentro."

"Let's go get the priest in the church. He may know something."

"De acuerdo. We've tried every other house and building in this miserable town."

Cursing and complaining, the searchers moved away.

Tom released the hammer carefully and slid the .45 into the holster on his left side. He shivered in the frigid air and went to Macha. In the still warm hollow where they'd spent the night, he found his wool-lined jacket, the one he'd placed on top of the blankets. He put it on.

When the pursuer had pushed the door back, Macha's full lips had parted in horror. Still shaking, she pushed her clinging hair back from her eyes and face, combing it absently with her fingers. She threw back the blanket and smoothed down her skirt which had rucked up in high wrinkles upon the smoothness of her long pale-brown legs. With one lithe movement she slipped her head through the slit in the Navajo blanket, allowing its coarse thick folds to fall down to her ankles. She slid fur-lined moccasins upon her sock-clad feet and looked up to see Tom watching her.

"A close call" was all he said.

"We've got to get out of here—they'll come back."

"No," he answered. "This is the safest place in Frisco. They just checked it."

Moving to the open door, he pushed it almost closed but kept his face at the crack of light at its edge. The wind had died down. No roosters greeted the gradual turn from charcoal to steel-gray in the east.

"There are three of them," Tom announced. "They're inside the church."

Later, after their pursuers had ridden off toward the Upper Plaza, Tom coaxed the fire back to life.

Macha sat on the crumpled mattress, holding her hands out toward the flames which rippled from the glowing log. She wore the extra blanket draped once more about her shoulders. "When will Francisco come to take Pancho and me to the north?"

"He'll wait until those men leave."

The fire hit a sap pocket and snapped out angry red sparks. Softly

Macha asked, "Will you come with us? We can start a new life—I'll be so good to you." A sense of urgency pulsed through her words.

He didn't reply at first. Taking this as encouragement, she said, "I've always wanted someone like you, a gentle person, someone I could love—who'd love me. It doesn't seem so much to ask." Her voice dwindled and the last phrase was scarcely audible.

Before Tom could answer he heard something. Moving to the door, he watched the priest struggle across the cemetery, winding through the shimmering graves and past the single aboveground sepulcher. A simple metal cross on it, now covered by a thick sheath of ice, glittered as a ray of sunlight pierced through the clearing clouds.

"Good morning," the priest said. "I've brought something to warm you." With that he tilted a blackened iron pot and poured from its spout a stream of dark coffee into heavy white crockery cups. A marvelous penetrating aroma rose with the steam and filled the tiny room.

After this, beaming at the opportunity to present such welcome gifts, he pulled away a dishtowel which had protected a platter laden with crisp bacon and slabs of hot buttered toast.

Moving back, he said theatrically, "A feast!" Then he lowered his head and prayed in rapid Spanish.

"Will you join us, Father?" Macha asked. But he explained that he had eaten at four that morning, the time when he normally began his day.

The priest wore a heavy coarsely woven coat over the black habit that swept just above his shoetops. A knotted rope served for a belt. Tom examined him carefully. He was a small man, not over five and a half feet in height, weighing perhaps one hundred and twenty pounds. His face looked emaciated and all the bones in it were apparent under thin crinkled skin. He had wispy white hair under an ancient black round-brimmed hat. His teeth were still his own in spite of his years and they were prominent, not quite fitting in his mouth, a fact which caused his thin lips to protrude slightly. But in spite of all of this, he had an earnest, sympathetic look—the face of a friend.

He had listened to confessions thousands of times each year; nothing men or women did or thought had been hidden from him. He had heard too many deathbed confessions, comforted too many grieving survivors, to worry a great deal about the small, human things called sins by others. The fact that this attractive young man and woman had lain together through the wintry night didn't attract his comment. He

knew the circumstances which caused Macha to be hiding, and that
Tom was her protection till she escaped. If they simply found warmth
together—or something more—was of no importance to him.

His name, Macha had informed Tom, was Padre Pedro Herrero. He
had been the only priest in Frisco throughout her life.

Padre Herrero couldn't conceal his distress at the violation of his
church. He spoke indignantly of the armed men who had forced their
way into the sanctuary, men who had uttered blasphemies before the
very altar in God's house. The old man trembled with emotion as he
related over and over what had happened. He said to Macha, *"Pis-
toleros,* sticking guns out at me, saying that they knew I was hiding
you, daughter."

The three spent an hour waiting tensely for Francisco's arrival.
Macha kept looking at Tom. Finally, when the priest went outside to
the dilapidated privy behind the shed, she asked, "Have you thought
of what I said?"

"Of course I have, but—"

She stopped his words by putting the fingers of one hand upon his
mouth. "Don't say anything more—words can be so final. I don't want
to hear them—don't want to remember them." She pressed her face
against his neck. "I'm really afraid."

"I know you are."

"Can't you at least ride part of the way with Francisco and Pancho
and me when we start for the Chama River?"

"Of course."

The priest returned, and spoke to them of the snowstorm. He
talked of the people of the village. After this he again denounced the
outrage he had endured—he couldn't stay away from this subject.
"When those three men broke in, they found me at my prayers. One
held a gun in my stomach and made threats. They said they would do
terrible things to me if I lied to them. But of course, I lied." A slight
smile crossed his lined face. "I'm sure God doesn't mind *all* lies. They
quarreled among themselves, then left." He seemed lost in thought for
a time before saying, "They're dangerous men."

"I know," Macha replied.

The priest sat in the silence with Macha and Tom on what served
as the only furnishing in the room, a wretchedly dirty crumpled mattress, and leaned with them toward the meager fire in the abandoned
caretaker's shack. "It's very cold," he said at last.

"Francisco should be here by now," Macha commented again.

"I'll slip out to see what's holding him," Tom said.

The priest rose to his feet stiffly. "Macha will go with me to the church."

A moment later, Tom stepped through the low door into the whiteness. The snow's surface had frozen, and when he walked upon it he heard creaking noises. At times the crust cracked, and when he kicked at it, pieces that looked like shards of broken white china plates scattered beneath his boots. Glancing over his shoulder, Tom saw the padre trying to protect his ears from the cold by cupping both hands upon them. He stood at the church's door as Macha went inside. The black-clad priest, looking stark as a raven against the solid white expanse of the cemetery and the shimmering church, followed her, closing the door behind him.

Tom reached the livery stable and went inside. Wiley's colorful wagon stood out front, festive snow pillows piled upon its red roof, and he saw the two big workhorses in the pens out back. They had shaggy winter coats and stood, heads down, with their tails to the light wind. Each breath from their widened nostrils turned to small white puffs of steam. His horse Deuce raised his head and perked his ears forward alertly on Tom's approach.

Tom walked carefully on the slippery ice and snow which lay in treacherous shallow angles on the torn ground of the corral to greet his horse—to pound him on the back and hold the animal's wondrously soft, whiskered chin a moment. Then he went to the office of the livery stable, seeing smoke coming from a pipe in the roof above it.

He entered and closed the door quickly against the wintry air before speaking to Wiley Callan.

"Mornin'," Tom said.

"I slept the sleep of the just last night, the sleep of an innocent newborn babe who is still a total stranger to all things evil," Wiley said in a friendly tone. Then his voice changed and he declaimed in his nasal Texas accent, "Sleep that knits up the raveled sleeve of care— chief nourisher in life's feast. That's what I always say."

Tom smiled. "It's no wonder that folks consider you to be half crazy."

"*Half* crazy? Is that how I'm described? I don't like 'half' measures and would far prefer to be thought completely crazy—as mad as a

march hare. It's good for business. Folks think they can outwit someone like me." He chuckled at the thought.

Wiley sat in a rickety ladder-back chair before a potbellied iron
stove which glowed a dull red. "I've been here all night," he said.
"Slept on the floor beside this heater. A wonderful invention, the
Franklin stove. Kept me warm as toast all night."

He briskly rubbed both hands across his close-cropped spiky orange
hair and stretched luxuriantly. "Well, let's get out and face a new and
better world." Wiley had an attitude of unflagging optimism, even
when no reason at all for this presented itself.

The new friends went to the pens and broke the ice in the trough so
the horses could drink.

While they watched them dip their noses cautiously through the
floating bits of ice, Wiley observed, "Your right arm seems better."

"It is. A lot better—don't need the sling any longer. In fact, I can lift
it up almost shoulder high today. Must not have broken anything."

"How do the busted ribs feel?"

Tom made a wry face. "About the same. Takes a while for them to
heal. I've had a fair amount of experience with this problem, mostly
from horse wrecks, and the best thing to do is ignore the way it hurts.
Not a thing you can do about it."

"I never ignore pain," Wiley stated. "Of course, pain hurts a sensitive soul like me infinitely more than it does the rough louts, the
ordinary unfeeling men out here in the West. Allow me to offer you
some of my tonic. It takes the edge off every ache, and I recommend it
highly."

"I'm sure you do," Tom said, suppressing a smile. "What does it
have in it?"

"The most important element stems from a careful combination of
the essences of sacred roots and herbs which I extract scientifically.
Which is to say, I boil them for their juices—the scientific properties
are lodged in juices. Naturally, no other living man knows of the exact
ingredients, and I'll carry the mystery of the recipe to the grave. It was
given to me under an oath of secrecy by a dying medicine man in the
Indian Territory. Taken undiluted, this potion is far too powerful for
anyone to handle. It also is a trifle sharp to the taste. So I've worked
out, with arduous trial and error, a perfect solution."

His last remark made him cackle. He stated in full round tones, as if
savoring them, "That is to say, I have arrived at a solution for a

solution." He smiled, pleased with himself, and not minding that
Tom's face took on a pained expression. Wiley was accustomed to
people flinching at his strained attempts at humor.

"There's a little licorish for flavor, some water to stretch it a mite,
and a good amount of that greatest of all purifiers, grain alcohol. It
may be the last ingredient that makes so many little old ladies swear by
it." His high laugh, almost a giggle, seemed a strange sound to come
from such a large man. "The same ones who hold forth in the
Wednesday evening prayer meetings against strong drink are among
my best prospects when it comes to Doctor Callan's Elixir. I've had
more than one tell me in confidence that after two cups of my tonic,
they often experience what they describe as a full-fledged bout of
religious rapture."

Wiley added, as if in apology, "I don't drink any form of liquor
myself, and I insist most emphatically that my elixir is in no way
related to any member of the low-down whiskey family. After all,
Doctor Wiley's magical potion is taken strictly for *medicinal* purposes."

Tom went to the saddle room and found most of his gear. The
saddle rode a vee-shaped construction made of two pine planks on a
long sawhorse, along with a variety of old saddles left there by others.
A smell of leather and liniment lingered in the air. His bridle hung
from the saddle horn. He took this off and carried it with him to the
office where he warmed the bit briefly at the potbellied iron stove so
the frozen steel wouldn't stick to the horse's mouth.

"Let me give you a hand," Wiley said. "Can't stand idly by while a
cripple like you does all the work."

Moments later, with some difficulty, Wiley got the bridle on Deuce,
who kept shying away, ears back, fighting the bit with clenched teeth.
Then Wiley led him to a shed where he flapped the saddle blanket
over his back, smoothed it, then lofted the saddle—skirts and girth
and stirrups flying—on top of the blanket. He jostled the saddle horn,
seating it properly, then cinched it tight with an extra tug, causing
Deuce to curl his neck and bare his teeth, obviously giving serious
thought to taking a bite out of Doctor Callan. Then Wiley gave a grunt
of satisfaction and said, "That is one fine-lookin' horse. I'm forced to
this conclusion in spite of the fact that the admiration is not mutual."

He stood to one side as Tom stepped gracefully into the saddle.

"I'll circle around to see if I can find Francisco. He should have
come for Macha by now."

The cold hard saddle felt good. The muscles of his upper thighs had a perfect fit under the contours of the saddle swells. He rocked in unconscious easy balance, back straight, heels down, his hat brim pulled low, shadowing his eyes against the blinding reflection of the sun rays sparkling off what looked like an immense scattering of diamonds on the surface of the endless snow. Far off to the west the butte loomed solidly against a sky turning slowly from gray to hazy blue.

The sharp snaps of pain from his ribs were bearable, and his shoulder hardly ached at all. Experimentally, he stretched out his arm and leaned forward. Lean and hard-muscled, he'd always healed rapidly.

Deuce moved well under him, his smooth powerful action carrying them over the plaza on the way toward Francisco's house. Off to his right Tom saw Milligen's Saloon. Smoke came from the chimney, but no horses were tied out front. In fact, the town seemed deserted.

When he pulled up at the cluster of adobe houses, Marta opened the door. Small children held to her wide skirt and peered around her at him.

"*Gracias a Dios.*" Marta breathed out her heartfelt thanks. "You're alive. Is Macha all right?"

"Of course she is."

"Francisco left about half an hour ago. He had the *alcalde*'s old buggy and said he'd get Macha and then come back here for breakfast. I've got the boy ready for his trip."

She knelt as she spoke and put her arms around the five-year-old affectionately. He looked past her with large bewildered eyes at the man on horseback.

"Get down," she said. "They'll be here any minute now."

Old Rafa bustled over from his nearby house with a woven bark basket which he supported carefully. When he came closer Tom saw that it contained brown speckled hen's eggs.

"Chickens ignore snow and ice and storms," Rafa told the children as he brought his gift into the house. "They just lay their eggs and hope for the best," he said with pretended wisdom. His mustache wiggled slightly as he smiled at the three youngsters.

Marta kept standing at the door. "The coffee's ready—I've baked bread—we have some bacon . . ." Her voice dwindled to silence. "Why haven't they come back? Francisco told me Macha would wait for him at the old hut near the cemetery."

Tom said, "Macha's with the priest. I went to get my horse. My plan is to ride with Francisco and Macha and her boy until they're safely on their way."

"That's good," Marta said absently. But a minute later she stated softly but insistently, "Something isn't right." She stood at the slightly opened door, ignoring the stabbing breeze which came through it.

Tom took his belongings from the alcove which held the oven. Smells of baking bread came from it—rich, swirling odors—causing his mouth to water although he was scarcely aware of it.

Anxiety gnawed at him. He retrieved his spurs and buckled them on his boots. Rising to his feet, he went outside and flipped the saddle-bags so that they rested on either side of the skirts behind the cantle. He tied them securely with the saddlestrings, then retrieved his Winchester and checked it. Very deliberately he levered a shell into the chamber, uncocked it with care—letting the hammer down slowly—then went outside and slid the rifle into the saddle scabbard.

"Where could he be?" Marta asked, standing in the doorway, eyes fixed on the village. Not a soul could be seen. But over most of the houses, white smoke came from short chimneys and trailed off in long lines, angling toward the south.

"I'd better go for them," Tom said. He mounted again, reined Deuce about, and set off at a brittle sliding trot, feeling his horse slip as iron-shod hooves skidded on the insecure icy footing. The forward motion caused needle-sharp wind to sting his face, causing his eyes to water, and his nose and cheeks began to tingle. His toes began to have the familiar dull ache that came before they went numb in weather like this. But he didn't really notice these things, for the old warning went off within his mind, and a swift prickling ran up the back of his neck.

Rounding the corner by Francisco's livery stable, he saw the church. In the cemetery a surrey with a slightly swaybacked horse hitched to it stood in dark silhouette against a white-clad sepulcher. The horse stood quietly, winter coat ruffled by the breeze, tail blowing to one side. Tom pulled Deuce back to a walk, then halted at the small shed-roofed storeroom built on the rear of the church. He dismounted, unbuttoned his coat, and loosened the Colt in its holster. Then he advanced on the balls of his feet, every sense alert, his hand ready to draw at the first eyeblink of trouble.

Thirteen

TOM PRESSED HIS BACK to the wall of the church when he reached the first window. Very slowly he leaned around and looked inside. No sign of movement. He ducked under it and moved rapidly to the steps leading up to the front door. Glancing to his right, he made out a number of tracks in the snow heading from the church toward the cemetery.

Every sense in his body told him something was wrong. Pulling the Colt with his bare left hand, he put his gloved right on the freezing brass doorknob—turning it very slowly. The instant it disengaged he forced it open, threw the tall door back with an echoing crash, and leaped into the opening, pistol waving from side to side.

Nothing. The sanctuary in the chilled morning light lay empty. Tom's bootheels made hollow thumping noises and his spurs clinked as he made his way down the center aisle past the red oak benches worn smooth by use. A large leather-bound Bible lay open on the elevated altar high above the pew-lined floor.

Primitive paintings of the stations of the cross hung upon both side walls. Behind the altar, facing the missing congregation, a very old carved crucifix was suspended. He looked at these reminders of the mindless cruelty, the viciousness, shown by men down through the ages to those within their power. The crucifix had been repainted recently, and bloodred paint glistened in vivid rivulets down the temples and across the face from the crown of piercing thorns. More painted gore dripped from the wound in the Christ figure's side, and shiny crimson covered the hands and feet through which heavy nails had been driven into a rough cedar cross.

Tom went to a small door at the left, behind the altar, and opened it. The priest's living quarters lay as bare as his church. A narrow cot with a table holding a Bible and one other book, a basin for water, and a single straight chair were the only furnishings in the room. At one side, however, a small pillow lay on the floor under a black cross which hung on the roughness of the plastered wall. In a corner of the L-shaped room he saw a long rope that led up to the bell tower on the roof.

Tom holstered his Colt and returned to the sanctuary. He walked past the altar to the other wall and stopped beside the wooden confessional booth. Stepping beyond it, he put his face close to a window—feeling the coldness seep through—and gazed out toward the cemetery. About a hundred yards away he saw a surrey with a swaybacked horse hitched to it. Long reins had been looped over a little wrought-iron fence that surrounded the sepulcher. Then he noticed something else, an arm lying on the other side of the crypt, palm up.

He ran from the church to the first large tombstone and went down to one knee in a crouch behind it, looking everywhere for a sign of Macha. He heard no sounds at all except the thudding of his heart. He rose, surveying the stillness of the silvery burial ground, and went forward, his boots crunching through the snow.

Tom stopped when he reached the body. He took several deep breaths, then forced himself to look down.

Francisco lay flat on his back, glazed eyes open, his skull crushed by a heavy blow. A long, heavy, rusted crowbar, the type gravediggers would need to chisel through caliche and limestone in this part of the country, lay half a dozen paces off to one side. Deep footprints gouged cavities in the begrimed snow all around the corpse. He moved closer, and saw frost-flecked frozen blood, an irregular red velvet crust, which clasped six or eight inches of the murder weapon's octagonal iron shaft.

Clotted blood collected in a gelid pool about the dead man's head—the scarlet liquid tinged with black—a darker red than that on the crucifix he'd seen. Images, not really thoughts, swept before his mind's eye.

Dread seeped through him. He ran to the old caretaker's abandoned shack where Macha and he had passed the night, only to find it empty. Returning to the burial ground, he looked at the confusing tracks, trying to pick out ones that might be hers. Then he saw something at the far end of the cemetery that he'd somehow missed: a still darkness propped against a headstone.

He stood before the grave for a long time. A child had been buried here, a very small one. The sandstone used as a marker had the baby's name chiseled in it, nothing else except the dates showing the passage of one and a half years of life. At the marker's top a lamb had been carved by loving hands.

Padre Pedro Herrero had been placed against this stone like a rabbit on a chopping block. He'd probably been held there by strong hands while another executed him. His eyes in death, unlike Francisco's, lay closed but not as they might in sleep. The skull-like face had already turned an ashen off-white color. His throat had been cut from ear to ear, like that of a slaughtered goat. An eruption of brilliant red blood had splashed far out upon the pure white snow.

The men who did this had Macha.

Julian Haynes stood before his captive. She sat in a tall straight chair, her feet tied to its legs, her arms bound tightly behind her. Macha tried to meet his fierce gaze defiantly, but her eyes betrayed her and dropped to her lap.

His voice was menacingly quiet. "I grew up with T. J. Hoskins. We were kids together on this ranch. When I took over, he worked as my lieutenant and saw that my orders got carried out." His voice had a conversational quality about it. It didn't sound as though he were really angry.

"When I sold most of the ranch, he went with me to El Paso where I made my first real stake. Later we had big plans for investments in the Concho River valley, and he went there with me. T.J. served as the judge out at Santa Rita. We made a good team," he mused. "A good team. It might have gone on for a long time. I never really liked him, but he was fair company. And after spending so much time together through the years, I guess that some would call us friends. Men like me don't make friends easily." His eyes as always were concealed behind slitted lids.

"Of course, I knew he'd always had a fancy for you—and I'll give him credit, he never hid it from me. We had no real secrets, what with growing up together almost like brothers. And in a few years, when you could be expected to start losing those good looks, I'd probably have told him he could have you. It's true that when I heard he'd sneaked out to your room, it irritated me. But then I thought, what the hell, T.J. was just as human as the next man. You and I know human nature—isn't that right, Macha? We know what men are like, don't we?"

She made no sound as she sat helplessly before him. Small beads of perspiration shone upon her face.

He reached into his coat pocket and took out the ivory-handled stiletto that the old *patrón* had given her on his deathbed. "This was what you used on poor T.J."

At that moment his forced calmness snapped quite suddenly, the way a dry stick might when bent too far. He whispered ominously, "You murdered him, you filthy slut. Knifed him in the belly, then when he was down you stuck it clear up in his heart."

He took a moment to get control. When he spoke again he did so in level tones, the ferocity gone, the trembling no longer apparent. "All he wanted was a few minutes of lovin'. What difference could that possibly have made to you? You'd 'a been none the worse for it, and maybe the better." A humorless smile ghosted across his face.

"I was terrified," she whispered. "It was dark . . ." Her voice broke for an instant before she could complete her statement. "Someone came in my room and tried to rape me."

"I know what kind of a shameless bitch you are. Jesus, I ought to know that better than anyone. Through all the years when I took you any time I felt like it, you only pretended to get mad. You sure as hell never pulled a knife on me. Yet when poor T.J. came to you, thinking about a little fun with you in bed, you *murdered* him. It passes belief that you'd do such a thing—and I can't let that pass. I've been telling you, Macha, T.J. was like a brother to me."

"You *are* my brother. Both of us know that. We have the same blood."

"Don't say that, God damn you! Don't ever say that."

Julian Haynes quivered as he stood over her, looking as though he'd suddenly lost all control. But then he recovered and said, "My dad was like an old goat. He spread his seed all over the range. That kind of thing doesn't mean I have to think of all his bastards as kin." Only a slight shaking of his hands belied his fury.

She waited, terrified. In a small voice at last she asked, "Have you forgotten all those nights when Chato brought me to you? You weren't always mean—sometimes you were gentle when I'd cry. It started when I was only fourteen! Have you forgotten Pancho—your son?"

With a sigh of exasperation Julian Haynes said, "The kid was just an accident. And you already know my opinion of bastards. Besides," he added with a slight sign of pride, "he's not the only one I've sired."

She ignored that. "What are you going to do to me?"

"Everyone knows T.J. and I were raised together. They'll be curious to see if I've turned soft. So I've got to show them, don't I?" He asked this as if it were the most reasonable question in the world. Then he said, "I'm going to kill you. I'll make an example out of you so others will know they can't cross Julian Haynes."

He came closer. "I strung a man up on a telegraph pole for no more than stealing a calf. So hanging or something quick won't make my point." He moved closer and pushed the shiny dagger at her face, watching her shrink away from it as far as she could. Thrusting out the razor-edged blade, he waved it a moment, then put the point against the smooth skin under her left eye, enjoying the moment. It gave him a perverse thrill of pleasure. He slowly increased the pressure until the yielding soft flesh broke and a trickle of blood ran down her cheek.

Macha gasped from pain and fear.

"The boys said that some gringo was trying to protect you. Who is he?"

"A stranger."

Haynes slapped her with his left hand as hard as he could. Her head jerked sideways and a flaming handprint appeared upon the side of her face. In a menacingly quiet tone he insisted, "Answer my question."

"You're acting like *un chiquillo*—a real man wouldn't treat a woman this way."

The needle-sharp point of the dagger jabbed down, penetrating into her upper arm.

"His name is Tom," she blurted out, her face a mask of agony. And then, as the blade pulled free, her head slumped forward and she began to cry helplessly.

When he didn't say anything, she raised her head and looked up. To her surprise she saw that he had gone pale.

He asked, "Do you know his last name?"

Before she could answer, the door of the big room flew open and a cowboy burst through it. She recognized him—one of the men who'd dragged her and Padre Herrero and Francisco from the church. He looked startled and said to Haynes, "A rider's on his way in."

"Is he alone?"

"That big wagon I told you about, the red one, is trailin' behind."

"Get the others—and be quick about it," Haynes barked.

Tom English slowed Deuce into a walk, then stopped, looking with surprise at the great mansion lying alone in the rocky land. It loomed before him, broad-shouldered, huge. Dull red Spanish tiles covered the roof although many had fallen to the ground. Their broken remnants lay in the melting gray snow. The white plaster on its two-storied sides had flaked away in places revealing an adobe block construction. To his right, small wooden and adobe houses clung to the side of a rough hill topped by large white boulders, some of them the size of railcars. He had a vague sense of a barn and pens in the distance behind the main building and the small sheds near it.

Three men stood in front of the mansion waiting for him. There'd be no question of surprise. One held a rifle cradled in his arms, the other two wore six-guns. Tom put his weight in his left stirrup and swung down. He dropped the reins—Deuce had been trained to stand —and faced them. He approached, expecting the man with the rifle to fire, but nothing happened. When he came within thirty feet, he stopped.

A thin man in the center advanced. Another, the one holding a rifle, sidled off to one side, and the third fell back a few paces.

"What do you want?" the lean man asked haltingly. He had a long narrow face with a reddish purple birthmark covering almost one side of it.

"You brought a woman here from Frisco. I've followed your tracks."

The man with the birthmark said harshly, "My name's Rigo—*Rigo el pistolero*. You may have heard of me." His right hand closed about the wooden butt of his pistol.

The man named Rigo sucked on a tooth and twisted his mouth as he waited, his face hardening. "I've faced seven men before you and I'm still alive. They're not."

He advanced a few steps, keeping his hand fixed on the six-gun.

His companions moved off to the sides, getting out of the line of fire.

Behind them, the wheels of Wiley Callan's ungainly red wagon clanged and clattered over the rocky trail. It groaned to a stop a hundred yards away.

Tom had unbuttoned his heavy coat earlier. Now he swept the coattail behind his left gun which canted out ever so slightly from his side in its tied-down holster. His hands hung low. Seconds ticked silently by with neither man making a move.

Tom said, "You could have taken her without killing the priest or her cousin. There was no need for bloodshed. But right now, all I'm asking is that you turn the woman over to me."

A cruel light came into Rigo's eyes. "No more talk."

An unbidden thought came into Tom's mind: *This has happened before.* Another stranger throwing down a challenge.

Rigo started to draw his weapon but hesitated as Tom's voice cracked out, "Don't force this fight! Don't try it!" Tom faced the arrogant man with the muddy purple blotch on his face, watching his hesitation.

He waited in the biting cold and saw Rigo's eyes narrow almost imperceptibly as he began his draw.

The bass-drum detonation of Tom's .45 rang out before the barrel of the stranger's gun cleared leather. The bullet slammed into Rigo's chest, and his arms flew wide as it blew him backward.

From the corners of his eyes Tom saw jerking motions made by the other two as they brought their guns up. Before Rigo hit the ground, Tom's Colt exploded three more times in such rapid succession that the violent vibrations rang together, echoing wildly through the hills, ravines, and boulders, the percussive hammer blows shattering the frozen glass of day.

The man who had begun to raise a rifle to his shoulder never got it that far. He dropped in his tracks, blood spouting from his throat. The other, his pistol whipping forward, caught a bullet in his shoulder that knocked him sideways but didn't down him. Before he got his balance, another struck his forehead, shattering his skull just above the bridge of his nose, and he dropped like a stone.

Acrid gunsmoke wavered before Tom's eyes as he stood in a slight crouch. He heard a crunch behind him and spun about with the left Colt hip high.

"*Careful,* Tom, it's me," Wiley Callan hollered in his peculiar high-voiced way. The two men stood upon the killing ground, before three crumpled forms and the paint-pot splatters that darkened the snow.

At last Wiley said, "If I hadn't witnessed this with my own eyes, I'd never have believed it possible. The whole thing couldn't have taken four seconds."

Trembling with excitement, looking at Tom with sudden respect, he said, "If it were done when 'tis done, 'twere well it were done quickly." Clearing his throat, he elaborated. "Well, Tom, you sure did that. You did it quickly." Then he explained, "By the way, that's what Macbeth said before killing Duncan, the king of Scotland."

Tom's brow wrinkled in perplexity.

"If Shakespeare had ever seen you in action, my new friend, I can only imagine the sorts of things he might have written."

They went to the massive front door. It swung back, scraping the floor, sagging from the heavy metal hinges. They entered the house and made a quick search, finding not a soul inside. When they went out the back way, a little girl stood off at one side. Speaking in rapid Spanish, Tom asked her if she'd seen the woman, the one named Macha.

The child nodded, her mouth clamped shut as if struck dumb by this apparition with his piercing blue eyes and the tall burly man with him, the one who took off his hat and ran his hand over hair like none she'd ever seen, as orange as new rust and with bristles like those in a store-bought brush.

Hesitating at first, she stammered that Macha had left with the *patrón* and with Chato. When Tom questioned her, she explained that Chato was the *jefe* when the owner wasn't on the ranch. The men had saddled three horses before all the shooting started. They rode off, she said, that way, pointing to the south toward a range of craggy mountains.

With bewildered fascination she told Tom that Macha's hands had been tied behind her, that a lead rope from a hackamore around her horse's head had been fastened to the *patrón's* saddle horn.

The sun had broken free of the clouds and its weak warmth fell upon them. The snow upon the corral's rail fence began to melt, dripping silently upon a lacy sodden carpet underneath.

The two men looked at the threatening peaks in the distance. "Do you know this part of the country?" Wiley asked.

"No, but I've studied a map. One range of hills after another lies

between here and Deming. I guess that Haynes is taking her with him
to El Paso, if he doesn't double back."

Reaching a decision, he went quickly to the front of the house.
Mexicans had emerged from the shacks and stood at a respectful
distance, looking at the fallen men and glancing fearfully at Tom.
They had obviously watched everything that had happened.

Tom gathered his reins and mounted Deuce. "Your wagon can't
make it where I'll be going, Wiley. I appreciate your wanting to help,
but I've got to go on alone."

He avoided the sight of the fallen men. A slow revulsion moved
from his throat down into the pit of his stomach. Anything would be
better than waiting here.

As though reading his mind, Wiley said, "I'll get these folks to help
me with the buryin'."

As Tom spurred Deuce, Wiley called, "Don't run into a trap—
they'll be watching to see if anyone comes after them."

He looked at the receding figure, riding resolutely toward the blue
mountains, hurrying before the snow melted so he could pick up the
tracks.

Wiley shook his head and asked himself, "What manner of man is
this!"

Fourteen

AT FIRST Tom had no trouble following the tracks in the snow left by the three horses. He urged Deuce forward, winding through and over rocky hills, cresting one only to see he had to descend and climb another. The wind shifted to the south as the sun climbed higher, blowing warmth which made the snow melt rapidly. By early afternoon, the unbroken white blanket had changed into light and dark patches of wet gray iciness, but the hoofprints of the horses he trailed could still easily be made out upon the muddy ground.

He rode through a protected meadow, a hidden place surrounded by mountains. The small pasture had a stream through it lined with slender trees which waved their delicate leafless branches in the gusting breeze. He paused to let Deuce drink from the swiftly running water, letting the reins hang loose, holding his left arm extended.

Shifting his weight in the saddle, he thought he saw something move in the stand of liveoak trees on a slope about three hundred yards away. And then a bullet's banshee cry blew past his head. He leaped sideways from his horse's back as a second bullet split the air inches from his ear. Hitting the ground, he lunged up and pulled his Winchester from its saddle boot and slapped Deuce's rear. The horse galloped away, dragging the reins with his head held sideways so he wouldn't step on them. But he'd been trained too well; he stopped— "tied to the ground" in the cowboy expression—and waited expectantly.

Tom flung himself behind a tree and, when the rifle on the hillside flashed, he answered fire, levering one cartridge after another, getting off four quick shots. As the shifting, bouncing echoes of the explosions died away he heard a rifle shot followed by a high squeal. Looking about, he saw Deuce rear up and buck wildly. Then the horse stopped leaping. He came to a halt and began stamping both front hooves and making low whinnies. When Tom reached him he could see blood seeping from a long furrow which had plowed across Deuce's muscular chest. Although only a deep graze, blood welled from it and ran down both forelegs.

He led Deuce into a thicket and took cover. Bark exploded from a tree trunk above him as he heard a rifle's sharp cough in the distance. The unseen attacker had him pinned down. But then silence fell. He waited for what seemed an eternity, nerves tingling.

It's a trick, he thought. His enemy must be trying to get him to venture into the open. But when twenty minutes passed without a shot being fired, Tom decided that his assailant must have thought shooting the horse would stop the pursuit. Tom led his trembling mount to the water's edge and, not knowing what else to do, slathered cold wet mud from the creek's bank upon the long, bleeding wound.

He held the jittery horse's head in his hands, then stroked his neck, speaking softly, soothingly to him. He took the reins and walked away from the bottomland, proceeding uphill until he reached a screen of trees where he could find shelter in case the bushwhacker should be waiting.

A sharp sound rang through the clear quiet air like a cymbal—a horseshoe striking stone. Tom raised the Winchester, feeling only a twinge of pain in his injured right shoulder, put his cheek against the smooth wood stock, and leveled the wavering sight upon a bobbing hat that rose above the rocks as a mounted man descended carefully down the slick wet hillside behind him.

He had known from the outset that he'd be outnumbered, that two men held Macha captive, but he hadn't expected this kind of trap. Looking about, he saw no sign of the sniper who'd been on the other side of the creek.

Once again he steadied the rifle, cocked it, and began a gentle pressure on the trigger. He had the sights fixed now upon the center of a tall rider's chest. The horse he rode came to a stop, partially screened from Tom's view by a spiderweb pattern of black tree branches which cracked gently against each other in the wind. He could barely discern some type of movement, and then the horse began to walk forward as the rider twisted in the saddle in order to reach behind him to a saddlebag in order to pull something from it.

At first Tom couldn't tell what it was, and then he saw it was a large bottle of some sort. The horseman tilted it to his mouth and took a big drink from it.

With a tremor of relief, Tom lowered his rifle barrel. He took a deep breath and allowed the curved metal buttplate of the Winchester to clink against the cold limestone ledge beneath his feet.

Wiley Callan sat uncomfortably astride an almost vee-shaped home-made Mexican saddle, wood showing through worn and tattered leather of the swell on both sides of the horn. He held the bottle of his elixir in one hand and a gentle smile wreathed his face.

"Surprised to see me?"

"Not half as surprised as you'd have been if I'd shot you."

Wiley looked startled. "Are you as jumpy as that?"

"Hell yes, I am. Didn't you hear the gunfire going on just before you got here?"

"Afraid I missed it. I was singing. It breaks the monotony of travel, and besides, I rather enjoy the sound of my voice."

"I've noticed that," Tom said wryly. Then he grinned. "To tell the truth, I'm more than surprised, I'm astounded that you're here. Before you tell me how you managed to come by that horse and trail me to this valley, I need to let you know what's going on."

He explained what had happened—how someone had tried to ambush him. He reasoned that it probably would have been Chato, the gunslinger who worked for Haynes.

Wiley said as they started riding, "I 'borrowed' this bony nag back at Julian Haynes's ranch. I've seen better horseflesh," he observed, "but he'll do until I can find a better." After a pause he added, "That's the least of my problems. If I don't get a regular saddle soon you'll witness a terrible sight, for I'll split right smack dab down the middle. Half of Doctor Wiley Callan will slide off on the right side of this miserable horse, and the other half will fall to the left." He grinned. "This Meskin saddle really isn't quite as bad as it looks. If I scootch clear to the back, there's a little flat spot."

They found a crossing upstream and went through the rushing water. It foamed about their horses' legs and licked against their boots. On the other side, Wiley began to speak again. "It wasn't any trouble at the outset to follow your tracks in the snow, but for the last few hours, after it began melting, I've been slowed up somewhat. But," he beamed, "my efforts have met with signal success."

"Wiley, I appreciate your coming, but since I notice that you're not armed, what would you have done if you'd found me in trouble? Haynes and his backshooter aren't likely to agree to a bare-knuckled boxing match."

"There is always a way for good to triumph over evil. My approach is to act extemporaneously, spontaneously, in achieving this natural outcome."

He widened his eyes slightly and began to speak in his somewhat affected stage voice. "Before proceeding further, allow me to acquaint you with some of my rules. There are three things I *won't* do," Wiley declared. "First, I refuse to eat pork, for in my opinion the children of Israel were right—the pig is an unclean beast. Second, I have never sought the comfort of a lady of the night, for that goes against my beliefs regarding the sanctity of the body—especially mine. And third, I have vowed never to use a firearm. For one thing, I don't believe in violence. It doesn't solve problems in the long run."

"You don't consider knocking men unconscious with your fists to be violent?"

"You're speaking of sport now, an altogether different matter. The object of boxing is not to kill or cripple an opponent, it has to do with skill and conditioning. But that's another subject for discussion. The purpose of a handgun is to slaughter a fellow human being. And that is an act to which I am unalterably opposed."

"Well," Tom said, wondering how to deal with his newfound acquaintance, "I'll agree to that, but when the other side intends to kill you, all those ideas tend to weaken."

"You have a point. Philosophy may not apply to our present situation."

They followed a trail which led upstream, riding carefully, having picked up fresh horse tracks. Tom held the Winchester with his right hand, balancing it across the crook of his left arm which held the reins. He leaned forward and looked down at the ground in front of his ice-encrusted right boot. His feet, which had ached so from the cold, had now turned completely numb.

"The wind has shifted back to the north, and I fear that the temper- ature has dropped below freezing once again," Wiley stated in a conversational way. Tom gritted his teeth at the obvious comment, and did not reply.

The scarred rocks of the path led them along the bank of the small river which narrowed as it went through a pass between steep mountains. Wind whipped spray and pinpricks of sleet out on them as their horses gingerly picked their way over icy moss-covered stones beside the raging foam-filled torrent. On the other side of the pass the water slowed as the stream widened. Shadows fell from the looming mountains as the hours slipped by, making the temperature drop even more.

The broad valley spread before them. As they left the stony trail for the firm dirt of the prairie, they spurred their horses into a slow lope, hoping to get their circulation going, trying anything to get warmer.

They slowed to a trot and Wiley said, "Listen to the sounds our horses make."

Tom looked at him, wondering what he meant.

His words took on a dramatic quality: "Hooves into the receiving earth." He noticed the nonplussed expression on his companion's face and attempted to explain. "That's from *Henry the Fifth*," he said, as though that meant anything to Tom.

They rode stirrup to stirrup for a while before Tom asked, "Does it worry you that folks might take you for a fool?"

"Never," Wiley responded with emphasis.

The two riders huddled inside their coats, feeling miserable. Finally they made camp when it grew too dark to follow the trail of the men they pursued.

After they dismounted and tended to their horses, Wiley stated with some deliberation, "It absolutely delights me to be racing to the aid of a maiden in distress."

Tom looked up in disbelief from his task of breaking small sticks.

The two men warmed their hands at a small fire over which they had suspended a metal canteen of boiling coffee. Wiley held firmly to a length of beef jerky and gnawed at it until he at last worried a piece of it free. Then he munched upon this for some time until he could swallow it. When he could finally speak again he said, "But it does not delight me to have to make my evening meal on leather. I derive no pleasure from that."

In a dark tree above them Tom could make out the ruffled shape of an owl. Its large eyes reflected the firelight.

They pulled their blankets about them and curled on either side of the fire, seeking warmth.

"Goodnight, Tom. If those villains should steal up under cover of darkness and slaughter us in our sleep, it won't be all bad. At least we can stop shivering from the cold."

"That's a comforting thought," Tom replied, burrowing deeper into the harsh scratchy wool of his blanket.

After a miserably long night, dawn finally flooded the valley. The sky turned silver with pink and golden streaks. And then it deepened into cloudless shades of blue. The mountains that had been absolutely black revealed the trees, ravines, and boulders on their sides.

The river had frozen for several feet from the bank on both sides, and the men broke this with heavy branches so their mounts could drink. After a hasty breakfast of more coffee and beef jerky, they saddled the horses and mounted.

The wind had died down and the tall trees by the stream stood without movement, looking like etchings made with India ink. Puffs of white vapor came from the horses' noses and mouths and smaller clouds showed by the faces of the men. Clear bright sunlight splashed among the shadows as they picked up the trail once more. Steel chimes rang as horseshoes clanged on clattering rocks.

They found the red mare an hour later. She whinnied at their approach, and their horses answered. The animal had a halter instead of bridle on her head. A ten-foot-long lead rope, fastened to the chin-strap of the halter, dragged beside the riderless sorrel.

Tom dismounted and walked toward a wide place by the river. He looked at the ground, trying to make sense of all the tracks in the patches of brittle brown grass. Then he saw the darkness at the foot of a tree. Bending to one knee, he reached down and touched it.

Scuff marks led to the water's edge. Dry-mouthed with horror, Tom followed these and then walked downstream. Wiley rode ahead, leading the mare they'd found. Half an hour later he called out.

Tom remounted and urged Deuce forward until he reached Wiley. They stood together on the river's bank, looking down at the thin sheet of ice that extended a few feet out into the stream. Beneath it they could see the paleness of Macha's body. It had wedged against a fallen log. Her hair streamed out in the current, moving back and forth.

The two men didn't speak to one another. They broke through the ice and pulled her stiff, nude, mutilated form up on the bank. Tom tried to close her open, horrified eyes but couldn't. He wrapped her in a blanket.

Then Wiley built a fire and the two men sat by the body, looking occasionally at one another.

The usual crowd gathered in Sol Racine's Saloon and Gaming Hall in Silver City, New Mexico. Blackjack Crosby shuffled the cards, sitting very straight as he always did. He had a military posture and, while not much over five feet eight or nine, he gave the impression of being a big man. He had a slightly aquiline nose, observant eyes, and an attitude of total confidence.

Across from him, in his accustomed chair, sat Big Sam Macklin, waiting expectantly. As he did so, he drawled out a complex joke in a reverberant baritone. Big Sam had a marvelous singing voice and it worked wonders for him when he wanted the attention of a crowd. The musical quality of his spoken words made people pay attention. He loomed above the table, a head higher than the other five men seated around it.

"And then the old cowboy said," he concluded his story, " 'They'll do that.' "

The men around the table almost fell off their chairs, laughing as they always did when Big Sam hit his punchline.

The saloon, a large square room, had pine floors which were somewhat splintery and rough cedar walls. However, it had a touch of elegance. Local Mexican craftsmen had made eight large silver candelabras, and these had been suspended by black silk ropes from the rafters. Above the bar itself and over the four round poker tables, coal oil lanterns cast their relentless yellow glare.

An unusual feature lay in the way a fireplace had been built in the exact center of the room. It was oval, about three feet high, some six feet wide at its center and at least eight feet in length. A local metalworker had built a large copper hood which exactly matched the contours of the fireplace. When great logs blazed fiercely in it, the smoke which roared up was captured by the hood which led to the chimney above it and out the shingled roof. The fireplace radiated so much heat that men could only sit on the wide stone wall around it for a few moments when they first came in. Those coming in out of the cold would then stand with their backs to the fire for a short time, gratefully, then swagger with stiff legs toward the bar. They bought whiskey as a sign of gratitude. The nighttime marvel of this remarkable saloon, so different from the grim rooms where they lived, gave the customers an unspoken sense of superiority: they had discovered a hidden secret place of pleasure.

A crackling fire, throwing out dancing lights, the firefly flickering of a multitude of candles, and the steady glow of carefully positioned lanterns gave the saloon a festive appearance; gave it, indeed, a carnival atmosphere. A surprising number of customers who favored Sol Racine's Saloon and Gaming Hall with their business spent all their disposable dollars there out of an overwhelming sense of gratitude for the color that had been so graciously brushed upon their gray and lusterless lives.

This result had been carefully calculated by Crafty Jack Dent, the man who actually owned the place. He had hired Sol Racine to run it, thinking that his many endeavors would keep him too busy to spend much time there. But Crafty Jack had himself been caught by the sticky strands of the web he'd spun, for he, too, adored the atmosphere, the smoky smell, the sparkling lights, and the sound of men's voices mixed with the clink of glasses. And, for Crafty Jack the dearest sound of all, the chink of silver dollars on the bar capped it all. He made good money out of all this fun.

So did Big Sam Macklin and Blackjack Crosby. In fact, their exploits at the gaming tables were the stuff of legend.

Big Sam leaned forward toward Blackjack and stated, much as he often had before, "Why stake out a claim and break your back diggin' silver out of some rockbound mountains when you can get others to do it? Not only that, but get them to convert their silver ore into good U.S. currency, bag it, and bring it to you while you sit in comfort with a fine bottle of bourbon close at hand?"

Blackjack looked at him with his clear, intelligent eyes. He did not waste words. "Draw or stud?"

"Well, we always play draw poker," Big Sam said as though pondering the decision. "And you ask me every night, seven out of seven during the week, if we should play stud or draw poker, and regardless of what I say, since you start off as dealer, we begin with draw. So my decision is that we'll play draw poker tonight."

"Good," replied Blackjack Crosby with the barest twitch of a smile hovering near his mouth.

A burly miner with glaring eyes and bushy black eyebrows sat down, huffing from the effort, and adjusted his chair. He drew out a large leather bag and put it down with a heavy clump with his right hand. It jingled as the silver dollars thumped onto the wood of the tabletop. "You'll not bluff me tonight, Big Sam. I'll not permit you to buy the pot the way you done two weeks ago." He scowled at his large adversary, adjusted his chair, and said gruffly, "Deal the damn cards."

"My experience has been that the cards are kinder, they are gentler and more understanding, to those who speak to them affectionately." Warming to his topic, Big Sam added, "I often use the word 'darlin'— sometimes I say 'sweetheart'—but never do I say the word 'damn' when describing playing cards."

The miner's meaty face, scarred, a fat broken nose in its center, did not show pleasure. He narrowed his eyes and said in threatening tones, "I'm here to play poker with you, Big Sam, and not to bandy words."

He pulled a large single-action revolver from his belt, cocked it, and pointed it at Big Sam's chest.

None of them had noticed that the front door had swung open moments before. Two men had limped in on cold-deadened feet and stood with their hands extended toward the fire. One of them, a tall fellow with a strange haircut which made his head look like a short-bristled orange brush, ambled over from the fire.

"Evenin', folks," the big freckled man with orange hair said. He slammed a ham-like fist on the miner's forearm, a hammer blow which caused the pistol to leave the miner's nerveless grasp, spin off the table, and crash metallically upon the pine boards at their feet. Then he drew the fist back a short way, not more than ten inches, and with a slight shift of his weight, threw what seemed to be no more than a hard straight jab into the miner's jaw. However, the force of the blow drove the man's head back as he somersaulted onto the floor. Several broken teeth lay near his head. Blood came from his mouth. He lay quite still upon his back as though suddenly in a dreamless sleep.

"Jesus Christ," exploded Crafty Jack. "Have you ever considered boxing for prizes? I'll back you if you're interested, and we'll go halves on what you win. Yes, sir," he said, a smile on his handsome face, "I think we can come up with a plan that would be very profitable."

"I disapprove of handguns," Wiley explained.

"I noticed that," replied Crafty Jack.

"Sit down, mister, if you'd like to take his place," Blackjack said to Wiley, nodding at the unconscious body on the floor. "The game is draw poker."

"Fine with me," Wiley declared with pleasure at being included in a circle of friendship. "It's been years since I played. You may have to refresh my memory about the rules."

Blackjack's eyes met those of Big Sam. Both men smiled. "We'll be happy to help," Blackjack said.

Fifteen

SADNESS put her arms around Tom's neck and for a moment he didn't feel so terribly alone. He heard a constant ringing in his ears and beyond that the sounds of muted conversation in the saloon. Someone dropped a bottle, glass shattered, men cried out. Guffaws greeted the mishap, but Tom didn't even glance toward the confused area where cowboys and miners leaped from their chairs and after a time settled back in them.

Sitting alone at a table as far from all the others as he could get, he very carefully pulled the cork once more from the clear bottle and poured amber liquid from it into his thick glass tumbler. Then, not rushing but savoring it, he let the whiskey's heat slide down. He felt a rawness in his throat that was not unpleasant, and warmth spread out pleasurably through his upper chest, making him conscious of an inner glow.

Time passed and his lips grew numb. Nature, heretofore so dependable, turned unexpectedly upon him, and the room tilted. The sturdy table no longer sat inertly before him but rather seemed also to betray him, giving way to weakness and wobbling. He put both hands on the table until it steadied.

Pictures came into his mind that he couldn't bear to see. And yet he couldn't force the images away: Macha's face, her smile. After seeing her so vividly within his mind he found it impossible to believe that she was dead. He seemed to hear her laughter, the melodic sound of her voice. Then memories welled up and he could feel her softness. It was as though she were at this instant somehow holding him breathlessly, and then she began caressing his cheek. His hand raised involuntarily and his fingers touched the warm salty trail left by tears.

I've come from my home in the Concho Valley of Texas, a land of light that I understand, he thought, *and somehow, here in New Mexico, I entered into shadows, into a way of life that seems so strange, so completely foreign. And I don't understand it. I don't understand myself—or why I'm grieving so for someone I've only known for this short time.*

There was a commotion in the room, and Tom raised his head. Wiley was on his feet stating, "I have been given permission by the owner of this establishment, Mr. Dent, known locally as Crafty Jack, to present *The Tragedy of Macbeth.* In exchange, I have entered into an agreement with him of one year's duration where I am to travel in some luxury at his expense while we pursue, in partnership, the business of boxing for prizes."

He began to move tables and chairs to one side and to gather all the lanterns with great intensity of purpose. He stood on a chair and tied them one at a time with care to the rafters, often getting down and examining the results with a professional eye, leaping back upon the chair to make an adjustment, then bounding down and back into the confused crowd to see if he had achieved the effect he sought.

At last he seemed satisfied. The four coal-oil lamps that normally were over the poker tables had been temporarily placed so that they were clustered together. The light they cast illuminated his stage, a cleared irregular area some twenty feet square. In front of this and to all sides the saloon was darkened except for the light that lapped out from the wavering flames of the logs which crackled and smoked as they burned in the fireplace. Sol Racine had turned down the wick of his lamp at the bar as a concession to culture, but left it glowing dimly in case a customer felt a sudden thirst.

When all was in readiness, Wiley stood up very straight and in a surprisingly deep and powerful voice he said, "The chronology is by no means assured, and we can only say with any degree of certainty that Shakespeare wrote his first play, *The Comedy of Errors,* at some time between 1588 and 1593; and he wrote his last, *Henry VIII,* around 1612 or 1613. Most scholars believe that he wrote *Macbeth* in 1605 or 1606."

The customers in Sol Racine's Saloon and Gaming Hall looked at one another in considerable bewilderment during all of these preparations. When the stranger began his speech they decided to go along with what was happening. They didn't mind watching folks make fools of themselves.

Wiley's marvelously retentive mind fed phrases to his capable tongue. He felt a shiver of excitement: at last, the greatest ambition he'd harbored in his life was about to be realized! Squinting into the darkness, trying to see his audience, he continued addressing them.

"In the more than two hundred and eighty intervening years there has never been a performance of this play attempted by a single actor. I have hoped against hope that I might have the honor to do this. To my amazement, this has come to pass. Thus it is, gentlemen, that *for the very first time in history one man will perform The Tragedy of Macbeth.* Not a word, not a syllable will be left out. Listen carefully and you will hear how Macbeth turns his back on goodness, how he is drawn toward evil. Think about this—about the subtle power of evil as you witness this tragic drama."

He paused and glowered out from the lights into the darkness of the saloon, hearing the sounds of glasses clinking and of chuckling and of conversation. His words then rang out a warning: "If there should be during this historic performance the slightest sound of any noise or laughter, I will personally crack the skull of the scoundrel who has shown such disrespect for the genius of William Shakespeare and the talents of Wiley Algernon Callan."

The saloon fell into a dead silence except for the snapping made by the fire and the moans made by the wind in the chimney.

The actor undid the top buttons of his collar, threw back his head, and strode to the center of the square of light in the darkened saloon where he immediately began to play three parts.

Wiley crouched down and, astonishingly, spoke in the quavering voice of an old crone, of a witch: "When shall we three meet again? In thunder, lightning, or in rain?"

He scampered over to the other side of his stage and assumed a different part. This witch answered, "When the hurlyburly's done, when the battle's lost and won."

With haste he leaped to a third position, and bending down even more, and using an even higher falsetto, he recited, "That will be ere the set of sun."

Tom watched, totally confused, as his friend leaped about, using false voices and strange postures. The incredible thing was that as he did this, he took on at that instant the personality of the character he played. A moment later he saw him stand up straight at the front of the lighted area with arms held wide and say in resonant tones, "Fair is foul, and foul is fair. Hover through the fog and filthy air."

"That," Tom said to himself, "does not make a great deal of sense. But neither does anything else that has happened to me in New Mexico."

For the next hour and twenty minutes Wiley capered about, taking a king's part, a captain's, a queen's, playing Macbeth and also Lady Macbeth, taking Malcolm's, Banquo's, and Macduff's parts as well as playing all the soldiers and several apparitions, not to mention many other characters. It was a tour de force. It also was, even for a scholar who knew the play and who paid it the greatest attention, most difficult to follow. However, there were probably no scholars in the saloon during the play's performance anyway.

Tom had never read or seen any comedies or dramas by William Shakespeare although he had heard of the man. He paid very little attention to Wiley's enthusiastic performance, and as his friend's voice droned on and on and on, he poured himself another drink.

However, the others in the saloon, the cowboys and the miners, seemed dumbstruck, riveted by Wiley's energy and glibness even though the actor might as well have been speaking in ancient Greek for all the sense they made of most of it. Yet at times they did attend the words. Their inexplicable appeal filtered into the minds of the lonely men in the audience, reaching them on some level and in some way that they themselves would have been hard pressed to explain.

The ringing in Tom's ears became louder and he put his head upon his arms. And then, with Wiley performing *The Tragedy of Macbeth* at the top of his lungs, Tom fell asleep. Or perhaps he passed out. But regardless, in one way or another, he slipped mercifully out of his suffering.

The miners and the cowboys, the drunks and hangers-on, the sad-faced young whores from the huts out behind Sol Racine's Saloon and Gaming Hall, all of these people rose to their feet in a standing ovation at this moment: the peak, the summit, of Wiley Callan's life.

The climax had been reached and passed, the final words still trembled in the air. Wiley stood still for an instant, soaking in what he interpreted—no doubt incorrectly—as adulation. Then he bowed with a sweeping flourish. He rose erect, a broad grin on his face, and at that moment a great log in the central fireplace broke apart, throwing a host of shimmering sparks to all sides. A wave of yellowish light flared swiftly across the thespian's beaming face, and it seemed to Wiley at that second that God and nature and these good folks all loved and approved most heartily of him.

He played this final triumph to the hilt, but while they still cried out raucously, he made a timely exit. With consummate dignity he strode through the cheering, good-humored people to the bar where Sol Racine offered him his choice of beverages—and was surprised to find the actor would accept nothing more than a large glass of water.

A short time later, still flushed by triumph, Wiley sat upon a barstool and told droll stories to people who liked to be entertained. The gamblers had by now reaffixed the lanterns above their tables and had returned to the seriousness of their vocations.

Wiley, still trembling slightly but with his excitement gradually subsiding, found himself face to face with a rather short, plump-breasted Mexican woman who appeared to be in her early twenties.

"Did you enjoy *The Tragedy of Macbeth,* my dear?" he inquired courteously of this lovely creature, obviously a new fan of his.

She absolutely beamed with pleasure at him. *"Ah, señor,"* she replied with feeling, stretching forth her hand and patting him on the hip.

"And did you see how a good man can fall into evil ways?"

"Desgradiamente, no entiendo ni una palabra de Inglés. Lo que quiero averiguar es si quieres hacer el amor conmigo. Solo te cuestas un dólar."

Wiley looked at her, still smiling, but a frown of puzzlement wrinkled his brow.

A man beside him commented, "She don't speak no English, she says, but she wants to know if you'd like to take a poke at her for a dollar."

Wiley's face colored and he backed away. Like so many Americans he found it impossible to believe that a language as pure and clear as English could not be understood if spoken carefully enough. And so he said quite slowly to the young whore, enunciating each word with an actor's precision in spite of his extreme Texas accent, "You—are—very—pretty—my—dear. But—I—cannot—accept—your—kind—offer." Biting his lip with embarrassment, he fled.

Wiley sought refuge in the midst of a host of men, taking again the seat he'd abandoned after his deal with Crafty Jack. The gamblers

looked up from their cards as he joined them. One or two nodded
briefly in acknowledgment of his presence.

Big Sam Macklin and Blackjack Crosby, however, were not so curt.
They smiled warmly at his return, for he had shown a degree of
ineptitude with cards that they had never witnessed in the thousands
of nights which they had spent in the practice of the art of poker. The
orange-headed, freckle-faced man with the great-knuckled, knobby,
scarred fists even had trouble holding the cards dealt to him. Time
and again, when they had first been playing, he had dropped several of
them on the table before fumbling as he picked them up. It didn't
occur to him, apparently, that the other players had seen some of his
hand. Each time, good-naturedly, he would grin as though this weren't
important. And each time the real card players would look at him in
bafflement.

Wiley had cheerfully lost time after time. Once he had stayed in a
hand against Big Sam who had opened the betting. Since it took a pair
of jacks or better in this game to begin this process, it stood to reason
that Big Sam would have at least this in his cards. Wiley had insisted
on raising Big Sam's bet, and even got permission to re-raise—although that practice was not followed at most tables. Wiley had
thrown down his cards, face up, after Sam had shown his pair of
queens. "You got me fair and square," Wiley remarked.

All the others looked blankly at the pair of sixes he had discarded
with his other cards.

The big miner who had been out cold on the floor had finally
regained partial consciousness and had been led groggily away by a
friend, leaving no sign behind except for a smudge of blood upon the
pine boards with several broken teeth which had suffered further
damage by men having thoughtlessly stepped on them. The two sat
together at the bar where the injured party medicated himself with
the harsh whiskey favored by Sol Racine. The friend had not known
of the cloth sack of silver dollars, and the poor miner had not fully
recovered his senses. As a result, these still rested on the poker table
at Wiley's right side.

"Come on, damn it, let's play," an old fellow beside Wiley snarled. A
ray of unclipped whiskers stuck out in all directions from his face.
Those that hung from his chin were absolutely white while those
which rimmed his cheekbones still had a darker cast. He had the

slightly cadaverous look about his eyes that many men have when they
reach their sixties.

Big Sam spoke in his musical voice. "While the winners smile and
nod the losers holler 'deal.' "

The whiskered man hunkered in his chair, glaring from under his
hatbrim at Big Sam.

All at the table pitched their clinking silver-dollar antes toward the
center of the table, and the cards slapped down before each man.
Wiley picked his up and spent some time, as he'd done each round,
clumsily arranging them, picking this one up and sliding it down, then
taking another out, waving it in the air before deciding where it should
be inserted. The others, weary of this, drew deep breaths of irritation.

"If they're all black does that help?"

Big Sam looked at Wiley before answering. "It does if they're all
clubs or all spades. You'd have a flush."

"No help if only one doesn't match the others?"

Big Sam didn't deign to reply. A man opened with a dollar bet and
the others, including Wiley, followed. Six men sat at the table and
none dropped out.

"How about," Wiley persisted, "if the cards are lined up in se-
quence?"

"Surely," Blackjack said curtly, "you know about a straight."

"Can't you have just a single card that's only a little out of line?"

Another silence. The other five players stared at Wiley. Finally
Blackjack said, "No."

"Well," Wiley said, "I'll take one card." He smiled cordially at the
other men. "In spite of trail weariness, I'm having a grand time. It is
the result, I tell you, of clean vigorous living."

The gamblers looked at each other blankly.

The discards were pulled in by the dealer; the ones each player
chose to draw were dealt.

Once more Wiley began arranging his hand, moving one card here,
another there. He dropped the ten of spades on the table, frowned,
picked it up, and then said, "Who gets the chance to bet first?"

Suppressing his pain, Blackjack said patiently, "The man who
opened will place his bet."

That person put down two dollars. Others "saw" the bet, putting
out an equal sum, but when Wiley's turn came he said, "I know that
table stakes are a requirement, and as you know I've lost about all my

money. But if I can manage to borrow a little extra, would that be all right?"

Blackjack and Big Sam sighed simultaneously. The latter said kindly, "Why, yes. If you can find a way to bring more money to the game, and if it can be done quickly, then by all means do so."

Wiley, a trusting man, left his cards facedown at his place at the table. He went quickly to the bar and those left behind followed him with their eyes. He was speaking to the miner he'd almost killed.

The whiskered man kept looking at Wiley's cards. "He must have drawn a card trying to fill a flush or a straight."

"Who knows."

"I'm tempted to take a peek," the whiskered man said, his fingers moving toward Wiley's cards.

"No," Blackjack's voice cracked out. "There'll be none of that. Besides, for Christ's sakes, you don't have to cheat to whip this poor son of a bitch."

"I guess that's true," the whiskered one replied.

At this time Wiley engaged in negotiations with the man with whom he'd had differences earlier in the evening. He asked, "Did you see me perform *The Tragedy of Macbeth?*"

The vacant-eyed miner, his bloody mouth hanging open and disclosing the stumps of several broken teeth, shook his head negatively. His memory seemed to be returning, for he recoiled and blurted out, "Don't hit me no more."

Wiley ignored this and, patiently, said, "I'd like to borrow that sack of your money to use in the card game. While I hate to sound cocky, I happen to hold a mighty fine hand of cards."

Once again the miner shook his head, but this time with more feeling. His black brows knit into a furious frown as he said, "Hell no."

Wiley drew back his right fist a scant eight or ten inches. "I sure wish you'd change your mind," he said almost wistfully.

Horrified, the miner jerked back. Then, speaking hoarsely, lisping because of his missing teeth, he stammered, "I done asked you not to do that. Take the damn money!"

"Thank you," Wiley said with genuine appreciation. He nodded courteously and started back to his game. As he strode away he heard the miner behind him say, "I sure wish they was a sheriff in Silver City."

When Wiley returned he said, "I got the loan." He dumped the contents of the sack upon the table, and the quantity of silver dollars made the others widen their eyes.

The man who'd opened cleared his throat, then said, "The bet is two dollars."

Wiley pushed out two dollars and said, "I'll see the bet and raise it by whatever I've got here."

He bent his head and began counting. After a moment he said, "I have seventy-six silver dollars and four fifty-dollar gold pieces, and I want to bet it all." With that he pushed the tumbling stack of coins toward the growing pot in the center of the table.

"Jehosaphat!" the whiskered man exclaimed. "I never seen a bet that big in my life."

"Nor have I," another gambler said with awe.

Blackjack Crosby glanced across the table to see Big Sam Macklin fighting against a smile. Both men turned to saddlebags upon the floor, and without another word they pulled out paper money and gold pieces and quickly met the bet. But the other three men folded, throwing in their hands in disgust.

"I don't for a second believe the son of a bitch drew that card he was after, but I ain't fool enough to bet that much," the whiskered player exclaimed before saying, "even if I had it."

A crowd had materialized. Men stood several deep all around the table.

"Well," Big Sam said in his fine voice, "let's see what you've got, stranger."

Blackjack sat even straighter in his chair, not ruffled in the slightest, showing only a mild amount of interest.

"There we are," Wiley said. "All of them spades, a flush like you say. Of course I don't know what you fellows have in your hands. For good measure," Wiley added, "all of these just happen to line up right, or so it seems to me. You see before you, gentlemen, the ten, jack, queen, king, and ace of spades."

In the extraordinary quietness that descended upon the saloon a pin could have been heard if it had fallen. While one of these did not, a large hand did. Wiley's palm slapped with great force upon the table and in the following echo he said, "I would not expect you fellows to try to top a royal flush."

Blackjack Crosby folded his hand and slid it facedown across the table. Big Sam Macklin did the same. He said as he did so, "Blackjack, has it crossed your mind that this fellow may have played poker before?"

The game had broken up, and the last of the customers of Sol Racine's Saloon and Gaming House were departing. Wiley tried without success to rouse Tom, then went to the front door and opened it. Flurries of unexpected snow fell softly on his face and he quickly retreated, going first to the fire and then to the bar.

Sol Racine, who stood behind it putting bottles away, stated, "We don't have a hotel in this town, and the rooms that are for rent have long since been taken. Some folks who pass by pitch their tents at Cumbie's stables. That Cumbie is a cutter," he said, chuckling. "Right now he's gone to Texas where he hunts blue quail regardless of the weather. He's a fanatic about it."

"I love to eat blue quail," Wiley said emotionally. "In fact, I'm hungry enough to eat the balls off a running studhorse. I've had little except beef jerky for the last four days and I'm starving half to death. After returning the money I borrowed to that miner who departed a little while ago, I find that I'm left with more actual cash than many men have ever seen. And though I've made many inquiries, I can't find anyone willing to rent me a room or sell me a meal. I would like to ask you, sir, what is wrong with the capitalists in this town? Have you reached such a sorry state that there is no greed left? Why should I have spent hours getting a great sack full of money if no one will accept any of it? All I want is a place to sleep and something to eat." As he spoke, his aggravation turned to rage, and by the time he finished his voice had soared, trembling, into the rafters and throughout the establishment.

"Mister," Sol said, "there ain't no use in your hollerin' at me. It's well after midnight. This saloon is the only thing that's open around here after dark and I'm about to close it."

"What about my friend who's sleeping over at that table?" Wiley asked in an aggrieved tone.

"For five dollars, I'll let the two of you stay in here after I close up. But I have a careful inventory of the booze, so you'll pay for anything that's missing."

Wiley looked at him with a pained expression. "You should not have stained your charitable offer with that poisonous insult. Besides, my friend has passed out and I, thank God, do not drink." He followed the bartender to the door and said, "Here is the five dollars you've requested."

When the front door slammed, Wiley walked through the bar, lit now only by a single lantern and by the central fireplace. He found a good supply of logs, and threw several on the fire. As these blossomed slowly into flames he felt somewhat better, but the hunger pangs had by now become unbearable.

Wiley walked out the back way toward a cluster of small frame huts. He saw a light at the window of one of them and he tapped insistently on the door. It opened cautiously and dark eyes inspected him. Then it swung wide.

The pretty young Mexican girl with plump breasts he'd met in the bar earlier greeted him with a surprised smile. She ushered him into the one-room hut and moments later Wiley found himself surrounded by the most entrancing odor he had ever smelled.

Upon an iron stove a very large blackened slab of meat sizzled in a frying pan. He hardly noticed the young woman who looked at him curiously, but rather he went down upon his knees before the stove and stared as though hypnotized. Then he took out two silver dollars and handed them to his hostess, pointing first at the meat and then at his mouth.

"Tienes hambre, mi amor? Pues bien, voy a darte a comer en seguida."

While these words held no great significance for Wiley, he appreciated the friendly sounds. And when the young girl carved great slices of meat and put them on a plate for him, he moved to a small table and ate with gusto. In fact he had three helpings before he quit.

"Ah, my dear, you've made me a happy man. I have never had a finer meal. Never."

"Me llamo María," she said, pointing to herself and repeating, *"María."* When he smiled, she added proudly, "I spik *Inglés* okay."

What a pleasant girl, Wiley thought. He asked her, "What kind of meat was that? As I said before, it was extraordinarily good." He saw he was not communicating well.

Speaking very distinctly, Wiley pointed at the small amount of leftovers in the skillet and asked, "Beef? Steer? Cow? Sheep?"

The girl's eyes brightened. "No sheep. Pig."

"Pig!" Wiley repeated. His face fell. *I have,* he thought, *violated a lifelong pledge.* But he could not feel revulsion. Rather, he remembered the way the pork had tasted. It had been charred on the outside and

within had been juicy and white and hot. It had been perfectly delicious.

And at this moment a revelation struck Wiley: *I have gone against one of my beliefs, and it has been a marvelous experience.*

As he had these thoughts, he sank back in his chair, wondering about the validity of his other vows, in particular the one which prevented him from becoming overly friendly with ladies of the night, ladies exactly like his hostess.

She came up to him, swaying her rounded hips. She stroked his hair and then led him to her bed. She sat with his head in her lap, leaning forward, pressing softly against him.

"You very tired," she said observantly although somewhat awkwardly.

"That is quite true, my dear," Wiley responded as gallantly as he could. "And there is no bed in that wretched bar. Perhaps I could rest here a moment?" He let the question linger in the air.

Miraculously she seemed to understand. Or perhaps she misunderstood. She unbuttoned and removed his jacket and then his shirt. She unbuckled his belt and unbuttoned his fly. She pulled off his boots and then his pants.

This, Wiley felt, was even more fun than eating that pork. He gathered the blanket around himself modestly, for he now wore only his red longhandled underwear.

The girl did not remove quite everything, Wiley noted with an unusual degree of interest. She left her rosary beads around her throat. The waving light given off by several candles on a table under a simple crucifix illuminated her. She stood naturally, not trying to hold in her plump stomach, and apparently unconscious of her healthy young breasts which tilted up perkily as if they had snub noses. They dangled momentarily as she bent over, looking down into a cradle that Wiley had not previously noticed, and pulled the blankets about a baby, and then she slithered under the cover next to him.

"You very nice," María said as her expert fingers began to undo the buttons that lined the front of his red woolen longhandled underwear.

And in a reasonably short period of time Wiley Algernon Callan had violated the second of the three vows he had sworn to uphold.

While he lay in warm comfort, he thought back on the day and evening he had spent. He and Tom had lost the trail of the men they pursued and had finally arrived, despondent, in the mining town of

Silver City. But then things had turned about. First, he had fulfilled his life's greatest ambition: he had performed *The Tragedy of Macbeth* all by himself. He had won an incredible amount of money at the poker table. He had then capped it off by becoming, at least for the evening, a voluptuary: he had savored forbidden fruits. And he didn't feel guilty in the slightest.

With a sigh of pleasure, Wiley pulled María closer, feeling her warmth, patting the swell of her smooth rump.

"I shall remember this night, María," Wiley said. But, looking down at the dark-haired head that nestled upon his shoulder, he saw that she had fallen asleep.

Wiley spoke one last time to himself. "I guess it's asking too much for a man to keep more than one vow out of three."

The candles guttered out. The heat from the iron stove filled the small single room, the baby cried once in his sleep but then fell silent. And Wiley slipped contentedly into a sleep filled with marvelous dreams.

A pure white snow fell all night long upon María's small shack, transforming it, hiding its crudeness.

Sixteen

THE ACHINGLY SAD ODOR of sour spilled beer and whiskey hung heavily in the seemingly mildewed and probably green-colored air. Tom decided that if he kept his head very still on the table in Sol Racine's Saloon he might not die. He'd been sick twice during the night, barely making it outside into the befouled snow. Now, with his heart beating by fits and starts, he kept one cheek down on the dusty wooden surface, not daring to move.

A short, slight-figured man, standing perhaps five feet tall, who appeared to be dressed in a pair of bizarre-looking baggy black pajamas, pitched some logs on the glowing coals of the huge oval fireplace in the center of the room. He hummed a singsong melody with not more than five notes, repeating the sounds over and over as he began to sweep the floor with a worn broom, stirring up veritable storm clouds of dust in the process. He marched through these, stabbing at the floor as if chopping weeds with a hoe.

Risking a heart attack, Tom gingerly assumed a sitting position. Spots danced before his eyes and then gradually disappeared.

A very old Chinaman, his yellow face covered by deep lines—as if his skin were dry stiff paper that had been crumpled and then unfolded—shuffled through the saloon with a bucketful of long tapered candles. His slanted eyes examined Tom suspiciously, then he backed away. He bowed stiffly and said, "I dipped these tallow candles myself. I am Fernando Wo Ching, the candlemaker. I also work for Mr. Racine."

Tom did not trust himself to reply.

Wo Ching pulled a folding ladder from its place in the shadowed recesses of the smelly bar, put it upright, shook its triangular frame vigorously to be sure its legs stood firmly in place, and ascended the steps to the nearest candelabra. He then deftly dug out the brittle, guttered remains of the previous night's candles with a table knife, made a cursory effort to scrape the drippings from the silver holders, and with infinite care inserted twelve new upright tapers which stood in white readiness. He dragged the ladder to the next candelabra, repeated the process, and kept working without pause until he had replaced twelve new white candles in each of the eight great, curving silver chandeliers which swung gently at his touch, revolving slightly from the black silk ropes tied to the rough-sawn boards of the rafters.

He bustled over to the bar, went behind it, and put a small pitcher under the beer barrel's wooden tap. He opened this, carefully drew off half a pitcher, then stopped the flow. He brought the foaming malodorous brew to Tom, put it down on the table, and said, "Beer."

"I can see that," Tom replied, drawing back from it in disgust.

"Drink," Wo Ching directed. "You'll feel better pretty quick." He paused as though pondering before saying "maybe." Then he stated, "I've seen men treat their hangovers for years, and this cure sometimes works. Most of the others don't."

Tom obediently picked up the small pitcher and drank from its side. He shuddered, feeling waves of nausea, almost gagging at its bitterness. Then he took several more tentative sips.

"Good," the Chinaman said, his face splitting into a wide smile, revealing stumps of teeth that looked like the blackened remains of a fire-gutted house.

Tom felt a spiral of anxiety and had a falling sensation. *I wonder,* he thought, *if my system can stand the shock.* He waited several moments, sipped more beer, then sat back, resolved to die like a man. But he noted some improvement; his heart's irregular flutterings seemed to be falling back into their old dependable pattern. With an indrawn sigh of relief, Tom waited dully.

Memories and pain caused him to close his eyes. He observed the diminishing supply of beer with the beginnings of mild concern, but then saw the great iron-banded oaken-staved barrel lying sideways at one end of the bar. He thought, *I believe I'll slip away from all this reality again.*

Addressing Fernando Wo Ching, he said, "Men often do the damndest things in the name of fun."

The old Oriental ignored the comment, for he was once more sweeping the floor, moving the dirt and dust from one place in the bar to another, and then whisking through it all over again. He slashed at it as though attacking an enemy.

The early morning horror that Tom had faced on awakening had left him. He sat in the empty saloon, choking on the dust and the stench of stale beer, still sick at his stomach and with a pounding headache. He knew that these feelings were temporary. But he felt a more permanent ache, an unseen spiderweb of anguish which spread across his chest. He knew he couldn't raise his fingers and free himself from its clinging, from its constant maddening presence. He felt it to be absolutely unbelievable that someone as lovely and vital and alive as Macha should be gone.

He tasted the bile of hatred, felt its acid sear his throat. Tiny sparks flared through his sick headache, and he closed his eyes in agony. The men that he and Wiley had been trailing had disappeared as if into thin air. But even so, he knew with certainty that he would never rest until he found Julian Haynes.

The Chinaman stopped his short jabbing strokes with the broom. He took a pouch of tobacco from his pocket and fished a flimsy cigarette paper from another recess in his voluminous black shirt. Curling the paper with his fingers, he expertly filled it with a stream of golden brown flakes without spilling any. After this he licked and sealed it, doubled the end, and went to the fire. Pulling out a glowing splinter, he lit his cigarette.

Wo Ching raised to his full five feet in height, put his back toward the growing flames which warmed the saloon, and began to smoke as intensely as the fireplace. Everything the old man chose to do, he did with energy. When he sucked at his cigarette the burning tip turned brilliant red. Wo Ching pulled the cigarette smoke deep down into his lungs and then blew it out in a whooshing blue-white cloud before instantly repeating the process. He got his money's worth from the tobacco. The cigarette pulsed its bright red-tipped light at each inhaling.

The front door banged open and instantly a gust of icy wind flooded in like water over a broken dam. Wiley Callan hurriedly slammed the heavy door behind him and bustled up beside Wo Ching at the fire. He stood head and shoulders above the Chinaman.

Wiley leaned forward and rubbed his hands together as though washing them in the welcome heat given off by the popping, flaming logs, then turned about in order to allow the fire's radiation to fall upon his back.

He smiled at Tom. "In the Good Book we read of 'the quick and the dead.' The word *quick* actually being a church word which means *living*. During last night it struck me that you certainly weren't 'quick,' although when I got near enough to get struck by your terrible breath, I wondered if you were dead and possibly possessed by demons or if you might possibly still be alive, and I hung my hopes on the latter interpretation. However, the last time I saw you it was touch and go. Didn't know if you'd make it to see the morning's light."

Tom didn't deign to reply to this. He took another drink from the side of the pitcher and wiped the foam from his mouth wearily.

"Never would have taken you for a drunkard," Wiley said with the usual smugness of a teetotaler. "While it's true that water—I refer to my favorite drink—does not get a fellow excited and red-faced—neither does it cause him to feel as if he's caught the bubonic plague. That's the actual name of the 'Black Death,' as they once called it, a scourge that killed some millions of people—men, women, and children. A rampant disease caught from fleas and ticks that carried it from infected rats, they say. It turned men black, made them spew dark vomit, caused great buboes to swell and burst in their groins and armpits."

"In the name of God, Wiley," Tom said harshly, his stomach churning.

"I am merely painting a word picture of the average bad hangover, a sensation that I have never experienced but have observed at first hand. And I gather that the comparison with the Black Death is appropriate."

Tom shuddered and closed his eyes.

Wiley sat in a chair across the table from him. "I tried to rouse you without success from your besotted slumbers and finally in despair managed to persuade the manager of this establishment to allow us to spend the night, although I had to make him a princely offer before he accepted. You were, my friend, out cold. The memory of it brings to mind a phrase you may have heard me recite last night: 'When in swinish sleep their drenchèd natures lie as in death . . .'"

A complacent smile spread across Wiley's freckled face. "Lord, Lord, but I was in good form last evening. I still can scarcely believe the majesty of my performance. What mastery of language! How the bard's words did flow!"

Tom spoke at last. "You're no slouch at word flow yourself."

Wiley slid off his chair and stood erect. He arched his back, stretched out his arms, and yawned. "I shall never forget any of the extraordinary things that took place." A secret smile touched his mouth as he fell momentarily silent, savoring the memories.

He had a habit of making pronouncements, Tom noticed, of laying such grave importance on his words that the simplest statement sounded as though it must surely be terribly important.

Wiley said contentedly, "You may not recall the plans I announced last eventide, but—to refresh your memory—I now have a patron, a sponsor. Crafty Jack Dent and I are going to travel by rail to the finest cities in the West. For the next year I plan to spend my time earning a stake as a prizefighter."

"Thought you'd decided to give that up."

"It isn't easy to change fields of employment. Especially when you're broke. By the time the mentioned year is done I hope to earn enough to enable me to find some job that fits my talents. As a matter of fact, I'm thinking of reading law. I can employ my theatrical experience, my histrionic gifts, to great advantage in the courtroom. And as I get older, I may even become a crusty old judge." He had a faraway look in his eyes. "I'd like that a lot."

Shaking free of his daydream, Wiley said, "In any case, my immediate intention is to go get my wagon and drive it to Socorro where I'll store it. After that, I'll take the Atchison, Topeka, and Santa Fe train to El Paso and rendezvous with Crafty Jack at his hotel. We hope to have a few profitable fights there before heading to California. Crafty Jack intends for us to make selected stops, however, in Arizona."

Wiley stared at him with a look that seemed to ask, "Now what do you make of that?"

Tom rose to his feet. "I want to wish you well. We'll be riding back the way we came together, but before we start, I'd like to take this time to thank you for coming to help me. I've enjoyed getting to know you, and I'd hate to think we wouldn't see one another someday in the future."

"Oh, I'll be coming to visit you on your ranch, out in the vast spaces of West Texas. Your few mentions of those spots struck my imagination, and I have a picture of your ranch house near the Concho River."

As usual, he couldn't restrain himself. "Out in the midst of nature, on the broad face of the earth, under the heaven's vast firmament—I must experience these mysteries with you."

He raised his orange brows. "A thought has come to me. There is a remarkable contrast which can be made between the way one man lives his life and how another does."

Tom looked questioningly at him, wondering what he had in mind.

"By this, I mean to say, I've known men whose world wasn't much larger than a thimble. I stayed with one like this in St. Louis some years back when I worked as an actor. This man, a jeweler, actually spent most of his days repairing clocks and watches. He'd put on a black eyepiece to magnify the tiny gears and cogs and springs, and with fragile tools of incredible fineness, he'd reassemble them. He'd repair and adjust and tinker until they worked perfectly again.

"The point I'm making is that his world lay in the palm of his own hand. There is, you'll have to admit, a vast distinction between his field—his venue—and yours."

"Wiley, when I'm at my best I don't know if I can keep up my end in a conversation like this one, and as you can probably see, I'm not feelin' real well right now."

"Fresh air, that's the answer. Let's find our horses and head back north. The men we pursued have vanished. It's pointless to keep wandering the way we've done the last two days after the trail got cold. Let's get on with our lives—and leave vengeance for the Lord."

Tom shook his head, unable to speak at first. Finally he muttered, "I can't let this drop. I think I'll go with you to El Paso—that's more than likely where Julian Haynes is headed. His home is there as well as most of the businesses he's bought."

"Suit yourself—and when we get there I'll be more than willing to give you a hand with Haynes."

"Thank you, Wiley, but that's something I've got to do alone."

Tom treated himself to one more curative pull from the side of the pitcher of flat, warm beer, then left some money with Fernando Wo Ching who bowed with great courtesy as a show of his appreciation.

An hour later found them retracing their steps. As they rode northward, Wiley talked about the joy of discovering new places. "I'll see Tucson and maybe Phoenix. Crafty Jack always keeps his eyes open for opportunities and he says he'd like to make some investments out there, for he thinks that Arizona has a good future. Well, after looking around and staging a few fights, it'll be off to Los Angeles.

"My, my. I'll be able to walk out on the sandy beach and look over the broad Pacific Ocean—clear out to the rim of the earth. I've never seen an ocean." He seemed lost in daydreams a moment before picking up the thread again. "There's bound to be quite a few big-money fights we can stage in a city like Los Angeles."

He stood in his stirrups, rising above the uncomfortable old tattered saddle, and an awful look of distress crossed his face. Finally he managed to push back against the cantle to a place of relative comfort. Then he resumed his patter.

"By a stroke of good fortune one of the gamblers at our table last night had been in Frisco when I staged that bare-knuckled bout which you saw. He talked about it and this completely captured Crafty Jack's attention. He is a shrewd man when it comes to financial dealings. At least, that's how he strikes me. Did you know that he once attended Harvard College in Boston?"

"No, I didn't. How'd he happen to end up in the Southwest?"

"Well, I'm not entirely sure. As you know, I've just met the man. But he did comment that he was passing through Texas when he met a perfectly lovely small blond girl, and he says that before he knew it he'd fallen head over heels in love. After he was lucky enough to marry her, he decided to stay. So he got in the windmill business, recognizing a good thing when he saw it. One thing led to another until he got his life so complicated that now he finds it necessary to travel around all the time looking after his interests."

A rabbit burst out of the snow immediately in front of their horses, his strong back legs kicking small clouds of powder into the steel-blue morning air.

Tom's horse had been moving along with an easy flowing saddlegait before the rabbit darted just in front of his hooves. Deuce shied violently to one side, then cavorted about for a moment. After this, he danced under his rider, nervous hooves skittering, muscular neck bowed, and with his tail furled high.

Tom felt the rush within him as Deuce first leaped. He collected his balance and felt the pressure of his legs and the hot, quick flow of blood. Looking about, he saw the world with a heightened sense of awareness.

Wiley watched the pirouetting horse with amused eyes. "Mighty glad *I'm* not ridin' a high-spirited animal like that one." He said, "It's always a pleasure to see a man who is a truly fine rider. I can tell by the look of you that you've handled many a bronc."

Flattered, Tom replied, "My first jobs when I left home had to do with breaking horses. I've gradually learned a little about it."

"I don't believe that a man learns things like that. To my mind, there are some who are 'born riders,' and you'd fit that description."

By mid-afternoon they had come to a long mountain. After ascending a twisting trail they reached the long flat top of the mesa and rode for several miles, peering off the edge of the white rimrock into broken canyons on the north side. In the distance they saw smoke rising in the air behind some knobby hills. They headed for this when they found a broad crevice through which they descended, leaning back in their saddles as their horses' hooves skidded on the loose rocks. They'd go deep into cedar brakes, picking their way down through brush and great stones before climbing again. At no time did they ride on level ground.

The drifting column of smoke served as their guide. They'd look for it when they reached a high point, and head in its direction. A few hours later they rode up to a cedar picket corral with a wide plank gate. A cowboy waved to them as they approached, and walked in their direction from a small frame house that had never known the touch of paint. The weather had turned its boards a streaked gray color.

"Howdy," the man called out as they drew near. He had an oily old hat with the brim on the right side curled up tight. "Step down and have some coffee."

A thick growth of stubble covered much of his leathery face. He wore a faded denim work shirt under a heavy jacket, and big-roweled spurs clinked with his every step.

After Wiley and Tom tied their horses they exchanged introductions, learning from the man that his name was Cap Cathcart.

Grateful for the invitation, even though that sort of thing was expected, they followed the cowboy into his house.

"It looks like I make my full-time home here," Cathcart said, "but the truth is, this grew out of a line camp on the Y Bar ranch. I been winterin' here now for nine years. Been alone for the past four months, and up till now I haven't had a chance to speak to another white man. I've seen six Indians and a dozen or so Meskins who didn't speak a word of anything but Spanish, and I been wonderin' if I'd remember how to talk."

"You're doin' fine," Wiley reassured him.

The house had one L-shaped room with a large storage closet. A small kitchen lay at one side; a table with two chairs, a bed, and a gun rack with several rifles lay along the other. Cathcart fussed about his sparsely furnished kitchen, pushing the blackened iron coffee pot to the hottest spot on the stovetop. He took a spiral-handled iron device and fitted its triangular tip into a slot in a round lid on top of the stove. Then, after shoving some shivered dry kindling wood down upon the crumbling orange coals, he replaced the heavy lid with a resounding clank.

"While this heats up," he said, "come look what I shot yesterday."

They followed him outside to a shed beside the corral and there upon the ground lay the bloody carcass of a dead mountain lion. The sinuous, tawny creature had a massive head and its body stretched almost five feet in length.

The cowboy hunkered down and pulled its mouth open, revealing two-inch-long curved white teeth. "Would you look at these?"

"Lord a'mercy," Wiley exclaimed. "I never saw a mountain lion near the size of that one. He looks like his kinfolk in Africa."

"He's a big 'un," agreed Cathcart. "I've killed eight of these cougars so far this winter. It's hunters like them that thin out our deer in these parts. Lions have a taste for them, and each kills at least one grown deer a week. Besides that, when the deer population goes down, these critters hunt our cattle. So gettin' rid of them is one of my main jobs during this time of year."

He touched the beautiful animal's head somewhat sadly. "Sometimes it seems a shame to have to shoot something that looks as fine as this, but you can't let killers run around free, can you?"

Wiley saw Tom's pale blue eyes turn icy. "No," Tom responded, "you can't allow that."

After they'd returned to the little shack and enjoyed their steaming coffee, they agreed with Cathcart that they couldn't get far before dark and decided that they might as well pass the night with him. He seemed pathetically grateful when they said they would stay. "A man gets lonesome once in a while," he managed to comment.

The two guests listened to the pent-up flow of conversation from Cathcart while they enjoyed a hearty meal of fried beef and frijoles along with more coffee. Tom took quite a few pulls from the old cowboy's large jug of tequila, then he and Wiley pulled their bedrolls loose, propped their heads on their saddles, and in no time at all were on the verge of going to sleep under the disappointed rheumy eyes of the whiskered man who wanted to talk some more.

He kept making comments just as they entered sleep.

"Sorry I don't have no extra beds."

Startled, Wiley raised his head from the saddle which served as his pillow. "What's that? Oh, well, don't worry, my friend. This floor is a sight smoother than the rocks I'd be sleepin' on without your hospitality. And it goes beyond saying that your fireplace beats a windblown campfire."

Cathcart chuckled, then said, "I always treat myself to a nightcap of old step-steady." He held the jug out to Tom who was leaning on one elbow.

"Well, just one more," he said as he took a final swallow and then fell back, coughing from the taste of the fiery draught.

"I feel sorry for Cathcart," Wiley said the next morning, after a few hours on the trail.

"No need to be, for there's no other life that suits him better; he'd go crazy living in a town." Tom straightened his legs, pushing the stirrups forward as he sought to relieve a small cramp. Then he continued, "My hunch is that he hopes to live out his days cowboyin'. When his time has come, nothing would please him more than to step off his horse and lie down on the ground. Just drift off with his horse standing nearby."

Tom felt embarrassed at talking like this. "At least, that's how I guess he might feel."

Wiley snorted at these remarks. "*I* certainly don't plan to leave this mortal coil that way. My choice is to die in a big feather bed surrounded by weeping friends and distraught pretty ladies. And as far as the rest of it goes, I won't accept less than a formal burial in a fine mahogany casket with bronze handles." He chuckled as he added, "I'll write a stirring testimonial speech to be read by the most distinguished orator in town. A man like me needs to go out with style."

Later that day, as they rode north, they spoke of the subject that had been on their minds. It began when Tom recalled taking the halter off the sorrel mare that had carried Macha before her death.

They both pictured the way the mare had wandered off into the hills alone. But free.

Then Tom spoke of Macha's past—Julian Haynes's bastard half sister, who had been raped by him and borne his son.

A volume of horror lay behind the few simple sentences. It took a time before Wiley spoke, and when he did it was not with his own words.

"Unnatural deeds do breed unnatural troubles."

They rode all day, camped, and at dawn set out once again. By mid-morning they came across a small stream. At its edge, at the foot of a tree, they saw a round pool about three feet across. The spring had clear water welling up in it and spilling over the edge into the stream. A few feet away, on a slender chain leading to an iron stake, they saw a rusted tin cup.

"I wonder who uses this?"

"Lord knows. I guess it would be the cowboys who work this range. They keep special places like this in mind."

The two dismounted. In the distance they heard a cow bawling, and high in the air they saw three dark buzzards hanging in the wind, soaring on updrafts, never moving their wide-stretched wings.

They had reached a fork in the trail. One path led west while the other went through the pass along the swiftly moving stream. Tom didn't want to ride past the place where they'd found Macha—or by the freshly turned dirt where they'd buried her. Although it would be out of his way, he decided to circle west around the mountains before heading north toward the Slaughter ranch. He and Wiley shook hands and agreed to meet in Frisco.

"Watch yourself," Wiley said. "Take care."

"I will," Tom replied. "I believe my right shoulder's about well, so I'll put on both guns and take the time to do some practicing."

He saw from the look on Wiley's face that he didn't understand why anyone would choose to waste his time in this fashion. And Tom didn't want to explain that this was how he tried to hold his old nightmares at bay.

"I don't see why a man would want to weight himself down with all that iron, but if it makes you happy . . ." Wiley's voice trailed away. Moments later he was out of sight.

Deuce splashed across a shallow crossing in the creek. The ice on the edges had almost melted, but along the bank in the shadows of trees a brittle film stayed on top of the water. A matching coldness shivered within the rider. An hour later he stopped and put on both holsters. He tied his horse, adjusted the two six-guns, and began.

Echoes of the percussive sounds bounced wildly through the canyon.

One of the three buzzards flapped his wings before settling once more into his wide, circling glide as he looked patiently for signs of death.

Seventeen

THREE MEN sat in comfortable chairs in the bright and sunny living room of the J. B. Slaughter headquarters ranch house. A Mexican woman came in with mid-morning coffee for them and, before leaving the room, added another log to the cheerfully burning fire in the blackened stone hearth.

The house sat on the long rolling skirts of a big-shouldered mountain. From its vantage point a small portion of the vast Slaughter ranch could be seen. It spread beyond the horizon, reaching west from New Mexico into Arizona.

Tom's hand trembled noticeably when he picked up his coffee cup. He tried to still it but couldn't, so he put the cup back in its saucer and glanced at his host and the other man to see if they had noticed. It relieved him to find they had not.

He listened as they talked, allowing his eyes to take in his surroundings. The room had Navajo rugs upon the wood floor, and the walls held a line of deer and elk antlers. Above the mantel hung a large portrait of a heavyset herd bull, standing proudly as if he owned the earth and defied any creature to question that point.

"I first met Tom," he heard his host say, "at the City Bank in Dallas some years back. That was when we'd added a good bit of land to our holdings, and I was looking for cattle to buy. He said that he'd let me know if he ever wanted to sell some. We've been dickerin' about the price for quite a spell now. How long's it been, Tom?"

"We started talking in earnest right after I sold my interests in Montana." Tom added, "J. B. is not an easy man when it comes to a trade."

The other guest, J. J. Hagerman, who had recently purchased John Chisum's ranch near Lincoln, chuckled in a husky way, sounding as if he needed to cough.

Slaughter continued his account. "Anyway, a while back Tom got in touch by telegraph with a final offer—we struck a deal—and his men made the long drive from the Concho River country in West Texas with a herd made up mostly of Herefords and some Shorthorns— Durhams, that is to say—as well as a mix of Mexican cows for good measure. I'm nervous about trying the English breeds out here, but the time has come to see if they can make it on this range."

Slaughter had the lazy, arrogant way some wealthy individuals acquire. He had long since banked what he called his "go to hell" money, and he didn't ever worry if his word might give offense. He felt most comfortable with the few men in the Southwest also in his position. That's why he sought out their company. For the last two days he had thoroughly enjoyed having Hagerman as a visitor, and when Tom English arrived the night before, he had been delighted. It was a rare treat to have two men as his guests whom he could treat as equals.

"I been waitin' an unconscionable time for this waddy to show up for his money." Slaughter's eyes twinkled as he gestured toward Tom. "But weeks passed, and then more than a month went by. Everyone knows that Tom is a rich man, but he'd sent me some thousands of fine cattle and had neglected to collect for 'em. I knew from talking to Osie Black and Ted Carrothers, his trail bosses, that he'd be here to get his check. When he didn't get to Frisco to meet 'em, they had to leave so as to get back to Texas. They sent me word that he'd get here sooner or later—but I was *hopin'* it had completely slipped his mind." He boomed out a sudden laugh and leaned forward, his shrewd eyes glancing from one of his visitors to the other.

Slaughter slapped his hands down on his knees before saying, "Well, he's been paid, and I'm stuck with a herd of high-bred cattle that may or may not be able to stay alive in these mountains. Most of 'em are down to skin and bones after the trail drive, so I'm takin' all the risk while Tom has a pocketful of my money."

Hagerman said, "I'm surprised to see you traveling alone, Tom. Your reputation has spread far, and I thought you had five Mexican bodyguards who rode with you at all times."

"I lived that way for quite a while, but a man named Julian Haynes, who was raised not far from here, had some hired guns who bushwhacked all of them." His voice hardened as he said, "The men who died spent most of their time as cowboys on the ranch—and only acted as back guards when I had to leave it." He paused before concluding, "They were good friends."

The others sat uncomfortably in the silence that followed his words. Then Slaughter commented, "I sure didn't know about any of that. Funny that you should mention Haynes." He said emphatically, "He's a cold-blooded bastard. Never saw a man with less feelin'. His daddy was blind and old, and I knew Haynes as much as stole the title to his ranch. God, I hated havin' to deal with him, but when he came to sell most of it to me, I knew that if I didn't buy the land someone else would."

He winced—which was as much of an apology as J. B. Slaughter ever made. "The ranch had been owned by Haynes's mother's family. Long ago old Joaquin Estévez built a house that must be the biggest in New Mexico, and for years I've longed for it. But Haynes refused to sell the house to me. He kept it and three sections, and sold me the other thirty-seven. In my favor, let me say that I did most surely want that land—because it bordered mine. The only land I covet is what lays next to my fenceline." He boomed out his deep belly laugh, for Slaughter always enjoyed his own jokes more than those of others.

"Anyhow, years went by without our hearing much from Haynes, and then, to my surprise, he showed up day before yesterday with the title to what was left—and offered to sell the house and acreage to me. So, naturally, I bought that too."

Tom had reached for the coffee cup again, deciding to test the steadiness of his fingers, but at these words it fell with a brittle crash to the floor. "Did you say that Julian Haynes was here?" His face had turned dead white.

Slaughter looked at him, bewildered by the question. "Yes, I did."

"Do you know where he headed when he left?"

"No—but if I had to guess, I'd figure he'd be on his way to El Paso. His horse was worn to the bone, so he certainly wasn't planning to ride there. And besides, Haynes has lived the city life for a long time. He didn't seem real comfortable on horseback, so I'd say that he's more than likely going to catch the train in Socorro."

"Was he alone?"

"No, he had a man with him, name of Chato. Mean-lookin' hombre."

Slaughter and Hagerman couldn't conceal their surprise as Tom shook their hands hurriedly and rushed from the room.

"What in the name of all that's holy is going on?" Hagerman inquired.

Slaughter sank back into his chair and looked far out on his ranchland. After a time he said, "I've always heard that Tom English would go out of his way to avoid trouble. But it surely looks to me as if he's spoilin' for a fight. I wouldn't want to be in Julian Haynes's boots."

Tom rode past the prickly pear and thorny waist-high brush on the hill before stopping. On looking down at the Upper Plaza in Frisco, the first thing he noticed was Wiley's big red wagon with the yellow wheels. It sat near a line of horses tied at the long hitching rail in front of Milligen's Saloon. He was surprised at how many people milled about in the town until he remembered it was a Saturday afternoon, the time the Slaughter cowboys would be showing up.

He touched his spurs to Deuce's sides and circled around to the northwest of the town until he reached the adobe house belonging to the widow of Francisco Naranjo. He stepped down and dropped the reins to the ground.

Old Rafa Hernández, the tamale maker, came from his adjoining house wearing his customary threadbare denim jacket over pants held up by cotton rope. He rubbed his hand over the white bristles on his face. Rafa stopped beside him just as the door to Francisco's house burst open and three children ran from it, laughing—playing chase.

Tom watched Macha's son run with Francisco's children into the draw and out of sight. Marta, Francisco's widow, came from the house and without speaking drew near to him, tears running down her cheeks.

"We found out how Macha died," Rafa said, explaining Marta's behavior. "Your friend, the one with the red wagon, told us. He's been here waiting for you since yesterday."

Marta brushed a sleeve across her face, drying her eyes. "I want to keep Macha's boy," she said. "Rafa and I are going to see Macha's mother next week to make sure it's all right. I love Pancho—he'll be like one of my own."

Tom found it hard to speak. Finally, after clearing his throat, he said, "I'll send you money from time to time. I'd like to help."

They didn't answer. Pride forbade this, but he knew without question that the money would be welcome. Without Francisco, Marta couldn't keep the livery stable, and she had no other income.

As Tom walked toward his horse, Rafa followed him, his old sandals slapping on the hard ground which surrounded the adobe house. "So many things have happened lately," the old man said. "Did I tell you about the return of Elfego Baca?"

Tom stopped at the news, surprised.

Rafa put his hands on his stomach where it sagged heavily over the rope which held up his pants and patted the paunch with a certain satisfaction. He said, "Yes, he's back. Rode in two days ago with that deputy sheriff."

"Ross?"

"*Eso es.* I can never remember those crazy gringo names."

"But—what about the trial?"

"Elfego was acquitted; they said he acted in self-defense. There's to be a second trial for some reason, but both of them said that the trouble would soon be over. I don't understand such things. Anyway, Ross said that the reason he had come was to get the law organized over here—he said it was too far from Socorro and he couldn't be riding over to help us whenever things got out of hand.

"The deputy and Elfego met with Guillermo Jones and the *alcalde,* and they made Elfego town marshal. After that, Ross left town."

Rafa beamed as he said, "What do you think of that? Elfego's finally got the thing he's always wanted—a real badge. He's our own lawman, the first that Frisco's ever had."

Tom stood with Elfego Baca in front of the livery stable. "I didn't expect to see you here."

The young Mexican's dark face broke into a broad grin and he answered, "Neither did those cowboys. When they came into town, I was in a cane-back chair on the board sidewalk right outside the door to Milligen's Saloon. Had a Winchester on my lap and this badge pinned on the outside of my coat for them to see."

"What happened?"

Elfego didn't answer immediately. "They've got hard feelings, but several said that their boss, Mr. Slaughter, had told them that he'd fire every man he had if a single one caused trouble in Frisco. None of them, I don't suppose, would like to think he caused so many to lose their jobs. Work is hard to come by these days."

"So you think everything is under control?"

"I did at first, but now they've had a few drinks and some are acting a little mean." He shrugged. "Guess I'll have to see what happens."

"I feel responsible—a good bit of what they're mad at you about is due to me. If there's to be a fight, I'll help you face it."

"I don't think there will be, but thanks. In a way I wish I *would* have to back a few of them down; it would be fun looking at their faces when I told them who my compadre was, that this was Tom English." He laughed at the thought. "But, as I said, I don't expect anything to come up that I can't handle."

His eyes dropped down to Tom's tied-down holsters. "You're wearing two guns. I guess your hurt arm's better."

Tom nodded.

Elfego touched his star. "Those cowboys have been brought up to respect the law." Somewhat nervously he added, "I sure hope they don't forget what they learned."

"The real reason I'm here is to look for a man named Julian Haynes," Tom said. "That is, if he and the hired hand with him haven't left town."

Elfego examined the grim face of his companion. "So—there's two you're after. Can I help?"

"My quarrel is with Haynes—and it's a real personal matter. If he's here, it'd be useful to me to know that you're on the lookout so the man with him won't try to bushwhack me—he tried that once before."

Elfego's eyes narrowed. "I can do that," he drawled after a moment.

The two men walked across the rutted way until they reached the hitching rail. Six cowboys had come outside the bar. They glared at Elfego and after that at Tom.

Then it happened—Tom saw a familiar figure at the door staring hard at him. A jolt seemed to hit him in the pit of his stomach as Julian Haynes ducked back inside.

At that moment Wiley Callan strolled up, smiling broadly. "Where on earth have you been? I got here about noon yesterday and have used the time wisely. Since I'm going off on tour, I've been having a two-for-one sale on my elixir—and have blame near sold out my entire stock."

"Wiley, I just saw Haynes at the saloon door. His man Chato is probably inside with him."

Very quickly, Tom introduced Wiley to Elfego.

"That bar," said Wiley, "is full to the brim with people. Watch your step, Tom."

The short Mexican adjusted his town marshal's badge and said, "Let me go first. The men you're after don't know me."

"This has to be my fight," Tom said.

Elfego nodded, showing that he understood. He went into the saloon, followed closely by Tom and Wiley.

When Tom entered he saw men lined up at the long bar, some leaning on it, others standing back and putting a boot on the brass rail at its base. Others played cards or drank at the tables. The shutters at the windows were open, and the late afternoon sunlight filtered into the large, drafty room. Tom waited a moment for his eyes to adjust so he could see in the smoke-hazed interior. Then he spotted the two men at a table close to the far wall. He glanced at Wiley and could tell that he had also seen them.

Elfego, ignoring hostile stares, went off to the right where he found an empty table.

Wiley patted a few backs here and there as he made his way through the room. He had already met a number of people in Frisco. He moved casually, trying not to be noticed, but these efforts couldn't be successful owing to his size and unusual appearance.

Wiley made his way toward the two men. As he did, a tall cowboy with a bony ridge over his eyes and a prominent jaw rose to his feet, blocking his passage. Wiley recognized the man named McCarty, the one who had dragged Tom at the end of his rope. A number of his new acquaintances had pointed him out and repeated the story of what had happened.

McCarty crossed his big arms over his chest and said in his deep voice, "I heard you're the one who busted up Lud Grossbach in a fistfight."

"Not now," Wiley said, trying to angle around him.

"Hold on, damn it. I want to *talk* to you."

Wiley heaved a sigh of disgust. He looked across the room, saw Tom hesitating, and then he addressed himself to the tall, angular man who obstructed his way. "I haven't had the pleasure of meeting you, mister, and right now I'm busy."

McCarty ignored this. "What I hear," he boomed out, "is that you wore brass knuckles under some gloves you put on before the fight. Hell, ain't no way you could of bested Lud otherwise."

"Cowboy, I don't know why you have insisted on this particular time to engage me in conversation, but—it's not convenient."

McCarty's face reddened. He had obviously been drinking and, drunk or sober, he normally got his own way. He stuck out a hand and shoved it into Wiley's chest, forcing him to take a step backward to maintain his balance.

This was not a carefully reasoned decision on McCarty's part. Wiley's straight left banged into his eye, a right drove deep into his stomach, and then—as the tall cowboy doubled forward—the left whipped in an uppercut which made a loud cracking noise as it struck the tip of his lantern jaw. Jarred back on his heels, he still acted as if he wanted to fight. He blinked his eyes and shuffled forward just as Wiley's bony fist crunched squarely into his prominent nose, shattering it. He fell moaning in a heap, putting both hands to his face.

Breathing hard, Wiley looked quickly across the room for Tom but didn't see him. Then he felt the unmistakable touch of cold steel below his right ear.

Chato Verdugo, the henchman of Julian Haynes, held the dagger at Wiley's neck, its point pressing into the flesh—almost breaking the skin. Chato grabbed his captive's collar and marched him toward the far wall.

All of the cowboys had been watching the violent fight, and were openmouthed with amazement at this turn of events.

Then they became aware of Tom, standing in the center of the saloon. A man cried out, "This is the son of a bitch who was outside with that Meskin." He glared first at Tom and then at Elfego. An ominous rumbling began as the forty or fifty excited cowboys began to mill about.

Elfego stood up and walked toward them. He drew his six-gun and pointed it at the ceiling. He fired it, the explosion shocking the men into quietness. Waving the pistol, he herded them back against the bar. Then he turned about and yelled at Chato, "Drop that knife!"

At the prospect of a free-for-all, several cowboys began to tug at their holsters, drawing their Colts, and Elfego roared at them, sounding like an outraged wildcat. He fired twice over their heads and herded the cowboys back toward the front of the room.

While Elfego held his weapon in front of him, waving it back and forth at the far from sober cowboys, Tom stood by himself in the center of the saloon, watching Chato force Wiley to move to one side.

The cowboys stared as if mesmerized, looking beyond Elfego at the spectacle that played before them.

Chato hauled Wiley over toward the table where Haynes sat. Chato held an ivory-handled dagger at his throat, and even at a distance Tom recognized it as the one that had been Macha's. With a shiver he realized that this had been the knife used to mutilate and kill her.

Haynes cried out to Tom, "If you touch one of your guns this man will die. Do you understand that?"

Tom didn't answer, but kept approaching until he'd reached a point some twenty feet away.

The few remaining men at that side of the room scurried to safety. Sounds were made by their boots, by chairs being shuffled to one side, by glasses falling from tables to the floor, followed by an eerie silence.

Tom concentrated totally upon his enemy. He waited, hands trembling by his sides, as he watched the scene before him unfold.

Haynes had risen and moved along the wall while Chato stood behind Wiley. Wiley's face turned red as Chato grabbed him by the collar with his left hand and with his right held the dagger's point at his Adam's apple.

"We got tired of runnin'," Haynes said ominously. "So we decided to wait right here and get this over."

But his nerve failed him. He began to edge down the wall toward the back door, holding his gun on Tom.

This left Chato alone with Wiley serving as his shield.

Wiley spoke as if to himself, "I can't believe this is happening. Everybody *likes* me. They always have." A frown crossed his face. "Ouch," he complained. "Careful with that thing." The knife's point scratched across his throat, and what looked like a thin red ribboned necklace formed. Red beads grew and then trickled down from it, staining his collar.

Chato, fearful of Tom English, crouched behind his captive.

Tom fixed his cold eyes on the man with the knife. After a moment he said, "I'm sorry, Wiley, but it looks like I'm goin' to have to shoot through you to hit Chato."

Wiley replied, "Well, I'm sorrier than you are about that. But you go ahead if that's what you've decided."

"*¡Dios!*" Chato was heard to utter in a hoarse whisper. He shrank even more behind his shield. Only his hand and the knife at Wiley's neck could be seen.

A hollow detonation exploded inside the saloon and the hand seemed to fly in pieces. Chato, wrenched back by the force of the blow, whirled off to one side and a second bullet, sounding like an instant echo of the first, rang out.

It looked as if the heavy bullet had slammed through a bucket of bright red paint—splashing it on the wall—instead of splitting through a man's head.

Wiley stood very still for an instant, gingerly touching his scratched throat, and then he turned about to see the awful sight behind him.

Tom whirled as the ringing sounds still crashed through the air and faced the place where Haynes had stood. All he saw was an open door. Then he heard the clatter made by a horse's hooves.

He called to Elfego, "Make sure no one follows me."

The last light of day brushed a final glow upon the dull red tiles which formed the roof of the house built generations before by Joaquín Estévez. The mighty villa stood as if abandoned except for a heaving horse standing near the entrance.

Tom pulled his reins and drew to a halt when he reached the main house. He was conscious of the huts on the surrounding heights and of eyes directed at him from them. But he knew he had no reason to fear those people.

The unlocked front door, made with four-inch-thick boards, swung back heavily on its iron hinges as he stepped into the planked entry hall. Alert, waiting for the trap to spring, he walked silently, having left his spurs in his saddlebags.

The door to the left was ajar, and light streamed out upon the hall's floor. When he stepped through this he saw, in the forty-foot-long room, that he was expected. Lanterns had been lit, illuminating the area where he stood. At the shadowed far end, Julian Haynes sat in a leather chair behind a desk. In his hands he held a Winchester rifle leveled on Tom's chest.

"I'm going to kill you," the man with slit eyes said. He raised his olive-skinned cheek from the rifle's stock and said, "I don't mind doing that. In fact I guess I like it."

He pulled the rifle up and aimed it carefully. "Raise your hands. Now, that's better." He lowered the rifle slightly and leaned back in the chair, apparently enjoying himself.

"You know, Baxter and his men killed your five cowhands. And you killed Baxter. Look at things from my viewpoint. My oldest and maybe my only friend was T. J. Hoskins. You remember him from when he served as judge of Tom Green County in West Texas. Well, Macha killed T. J. and Chato killed Macha. And then you gunned down Chato. Don't it seem to you that there's no end to all of this? I'm tempted to let you go," he said, a teasing note in his voice. "But of course, I'm not goin' to do that."

Tom's left hand raised as high as it could. He had to lean slightly to one side as it strained out over his head. Involuntarily Haynes's eyes shifted to it for a fraction of a second—but it was enough. Tom threw himself sideways as his right gun jolted in his hand.

He hit the floor hard, rolled over on a wrinkled rug, and came to his knees. He held his Colt ready to fire again but couldn't see his enemy. Then he heard an awful gargling noise. In a crouch he advanced until he saw Haynes lying on his back, his face drawn back in agony. The bullet had entered his side but apparently missed his heart. There was a sodden torn red entry hole, but not the rush of blood seen when an artery's been hit.

The high choking noises stopped, and Haynes stretched his strangely closed lids until Tom could see the man's frantic eyes.

"I can't move! I'm paralyzed. Your bullet must have hit my spine." He choked again.

"Don't leave me this way," he begged.

Tom thumbed back the hammer until it clicked in place, its firing pin poised like a serpent's tooth. His finger felt the curved steel smoothness of the trigger. Only a feather touch was needed, but this seemed beyond his strength.

Haynes whispered, "My revenge is that you'll feel a terrible guilt the rest of your life for what you're about to do."

Tom let the barrel drop. He couldn't go through with it.

Haynes whispered again, "You've got to finish me. I'm begging you." When he saw Tom hesitate he added, "I did the knife work on Macha."

Haynes moved one arm with a sudden effort. *So,* Tom thought, *he isn't completely paralyzed.* Haynes fumbled at his waist, then a hand came free holding a hideout gun, a blue steel derringer.

Relief flooded through Tom as his finger twitched.

The six-gun erupted and the bullet's impact threw out a fine hot spray which stung across Tom's face.

He holstered the gun and backed away, feeling a strange exhilaration mixed with revulsion.

When he reached the door he saw at least twelve Mexicans in front of their huts, staring at him apprehensively.

One of them, an old woman in a black dress, asked in Spanish, "Is the *patrón* dead?"

"Yes."

"Good," she pronounced with solemn emphasis.

Tom looked at the gathered people. "Will you bury the body?"

A boy said, "When we kill rattlers, we throw them on a fence. We'll do that with him."

But Tom said, "No, don't do that." Then he mounted. He would ride to Frisco and pass the night. Tomorrow he'd say goodbye to Marta and the children and old Rafa. He would say goodbye to Elfego Baca, that extraordinary young lawman. He had a feeling that he'd see all of them again in the future.

Then he'd ride to Socorro with Wiley Callan before heading out on the long trip home.

He needed that time alone, he decided.

•

Eighteen

THE RANCH HOUSE on the Lazy E sat on a rise overlooking the meandering North Concho River, a long narrow oasis that lay like a ribbon in the arid land. Tall pecan trees lined the stream, waving stark branches in winter but with a promise of greenness and shade for the hot summer months. Those who knew this part of the river had their favorite fishing spots and even gave them names, like the Brown F. Lee hole at a bend where the water deepened. Sun perch, bass, and long-whiskered catfish wandered under the sun-dappled surface, a constant temptation to the occasional fishermen who waited on the bank with mixed feelings of frustration and hope. Many spent long Sunday afternoons in the summer holding cane poles or, getting tired of that, sticking them into the mud and allowing the corks to bob in the sleepy slow current of the dull greenish water.

A screened porch lined the front of the two-story gray frame dwelling, and stone chimneys rose from the shingled roof. The revolving wooden blades of a windmill showed through the trees in the background. Soothing, regular clanking noises came from it. Around the house, a wood picket fence, painted white, protected the yard from hungry cattle that might graze on the flowers that Sally English kept trying to grow every spring.

A woman and a young girl came out on the porch and pulled chairs forward beside a table holding a teapot and cups. Sally sat in a tall rocking chair and felt gusts of unseasonably mild wind blow past her face. She pushed a strand of hair back as she said to Rebecca, "Your dad's been back from his trip for almost four weeks. Something happened in New Mexico, but I can't imagine what it could have been. He's different somehow." A touch of anxiety showed in her eyes.

When Sally went to town, men turned to watch her pass. She had a lovely small body, softly curved, and she had an effect on cowboys that was almost like pain. But she was totally unaware of this as she hurried about her tasks. She found the world to be a funny place and had the gift of laughter. But for some time she'd been troubled.

"I've never seen him like this. He hardly says a word."

"He's fine," the daughter said. "Maybe tired or something. He looks thin to me." Rebecca adored it when her mother spoke to her the way she might to one of her grownup friends. She held her teacup carefully, taking part in an adult conversation. "Yep," she said, "he's lost some weight."

"You're right," the mother responded, "we just need to feed him." Her laughter brightened the day. "You and I'll fatten him up—and make him see that this is a pretty good world. We'll have fun. Things will get back to normal soon."

She smiled at her pretty daughter. "I'm glad that you and he made up."

Rebecca's face broke into a roguish grin. "I never was all that mad at him—just trying to get him to stay out of trouble." She sighed. "Sure wish he was just an ordinary rancher. Seems like he's got enough to keep him busy looking after the stock. It would be nice," she said, making a childish face in spite of herself, "if people would leave him alone, if everyone would just *forget* the past."

Sally closed her eyes for a moment. "Maybe that'll happen now."

The girl curled her legs under her and leaned against the woven cane back of her chair. "I hate it so when I'm with him in town and new people come up. You can tell by looking at them that they've been told who he is. They have that awed look—and they act kind of scared, and . . ." Her voice dwindled into silence.

"I know," Sally said distantly.

The baby rushed out on the porch followed by Lupe Acosta. The old Mexican woman, Santiago's widow, helped tend to him when she wasn't working in the kitchen. Ben Westbrook English, for all the dignity of his name, staggered in his haste, lurching forward on chubby legs. Losing his precarious balance, he stumbled and fell abruptly. After rising awkwardly, he moved toward his big sister who held her arms out to him.

Rebecca picked up the baby, fussed at him for being so clumsy, kissed the hurt knee, and finally got his mind off his injuries by tickling him.

Sally watched the ordinary scene while time passed slowly by, and told herself, "Everything is going to be all right. It has to be. He's home—and he's safe."

Tom rode old Judge again, not hurrying on the thirty-two-mile journey to Santa Rita. He had plenty of time since he'd left before dawn. He sat in the saddle thinking of the long trek home from New Mexico, remembering particularly an early morning near Marathon some forty or fifty miles from Mexico. He'd been feeling good and had allowed Deuce to rock into a slow, easygoing lope. Without warning, the horse went out from under him, falling violently, head over heels, after stepping in a prairie dog hole. Tom had fallen free and fortunately hadn't reinjured his shoulder. But Deuce had broken a leg, forcing Tom to shoot him.

He lugged the saddle for hours, dragging it behind him until a Mexican cowhand came along. They left the saddle on top of the blanket and bridle, and Tom clambered up behind the youngster. Then they rode to pens clustered in the flat below some mountains. A cloud of shadowy blue birds rose from a big rock water trough and circled. Behind, on the rocks, they'd left a neat line of reddish rust-colored litter.

Tom found that he had ridden onto land owned by old man Harte, known far and wide by reputation. He was a crusty, aging rancher with a piercing voice and a deceptive manner. Tom spent two days there trying to talk his crotchety host into selling him a horse. To his surprise he learned that Harte found it to be exceptionally painful to part with any of his property. It took Tom the better part of his waking hours to persuade the cranky old man to sell him a ewe-necked, spavined mustang mare with a swayed back. In desperation he finally offered a price that would have pleased the seller of a Kentucky thoroughbred, and the owner reluctantly accepted.

"That is a fine animal," old man Harte kept insisting in a high-pitched slightly nasal tone. "I can scarcely bear the thought of parting from her."

The Mexican cowboy who'd brought Tom to the ranch had been thoughtful enough to go back for his saddle and other gear. Tom bridled the docile mare, threw his saddle upon her sharp spine, and, after cinching it, mounted.

"I'll ride with you for a spell on your way out of the ranch," Harte stated.

Tom thought, *He's not as mean and ornery as folks think. In fact, he looks a little lonely to me.* They rode for a time around the hills in the valley that lay under the tall cliffs just to the east. In the other direction, off toward Mexico, blue peaks loomed.

Harte made abrupt observations from time to time. He had a peculiar way of speaking—perhaps his teeth bothered him, Tom thought. His lips went forward, puckering slightly as if kissing the words, although he only did this occasionally when he seemed to be poking fun at the listener.

They rode up to another of the big rock water troughs of which Harte was so proud. A blur of gray-blue birds wheeled up and off into the cloudless sky, hundreds of them in a graceful flurry. The same kind he'd seen when he was riding double behind the Mexican cowboy after shooting his horse.

Harte said, "Those are indigo buntings, that's their name. Look at a distance like Mexican jays, but their color's different; so's the shape of their heads." The observation surprised Tom.

"I miss my brother Ed. He's the one who taught me about birds," Harte said gruffly.

Tom shook his head in wonder. This man, who had been known to lead posses after horse thieves and rustlers, hunting them down even if it took months, and who then summarily hanged his captives, had an abiding love for birds. Like many men, he was filled with contradictions.

Tom heard Judge nicker, fluttering out a greeting, and the sounds called him back to the present. He'd been so lost in thought that he hadn't realized he had ridden back onto his own land—having reached the Lower Ranch.

He saw the familiar sight of his old friend Calvin Laudermilk approaching, riding his massive dappled gray Percheron, the one he called Sully. Long hair feathered down from the horse's fetlocks over his pie-plate hooves.

"Welcome home, stranger. I'd heard you were on the Lazy E. With all the gossips we got out here on the range, there ain't no way a man can slip around unnoticed."

The two rode toward the house Tom had built at the river's edge. It sat high on a bank which sloped sharply down toward the Concho's shallow riverbed. Gravel peninsulas had formed, peeking through the surface, while small isolated mossy ponds at the edges stagnated.

"The river looks low," Tom said.

"It is. Lucky you sold off most of the cattle," Calvin grunted as they reached the house and dismounted.

Tom and his broad-bodied friend went inside where they gratefully accepted glasses of cool water from a Mexican woman. Then they sat in leather chairs while Calvin brought Tom up to date on horses he'd been training and other horses that had been sold.

Calvin didn't ever use the word *work*. He did pass his time on this ranch. And he appreciated the fact that Tom made a deposit in his account at the bank now and then, although he didn't look on this as a salary but as a friendly gesture. He considered no man to be his employer. Calvin had convinced himself that he was doing Tom a favor by reluctantly agreeing to help run this ranch. He especially enjoyed being around horses and knew quite a lot about them. But it seemed indecent to him to take money for doing something that he enjoyed. Both of the men recognized the nature of their pact and were comfortable with it.

Tom took the time to tell Calvin everything that had happened in New Mexico. Or almost everything. He touched on things he hadn't mentioned to Sally or to any other living soul as the afternoon slipped by.

"It seems a miracle," Calvin said, "that all that bloodshed hasn't been spread all over the newspapers. The one-man stand of Elfego Baca's that you told me about—well, that's got to get a lot of publicity. What a story! Maybe it'll be the only thing that'll come out. You need some good luck for a change, and maybe those gunfights of yours won't come to light."

"I've been going through all the newspapers that have reached me since I've been home, and so far there's been no mention of them. Lord," Tom said, "I hope no one ever hears that I've gunned down all those men. I haven't mentioned these things to anyone but you, Calvin."

He excused himself and came back a few minutes later, smelling suspiciously of whiskey to Calvin.

Tom sat down again and said, "I'm going to hire a lawyer in New

Mexico, Calvin. A good one will be able to convince a judge that
Pancho Cordero, Macha's little boy, is the son of Julian Haynes. When
he has established this fact, I'll get the lawyer to go to El Paso and find
out what Haynes left. I expect that it'll amount to a substantial inheri-
tance. After all, Haynes never married and his son ought to be heir to
whatever he had."

"What about the other bastard kids Haynes sired, the ones you
mentioned?"

"I don't know," Tom replied. "Maybe the best thing will be to get an
honest man out there to act as Pancho's guardian, to help him until
he's of age. Maybe the lawyer can set up a trust that could help
Pancho's half brothers and sisters to get a start. I expect that most of
the mothers will have married by now and you know how touchy
Mexican men can be. They might not be willing to admit that the
youngsters aren't theirs. It'll be a delicate thing, but that's something
for a guardian and the lawyer to work out. But, as I said, I'm going to
stay on this until we get it settled. In the meantime, I'll send out a
regular check for Marta Naranjo—the woman who's looking after
Pancho. Those people were good to me in a time when I needed
help."

Calvin studied his friend, knowing that a great deal must have happened, things that he'd never really know. But Calvin didn't worry
about that. In fact, he felt he had more than enough information
crowding in his head, and hardly saw how he'd pack in much more. At
times he felt that his brain was like an old house that has filled beyond
its capacity with possessions. A vigorous spring cleaning might rid a
house of its clutter, but he had not determined an effective way to
sweep bothersome things from his mind. He took a deep breath and
said, "The hell with it."

"I think that one of the grand traditions established by the British,"
said Calvin, "is the custom of serving high tea. I do think that three
meals a day aren't quite enough, so when we came in I took the liberty
of ordering a little snack."

The Mexican woman came in with a platter at that moment and put
it before him.

"High tea," Calvin announced with a satisfied look on his face. He
turned to the business of devouring the stack of fried potatoes, offering some to Tom and acting relieved when this was refused.

"Eating is my main form of entertainment," Calvin apologized.

Tom left Calvin by mid-afternoon. He wanted to reach Santa Rita before dark as he'd been invited to have dinner with Max Hall, his friend who headed the First National Bank. He had declined Max and Cele Hall's invitation to stay with them, saying he'd be leaving early the next day. Actually, he wanted some time alone, so he planned to take a room in the Taylor Hotel. He'd stop there in time to freshen up before supper time. He put his spurs in Judge's sides, urging him into a trot.

When he reached the mesquite flats on the north side of Santa Rita, he rode through the familiar scattering of Mexican shacks. On arriving at the center of the community, he checked into its only hotel. After bathing and putting on fresh clothes he walked into George Henry's café next door.

Tom often wondered about the men who spent most of their time in town. They made it a point of honor to rise at dawn every morning in order to meet at this café. After exchanging rough jokes for an hour, each would wander off, only to gather again as soon as it seemed respectable. They didn't think it proper to go to a saloon during the middle of the week since they held responsible jobs and had to think of their reputations. But time hung heavily on their hands.

The regulars at George Henry's café saw Tom coming. They knew he'd been off on a trip and supposed he'd want to talk about it. All of them had been bored half to death by travelers coming home who insisted on giving them full particulars about everything they'd seen and done on their journeys.

"Howdy, Tom," a large-bellied man said morosely. "We heard you got back from New Mexico."

Several at the table sighed.

Then, bracing himself, the large-bellied man said, "Well, tell us about it. Tell us about your damn trip."

Images and sounds and feelings passed through Tom's mind: being dragged at the end of a rope, bodies kicked back by his bullets, the soft warmth of Macha's body against his during that long night—and then the sight of her hair waving in water that moved under ice, the sound of gunfire and the smell of burning cordite, and he seemed to feel his finger on the trigger as he stood over Julian Haynes. His mind went blank. Some things should not be recalled.

Tom replied, "Well, you know how things are this time of year in New Mexico."

H. B. Broome was nominated for the Medicine Pipe Bearer's Award for Best First Novel by the Western Writers of America for *The Meanest Man in West Texas,* the first novel about the reluctant gunfighter Tom English. His subsequent novels include *Gunfighters, The Man Who Had Enemies,* and *Violent Summer.* His great-grandfather was a U. S. Marshal in West Texas. His grandfather was a director of the Texas Sheep and Goat Raisers Association as well as an early member of the Texas and Southwestern Cattlemen's Association.

W
Broome, H. B.
Dark winter